MY NAME IS EMILY RAY

MICHELE DOMINGUEZ GREENE

Storm

Ebook ISBN: 978-1-80508-809-7
Paperback ISBN: 978-1-80508-811-0

Cover design: Blacksheep
Cover images: Getty Images, Shutterstock

Published by Storm Publishing.
For further information, visit:
www.stormpublishing.co

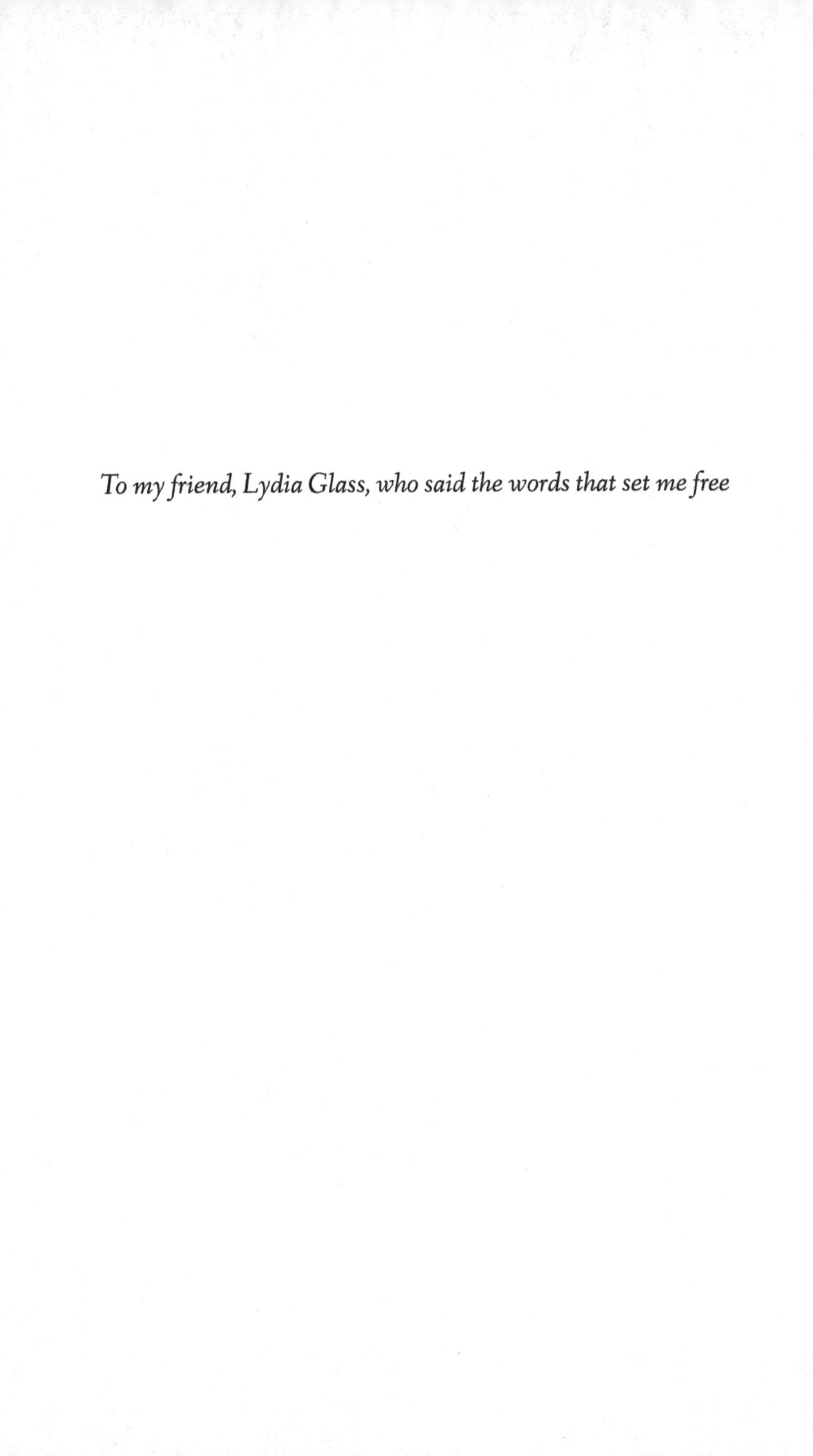

To my friend, Lydia Glass, who said the words that set me free

PROLOGUE

He felt alive, for the first time in a long time. That old, familiar undercurrent of energy radiating through his body. But he forced himself to wait in the sedan, parked in an empty aisle of the parking lot. He had planned everything so carefully; he made no mistakes. How many months had he spent searching for the perfect prize to set everything in motion? He felt a sharp pain in his lower abdomen. It happened regularly these days. He opened the Advil bottle in his glovebox and popped three pills into his mouth, swallowing them dry.

The security cameras in the area weren't working; Edison had a planned outage scheduled for six hours that afternoon. But he knew that already. He checked his watch again; they would be here by now. They were here every Saturday at the same time, so the pretty redhead could meet her lump of a boyfriend, the one who brought dogs to the park. Fucking loser. What could she possibly see in him?

He hated dogs. Hated their big eyes, always looking for approval. Hated their energy, their tails wagging, their dirty paws. He hated the pretty redhead's asshole boyfriend, too, even though he didn't know him. Or her. But she would be here today, with the prize he was after. He adjusted his medical face mask, a useful holdover from COVID-19. No one thought anything of it since the pandemic. He drew the baseball cap over his newly shorn hair. But no one would notice him. No one ever did. There were not many visitors now, due to the shift in the weather. But Red would be here, to meet that idiot dog walker who wore what was called a man-bun. What kind of pussy wears his hair in a bun?

He scanned the parked cars across the lot. The silver Jetta. They were here. He walked quickly along the path to the playground. The eugenia bushes blocked the view if you didn't know what to look for. Through the foliage, he saw her. Playing on the spring horses, like she always did. She was perfect. In every way. Her honey-blond hair in a messy ponytail. Her pink leggings and matching T-shirt. She smiled and waved at the redhead who stood far across the park, near the old library building, flirting with Skittle Balls and his filthy dogs. Red wasn't even watching. He held the balloons tightly by the strings, their shiny globes bobbing in the wind, visible just over the tops of the bushes. He waited. She would see them. She loved balloons. He had chosen well. Silvery mylar, fat with helium. *Frozen.* My Little Pony. *The Owl House.* He knew her favorites. He had studied her, leading up to this day.

She was getting up now, walking toward the path. Her little sneakers lit up with every step. Her eyes were on the balloons, wide with expectation. She came around the bushes, just out of view of the others. He untangled a balloon and she reached for the string he held out to her. Her wrist was so tiny in his hand. That was all it took.

The balloons floated on the wind, separating as they rose into the gathering clouds.

ONE

DAY ONE: 3:23 A.M.

The house is silent. I am the only one awake at this hour, as usual. By force of habit, I scan the security cameras linked to my phone. I have eyes everywhere, strategically placed to catch every blind corner, every shadowy passageway. From the kitchen I see the red light blinking on the alarm panel, like a heartbeat, letting me know that the system is set, that we are safe. Our giant mastiff mix, Moose, is curled up on his cushy bed in the corner of the room. No one can enter this sanctified space uninvited. Unless they want to come face to face with a nine-millimeter Glock. And a dog that stands six feet on his hind legs with a bite that can take an arm off. He was trained that way.

I reread the text that came through ten minutes ago, pulling me from the comfort of my bed and my husband's sleeping body next to mine.

CARD requested for child abduction from Redondo Beach, April 22, 2023, at approximately 4:30 p.m. Details sent via email to emily.ray@fbi.gov. Contacts: Andy Ryan, Redondo Beach PD 310-576-1410; Ed Whirt, Palos Verdes Estates PD, 310-385-9182

I've already read the email. Messages that come before dawn from our Los Angeles office of the Federal Bureau of Investigation rarely bring good news. I've made strong coffee to wake me up since there will be no return to sleep this morning.

A seven-year-old girl, Josie Vance, had disappeared a day and a half ago at approximately 4:30 p.m., from a park near the Redondo Beach Marina in the South Bay. She was in the company of her live-in nanny when she went missing. The email included all the preliminary investigative information, which was pretty basic. They had done everything they should have. And they had nothing.

I scan over the text of the email to the photos.

I feel a familiar tightness in my gut as I look at her dimpled face, honey-blond hair in braids, grinning with her hands on her hips. She looks so small standing on a sandy strip of beach that I recognize from the curve of the shoreline, the green cliffs above. It is Lunada Bay in the Palos Verdes Peninsula. My childhood home is perched on one of those cliffs, overlooking the ocean. I have walked that beach a thousand times.

A little girl from Palos Verdes, abducted from a neighborhood park, in broad daylight. The muscles along my upper back tighten into a painful spasm. It's so strong, it makes me want to curl up into a ball until it passes but instead, I take a long sip of coffee and breathe the pain out. My body always knows when I'm getting into dangerous territory. There will be full court press at the crime scene today making everyone's job harder; especially mine, as the head of the FBI CARD team that covers the western United States.

CARD. Child Abduction Rapid Deployment.

We are invited into the cases that require the full resources and expertise of the federal government to find a missing child. I've already spoken to the special agent in charge, Robert Powers, from our L.A. office, as well as our unit chief, Jeff Edmonson. I'll be the supervisory agent on the case and answering to them every day until it is solved. I have called the other members of our team; we will meet at the family home in Palos Verdes by daybreak. Our team is based in Los Angeles. Given the wealth and prominence of the family, there will be a ton of pressure to resolve it quickly and deliver a positive outcome.

A positive outcome. That can mean finding a child safe and sound, in the best-case scenario.

A positive outcome can also mean locating identifiable remains of a body so the family can have the mythical closure that people talk about.

But sometimes the outcome is not positive. It is silence. Unanswered questions. A wound that never heals.

My brain is already orchestrating the search for her. We will find her; we must. Because I know what happens when we don't. Most people in my line of work only know what kidnapping feels like from the stories of survivors. They've never been taken, never been tied up in the back of a van, never been thrust into the abject terror of being powerless over their fate.

But I know.

I was kidnapped as a little girl and held for eight years by the kind of monster that you read about in news stories, the bogeyman every parent dreads. Eight years that turned me into something altogether different from other little girls and ultimately, different from other adults. I'm a member of a special club that no one wants to join.

I'm the fear that catches in a mother's throat when she loses sight of her four-year-old at the mall. Or in the pit of the stomach of a dad who can't find his son in the group of kids playing at the beach when he swore the little boy was there a moment ago. That disorienting, dizzying moment when time stops, and panic comes hurtling toward you like a tree felled by a lightning strike. The kind of panic that threatens your ability to reason, to stand up, to breathe.

Usually the moment passes, the child is found. But that fear lingers, like the smell of a wildfire hanging in the air. It is terrifying to have it brush too close to you. But sometimes the child is not found quickly, if at all. Sometimes it is as if she has fallen into a void between this world and the next and her absence is an unwelcome, yet ever present, visitor.

We imagine a million nightmare scenarios and we bite back the questions and answers that we cannot bear to say aloud, for fear that they might be true. We realize that despite all the constructs we have put in place in our modern lives to make us feel safe, we are always two steps from the abyss. Two small steps. I am someone who fell into that abyss and climbed back out. I escaped. I returned.

I am also the living, breathing example of what every family hopes for when a child is taken. When we arrive to talk to distraught parents, mine is the face they focus on, clinging to the hope that they will have the happy ending that I had. Because I sit in front of them, no visible scars, exuding an aura of control. In me, they see the best possible outcome: a child returned, seemingly unscathed, ready to resume her life.

But it isn't like that. Being a kidnapping victim is something that never goes away. The broken parts can be fitted back together, like a shattered piece of porcelain meticulously repaired with invisible glue. But those fissures will always be ready to crack under pressure. Because there is nothing that can ever prepare you for what captivity means, how it feels. The uncertainty. The helplessness. The internal struggle between fighting back and giving in. A child stands no chance against an all-powerful adult. There are trauma pathways etched into your brain circuitry that cannot be erased, only managed.

And then there are the secrets that you never tell. I have mine. I have never shared them with anyone and I never will.

TWO

DAY ONE: 4:27 A.M.

The sky was still dark when I stepped off the elliptical trainer, my workout clothes wet with sweat. I didn't hear my husband, Antonio, come to the doorway. I moved to him and felt his arm circle my waist and pull me in to him.

"What time did you get in here?" he asked.

"About forty-five minutes ago. New case. I had to get the workout in early."

No matter the hour, I must exercise every day, without fail. I do it to keep my sanity, to banish that gun-metal gray cloud that often hangs over me upon waking. It is like a mental scar that I can't get rid of, I can only manage. I've had it since the day that my life changed forever, at the hands of my kidnapper, James Tibbs.

"I got a text around 3:15. We've been asked to join an investigation in the South Bay. A little girl, from Palos Verdes, missing from a park," I said evenly, waiting for his response.

"How old?" he asked.

"Seven. They don't seem to have anything. I don't know why they waited so long to call us in."

"Maybe they thought they could solve it without the big dogs," he suggested.

"Well, they sure as hell had better been doing something incredible these past two days," I said, wiping my face on my T-shirt.

"There will be a lot of press coverage, I'm guessing?" His tone shifted, no joking now.

"Yep. The family is quite wealthy, husband works in media."

"And someone is bound to see the similarities, don't you think?" he asked.

I sighed. "Perhaps."

He paused and brushed his lips against my forehead. "Are you going to be okay with this one?"

"Sure," I said.

Silence.

"It's not going to hit too close to home? A child from your old neighborhood? Taken from a park? Any siblings?"

He knew all the questions to ask. We'd been together since college and he had walked every step with me as I navigated the difficult road to adulthood, law school and then recruitment into the FBI. He knew my triggers.

"Only child," I said. He just nodded.

An only child, just like I am. Taken from a park, just like I was. The details of the Josie Vance case were strangely similar to mine, which was unsettling.

I answered the question he hadn't yet asked. "I'll be fine, it's my job. I can compartmentalize."

He ran his hand through my hair and said, "I know that, honey. Just make sure you stay on top of it with Lydia. I don't want you to go through another Shiloh situation."

He was referring to a case from two years earlier, where ten-year-old Shiloh Smedley was abducted and murdered. We came so close to saving her, but we were too late. I found her body in an Arizona culvert, still warm and pliable. I went into a major depression afterward and spent a lot of time with Lydia Walsh, my therapist. I had first gone to her in the weeks after I returned home, as a teenager. And I still saw her regularly to keep myself sane and stable.

"I'll be very diligent. I have to be in Redondo Beach by sunrise, so I won't be able to take the girls to school with you today. Will you explain?"

I hated hearing myself say those words. On an active case, I was always gone, missing so many daily milestones with my six-year-old daughters. Antonio wanted me to move to a different division of the FBI, but I wasn't ready. I wasn't yet able to let go of those lost children.

"Sure. I can go in a little late; we're demonstrating a new rover today at eleven," Antonio said.

He was an aerospace engineer at the Jet Propulsion Lab, in our sleepy suburb of La Cañada, just northeast of downtown Los Angeles. The JPL engineers built robotic planetary space-craft and ran the NASA Deep Space Program. I could see the white JPL buildings perched on the hillside from our bedroom window. Antonio was the constant, the sure and steady foundation that grounded our lives as a family. I pulled back and looked at his handsome face, his deep coffee-colored eyes, the mop of black curls.

He smiled. "What?"

"Nothing, just looking..." I murmured as I pulled away.

He stripped off his T-shirt and snapped it at my butt as I moved off to shower and dress. I felt the sharp sting and jumped.

"You'll pay for that," I warned.

"Talk, talk..." he muttered as he disappeared down the stairs to make his morning coffee.

I padded quietly toward the master bathroom, stopping to stick my head into our daughters' room on the way. They were still asleep, both sprawled on their matching beds with pink coverlets. Twins, Juliana and Eliza, they had just started first grade. Almost the same age as Josie Vance. Just to imagine them missing was like having a knife at my throat.

I leaned in and kissed them both, brushing their light brown hair from their little faces, savoring time with them before I stepped into the high intensity work of a new investigation. It would dominate my time and energy, pulling me away from my home and family. But I had to find the children *not* sleeping safely in their beds.

Half an hour later I was unlocking my Glock from the safe in the laundry room, watching Dolores, Antonio's aunt, move quietly through the kitchen. Tiny, with a sporty gray bob, she was wearing one of her many velour tracksuits. Today it was bright orange.

"Dolores, what are you doing up at this hour?" I asked.

"Honey, I sleep lightly. I heard you and Toño in the hall and I knew you must be leaving early for work. I tried this rocket fuel coffee you made. You should carry it in a red gas can in your car in case you run out," she said. "And here's your breakfast."

She slid a bowl across the counter to me as I holstered my Glock.

"You didn't have to get up early to do this," I said, secretly grateful that she had.

"And I packed your lunch. I added some walnuts and almonds, they are good for your heart," she said, closing the lid of my lunch pack.

I eat the exact same breakfast and lunch every day. Oatmeal with blueberries, black coffee and toast in the morning. A watercress and cream cheese sandwich on wheat bread, baby carrots and a hardboiled egg for lunch. Two bottles of water. I love my routines, I have many. I need them to keep the edges of my life knitted tightly together. Small details that I can control, no matter what else happens. Mundane certainties that take on greater importance. It is diagnosed as manageable OCD. I control it, not the other way around.

"You have a new case?" she asked.

"Yep, South Bay, Redondo Beach area," I replied.

"Will you be home for dinner? I'm making lamb chops with cheesy potatoes."

"I doubt it. I packed a bag in case I end up staying over. It's always kind of intense the first few days."

"I'll pack you some sandwiches, won't take a minute," she said as she set to work.

I watched her move through the kitchen with a deftness that I would never have. She looked like an Energizer Bunny as she whipped up tuna salad and rinsed lettuce leaves, giving a squirt of Kewpie mayonnaise to the multi-grain bread. I was a crack shot with both a handgun and a rifle, I held a seventh-degree black belt in martial arts and could take down a 250-pound man in two moves, but I was incompetent in the kitchen.

Dolores came to live with us when the girls were born; her own children were grown and living out of state. Antonio's mother died when we were in graduate school and having Dolores made our lives manageable. She handled the house, everything related to cooking, cleaning and organization. We wanted to hire a housekeeper, but she refused. Said she didn't want a stranger moving around the house *"como un topo,"* like a mole. And she always picked the girls up from school if we got held up.

"I'll leave your plate under foil in the fridge, just in case you get back," she said as she handed me a plastic bag of sandwiches.

I loved her immensely, not only for the invaluable help that she gave to our family, but she knew which questions to ask about my work and which to leave alone.

Antonio came out to say goodbye as I was putting my bag into my car.

"Dolores says you might spend the night?" he asked, putting an extra Patagonia fleece sweater in the backseat without a word; he knew it got cold near the ocean at night.

"Maybe. It's such a long drive back here and if I have to return first thing in the morning it will be easier to stay," I explained.

"I know, the first days are always tough. Promise me you'll call Lydia, *today*. I want you checking in with her regularly on this one."

"I'll call her from the road. I'll be driving forever!"

I leaned in for a quick kiss and adjusted the windshield wipers into the right position. I couldn't start to drive if they were not in the exact right spot. Same with my to-go coffee mug, with the drinking slot directly across from the handle. And my phone charging cable that had to be coiled with the ends lining up on the right side and stored in one of the cupholders.

I clicked the wrought-iron security gates open and watched as I always did, to be sure they closed behind me. Everyone was safe and sound, inside. I sent a quick text to Lydia.

> New case. I suspect a lot of triggers Let's talk soon

The streets of La Cañada were like a postcard of the suburbs, pinned in time. Our house was a taupe-colored Cape Cod style from the turn of the century with a carriage house and empty stables. It was a large property that extended into an overgrown arroyo, with a creek running through it. It was way out of reach of our salaries, but my father had set up a trust fund for me as a child after he made millions in real estate development. It generated a sizable financial cushion and safety net; it allowed us luxuries we would not have been able to afford otherwise. The La Cañada house was a property that my parents bought as an investment decades ago. When we got married, my dad gave it to us as a wedding present. When Antonio started work at the Jet Propulsion Lab nearby, it made sense to move in.

I made the connections to the five different freeways it took to get to Palos Verdes, which curved and jutted out into the sea, a dividing line between worlds. It was an exclusive seaside paradise that didn't welcome strangers easily.

As I drove, I ran over the details of the case again and again. The worst possible crime scene, open air and uncontained. A crowded public space with a large parking area, multiple strangers with no connection to each other. The sky was blue-gray and overcast, a slight wind rising from the west. It had rained over the past few days, a welcome break from the dry heat in Southern California, where the sun always shines but invariably burns too hot and people get scorched.

I passed a Salvation Army thrift store and suddenly remembered a vintage velvet coat I bought there when I was sixteen. It was black with a silk lining, a pattern of deep red roses. I hadn't thought of that coat in years. What had happened to it? Was it in storage with everything else from the Palos Verdes house?

I felt a surge of heat rising up my back and neck as I approached the Redondo Pier. The sweat spread to my sternum, clammy and damp. It was a panic attack, coming on strong. I pulled the car over, the engine idling. I drew in several deep breaths as a barrage of images filled my mind:

On the pier dangling my legs over the water where I sat next to the old men who fished all day, cigarettes absently balanced on their cracked lips.

Feeling the weathered wood against my shorts, the prick of a splinter breaking the skin on my thigh.

The smell of the fish in buckets, the fried oil wafting through the air from the Mariner House restaurant.

In the back of a van, my wrists and legs secured with zip ties, a gag in my mouth, frantically trying to keep my balance. The windows were covered with old aluminum foil, torn in some places. As I struggled to stay upright, I glimpsed the Salvation Army store through a sliver of the window before it disappeared as we drove away. I knew I had to get away from him. I thought that if I didn't yell or scream or cry, maybe he'd let me go?

I kept telling myself that it was all a big mistake. He would take me back home and the next day everything would be back to normal. But nothing would ever be normal again. I remember craning my neck to look at him in the cab of the van and I'd see his pale eyes glaring back at me in the rearview mirror. And that's when time started to get strange. When the minutes and hours and memories started running together. And the days became weeks. And the weeks became years...

I continued breathing with my eyes closed. I didn't usually have this kind of reaction when we took on a new case. I had cultivated a way of distancing myself emotionally from my work so that my own experience as a survivor was a positive instead of a negative. I didn't get panic attacks en route to a crime scene. But this one was different.

I wore a rubber band on my wrist and snapped it a few times, to pull me back to the present moment. The mild nausea passed, and I released my grip on the steering wheel. I had no recollection of having seen the Salvation Army from the back of the van the day I was taken. That detail was lost. Until today.

That's how the past can come crashing in on me, with some forgotten trigger that takes me right back in time. I drove on until I came to the parking lot of Veterans Park, but I kept going down the Esplanade for a few blocks. I wanted to settle before I arrived to face the weight of everyone's expectations. I was the FBI specialist. I would find Josie Vance.

THREE

DAY ONE: 6:34 A.M.

When I pulled up at Veterans Park the media circus was all set up, jockeying for position. The police presence was considerable, with Redondo Beach PD and L.A. County sheriffs in full force. The sky was pale lavender, refusing to relinquish the cover of night until the last possible moment. Before I got across the parking lot, two detectives came to meet me. One was young, with a buzz-cut hairstyle and a suit jacket that fit too tight across the shoulders, clearly a body builder. His face was red and slightly flushed as he extended his hand to me.

"Special Agent Ray, I'm Detective Andy Ryan, Redondo Beach PD," he said. "This'll be my first case in collaboration with the FBI. I'm looking forward to working with you and your team."

The other detective, clearly a veteran with his boxy suit and graying hair, stepped in.

"I'm Ed Whirt, from the Palos Verdes PD, we talked on the phone last night. Or this morning, rather. We're working this case also since the Vance family live on the peninsula, in Rancho PV."

"I know it well, I grew up there," I said, as I scanned the

children's play area, now cordoned off with yellow crime scene tape.

"I know," said Whirt, "I worked your case." He looked at me with expectation, as if we were long lost friends. I guessed him to be in his fifties, with the dull pallor of a smoker.

"Which case?" I asked. I had no recollection of ever meeting him.

"Your abduction, years ago. I'm retiring at the end of the year; it was one of the first cases I worked on."

I wasn't expecting this, and I tried to cover my surprise. It had been years since I had spoken to any police about my abduction and never in relation to my work with CARD. It was in my past and that was where it belonged. I could see that Whirt wanted to elaborate on the topic, but I didn't. Plus, I couldn't recall any Ed Whirt, just the two lead detectives, Herman Weg and Brandy Schultz.

"Well, thank you for your service. I know it was a difficult case," I said.

Ryan joined in. "Yeah, he told me that when they got the call about Josie Vance it was like déjà vu. You know, taken from the park, out with her nanny, same as you."

"Yes, there are definitely similarities," I said, stepping away from them. "Could you show me what you've discovered so far?"

Ryan led the way, Whirt hung back with me as I followed.

"Really, when you came home, alive after all that time, it was one of the high points of my career. No one expected it and that psycho, Tibbs, wasn't even on our radar," Whirt said, shaking his head.

"It was a surprise to everyone, including me," I said with some finality, ready to move on. I didn't want my history to play any role in this case. I moved to Ryan as he walked me through what they had pieced together.

"Josie and the nanny came here several times a week. She

played on the jungle gym, she knew some of the kids. There were a few other families here that day. We've talked to everyone, all the parents, visitors. No one saw anything or anyone suspicious. There was a classic car parade over on Hawthorne that afternoon and a lot of officers were working that," Ryan said.

"We found a couple of things nearby. The bracelet's the only one that's significant. Josie's parents confirmed it as hers. It was on the walkway," Whirt added.

He handed me a plastic evidence bag that held a pink, stretchy bracelet for a small child, the kind made from a plastic coil, like an old-fashioned telephone cord. It usually came in a set of three; I bought some from Target for my girls last month.

"What else did you find?" I asked.

Ryan handed me another bag that contained a small, thin volume of a children's book. *The Little Red Caboose.* The edges were tattered, and the front cover badly faded. It was soggy and damp, which meant it had been out in the overnight rain. I was familiar with the book. I had read it as a child, before and after I was taken. It startled me, to see it again after so many years, the weight of the thin volume familiar in my hands.

James Tibbs had a collection of children's books and toys, which was weirdly perverse given that he was a child predator. He had them to keep his prey entertained once they had been caught. This book had been a favorite of my early childhood, and I reread it countless times when I was in captivity; it was like a thread connecting me to my previous life. Through the plastic evidence bag, the tattered gold edges of the binding took me right back to Tibbs' house of horrors. I stared at it, my heart beginning to beat rapidly, transfixed by its appearance at Josie's crime scene. It felt wrong, a bad omen.

"Agent Ray?" Ryan asked, breaking me from the memory that had overtaken me.

"Does the book have any significance with the family? Was

it a favorite of Josie's or something?" I asked, working to keep my composure.

"Nope. They'd never even heard of it and they definitely don't have a copy of it. I'm guessing it was dropped by accident by some random family," Ryan said.

"We'll keep it with the other evidence in case it becomes significant later," I said, handing it back to Ryan, like a poisoned apple.

The walkway between the north parking lot and the park was lined with tall eugenia bushes, blocking it from view.

"Josie probably walked away from the play area toward the parking lot on the other side of the Elks building and disappeared," Ryan said.

"And the nanny?"

"She said she was distracted for a minute, looked away and then she noticed that Josie was gone."

"So, what's the deal with the surveillance cameras?" I asked. "Your notes said there was a power outage?"

Ryan's face tightened into a grimace. "Yeah. Edison had a planned outage. Notification was sent to all area residents and businesses so I think the offender must be local."

"Maybe. But I assume it was posted on the SCE website as well? Anyone could have found that information. What's up with that?" I pointed to the Elks Lodge. It had scaffolding around it.

"Thank God, it's closed right now. Otherwise, we'd have a huge pool of suspects to go through. It's a community center, too. They have a schedule of classes and stuff for seniors, teens, kids. It's seven pages long!" Ryan said, opening a bottle of 5-Hour Energy and drinking it down in one shot.

"Doesn't that make your heart race?" I asked.

He shook his head. "I'm used to it. I have to switch up with coffee. If I drink too much, it gives me acid reflux."

Whirt smirked. "Kids these days. Everything has a special

name. Remember when it was heartburn and people took Alka-Seltzer? Or when a narcissist was just an asshole?"

Ryan clapped him on the shoulder in mock remorse. "It's a whole new world, Whirt. Gotta put down that *Westways* magazine from Triple A."

Whirt spit out a fleck of tobacco from his unfiltered Camel and cracked a grin, but his eyes were clouded with concern.

"We've done everything," he said quietly. "The Redondo PD's put extra detectives and blue suits on it. We have county sheriffs to expand the ranks. L.A. would send some help, but they have a serial killer targeting sex workers in Hollywood."

"I know," I said. We had agents working that case and it was a shit storm.

Whirt continued. "We ran background checks on all the park employees, came up with two red flags but they didn't pan out. Solid alibis, no priors related to this type of thing at all. Just low-level drug busts. We did the neighborhood door-to-door around the park; there are some houses where no one was home."

Ryan jumped in, eager to show their due diligence. "And we checked everyone in the area on the Megan's Law registry. There was one guy, Dan Heisler, an out-of-work handyman on disability. We brought him in for questioning but he was at an Urgent Care center when Josie went missing."

"Did you get anything from the residents in the Village apartments? There are a lot of units, a lot of eyes and they look down directly on this park," I asked.

There were apartment buildings adjacent to the park along the Esplanade, a fancy name for a few blocks of beachfront apartments and condos. The Village apartments stood four stories tall with balconies that had a perfect view into the south parking lot and the play area.

"We went to every apartment, spoke to the people who

were home, left messages for the ones who weren't. We have officers and sheriffs interviewing them now," Ryan said.

"Same with the senior apartment complex across the boulevard. We also talked to the neighbors up in PV, the families from school. Nothing jumped out as suspicious, they're totally freaked out," Whirt added.

I scanned the park and the pier where I saw a few early morning hopefuls dropping their fishing lines into the dark water swirling around the pilings.

"Did anyone check with the local fishermen on the pier?" I asked.

"Those old guys are so far away, most of them are winos anyway, they're not even paying attention," Ryan said with youthful disgust.

"We have no idea where the person who took Josie went with her. We have nothing. Those old guys are there day and night, someone needs to talk to them. They notice things, even if they are winos," I said.

"I just meant—" Ryan started to defend himself, but I stopped him.

"When I was a kid there was a guy who fished on the pier every day. I never saw him catch anything, but he came, and he set up his poles. I would visit with him sometimes in the afternoons. He was a Vietnam vet, his nerves were shot to hell, couldn't hold a job but he said that the routine of coming and setting up his poles calmed him down. And he had his finger on the pulse of everything that happened around the pier and this stretch of beach."

"I'll go talk to them myself when we're done here. I didn't realize they could be helpful, I thought they were too far away," Ryan said sheepishly.

"I'll put one of our agents on it, you two need to be at the Vance house when the rest of the team arrives, to bring everyone up to speed."

"You know what I can't believe? That your parents let you talk to some old fisherman on the pier!" Whirt interjected with a dry laugh.

I walked the crime scene, now cordoned off with yellow police tape. I'd played here countless times as a kid – climbing the jungle gym and jumping from the swings. I'd also been abducted from this park. Why had Josie left the play area for the walkway where her bracelet was found? What child would walk from the jungle gym to an empty strip of concrete? Something caught her interest. Someone lured her away from the main play area to this particular spot, which meant he had done his research. He was organized, patient. Not good for us. We preferred them messy and impulsive, leaving a trail of evidence in their wake.

The children's book was bothering me. I had never read it to my own daughters after I escaped Tibbs; it reminded me of him. But now it had appeared again. It had to be a simple coincidence. It was a classic children's book, many people had copies —at least that's what I kept telling myself.

"And you said you found the book on the walkway, near the bracelet?" I asked.

"No, it was in the parking lot. It was next to a trashcan, by the bottlebrush trees," Whirt said, describing the exact area I was taken from.

The bottlebrush trees... The Little Red Caboose...

I pushed a growing sense of unease away. I needed to see the book again, to hold it in my hands. Without a word, I took the evidence bag with the book from Ryan and slipped on a pair of protective gloves. I gingerly took the book from the plastic bag. I turned the pages slowly, reading the text that I had memorized as a child. The musty smell of the damp paper, the smears of mud at the edges, the feel of the pages, it all pulled me back in time.

The little red caboose always came last...

It was a Little Golden Book. The gist of the story was that the little red caboose at the back of the train was always ignored by the boys and girls who stopped to watch and wave as the train cars drove by. The little red caboose wasn't important enough to warrant any attention. Until the day that she saved the train from slipping off the track with her sturdy, solid little body. I loved the story as a child. I understood exactly how the little red caboose felt.

"How I wish I were a big black engine, puffing and chuffing way up at the front of the train! But I am just the little old red caboose. Nobody cares for me..."

James Tibbs knew it was my favorite. I flipped through the book, remembering a time that I had colored in the pages, making a brown bear blue with a crayon. That had angered Tibbs and he had taken the book and hidden it for weeks, after beating me with a switch that he kept by the kitchen door for punishments. At that memory, I scrolled quickly through the pages to find the drawings of the bears. My heart dropped and I couldn't breathe. I couldn't be seeing it correctly.

There were several brown bears in the drawing, but one was clearly blue and had been colored over. With a crayon, not a pencil or marker. I closed my eyes and checked again, hoping it was simply a trick of the morning sunlight. But it wasn't. The bear was blue. My stomach turned over; the bitter taste of my morning coffee threatened at the back of my throat. I took in a deep breath to settle my system; I could not lose all composure in front of the detectives but inside, I felt like an alarm sounding at a nuclear reactor.

How had this book ended up in the spot that Josie had most likely been taken from? Just a few feet from where I had been snatched? My hands shook as I slipped the book back into the plastic bag. I kept it with me this time.

"I'm going to hand this off to forensics when we meet up

with the team, just to double-check for touch DNA or anything else," I said, trying to hide the panic I felt rising up inside.

My head pounded right behind my eyes, and my sudden nausea hadn't subsided.

The park was deserted. It had rained hard for the past two days and the playground equipment was barely dry, the sand still damp and slightly mushy. A few mothers with small children waited and watched at the periphery. No doubt they had come for a playdate but now couldn't pull themselves away, drawn by the voyeurism of someone else's tragedy. I could read their troubled expressions, a child taken from a trusted play area. It is always the same, that look of fear and disbelief.

How could that happen here?

Two steps from the abyss.

I traced the steps Josie must have taken. Out of the play area, along the cement walkway with tall bushes and a blind spot that was not visible from the play area. A couple of deflated helium balloons were stuck in a big magnolia tree, all sense of celebration gone. In the lot, there were the red bottlebrush trees, in cement planters every ten feet or so, dividing the rows of parking spaces. I remembered stepping on the little hard berries that fell from those trees as a child, the crunching noise they made under my shoes. This was the location of a scene that I have replayed countless times. It popped into my head uninvited, but I was ready for it this time.

A handful of twigs, a discarded soda cup of sand...

The bottlebrush flowers, red and feathery in the branches above my head...

Me, walking in circles, crushing the berries with a loud pop as my shoes crushed them into dust...

Seated on the concrete planter, I was building a structure and looked up when the skinny blond guy came and stood in front of me, casting a shadow over my masterpiece. He smiled, a warm, sunny smile, and asked what I was making.

"A fort," I replied.

"Not a castle? I thought all girls wanted to live in a castle, and be a princess," he said, crouching down to my eye level. His eyes were blue.

"Whatever," I answered. He sat down on the pavement.

"You know, I studied engineering," he said. "I can help you make this."

"Really?" I asked and handed him a pile of twigs I had been hoarding. He started helping me and I let him. I didn't know what he was. He said he usually brought his younger brother to that park and was looking for a lost soccer ball. Had I seen one?

I had no idea when he asked me if I wanted a hot dog from the guy with the cart in the parking lot that there was no guy and no cart. And no one else there to see when he grabbed me by the neck, popped open the doors to his van and shoved me in, all in one lightning-fast move.

I was inside with his knee in my chest and a gag in my mouth before I even knew what happened. No one saw. No one heard anything. And then he was driving away with me. My child's brain shifted into survival mode... how to get away... how to stay alive...

I was in the tunnel of that recollection when my phone

rang, pulling me back to reality. It was John Grice, my second in command on the CARD team.

"John, I'm at the crime scene now."

"Anything? I'm on my way to the family's house," he said.

"They found a bracelet that belongs to Josie. I'm giving it to Lila and Marty so they can take another pass with forensics. Evidently there are several guest houses on the property so we can use one as our command center," I said.

"Brinkman will be there within the hour, he missed a connection in Tucson," he said, referring to our polygraph expert who had been helping on a case in Arizona.

"See you in a bit," I said, hanging up.

According to the case file, Josie had two very wealthy parents and a devoted live-in nanny. Louis Vance worked in media on the finance end of things rather than the creative side. Melanie Vance was a society housewife who had brought considerable assets to the marriage from her family's business in Houston. Now they were a well-known couple involved in philanthropy, regularly attending celebrity events and fundraisers. No custody issues with a divorce, no suspected relative who could have been involved. The Vance family's wealth made the possibility of a ransom kidnapping more likely, but we had no evidence of that yet. And no word or contact since she had gone missing. As hard as a ransom kidnapping could be, at least we would know why she had been taken. The motive was clear, we knew what steps to follow. The other possibilities were never good.

Ryan stepped closer to me and lowered his voice. "I mean, I thought it would be ransom, since the family's as rich as shit, but there's been no call, no letter, nothing. We're just looking for something to run with." He sounded apologetic.

"How long have you been a cop?" I asked.

"I was on patrol for five years and I just made detective eight months ago. I've been working vice. We don't get a lot of kidnappings here in the South Bay. The sheriffs came in the day she went missing," he said.

"Most kids are taken by someone they know. A stranger abduction is rare. And we have nothing to build on, right? Who has a motive? Who has access? Who wants what and why? It could be ransom, sometimes they wait to make contact. Drag it out, make the family more willing to pay," I explained.

"And the ones like your case, where some freak holds a kid for years, are even more rare," Whirt said, lighting up another Camel cigarette. I wondered what his lung X-rays looked like.

That he kept bringing up my own abduction was starting to bother me. But he was right. Cases like Jaycee Dugard or the three girls held by Ariel Castro generate a ton of press coverage when they come back alive, but they are very uncommon. Sometimes the children are assaulted and then freed. Sometimes they're held briefly and released unharmed. Our team had found children safe and sound. We had also found small, lifeless bodies whose images were scorched into our memories, like Shiloh Smedley.

"What do you think, from what you've seen?" Ryan asked. He was so earnest, he wanted answers that I wished I could give him.

"I don't know. We have to find that thread. It's like a loose piece of yarn on a sweater and the more you pull on it, the more it unravels until the truth is exposed," I said.

We had no suspects, no witnesses, no trace evidence. The detail of the power outage was not a coincidence. Our guy was organized; we liked them impulsive and disorganized, leaving a trail of evidence behind. Whoever took Josie Vance wasn't an amateur; he'd done this before, which was always terrifying. How many had he taken? What did he do with his victims? Was there even a chance that Josie was still alive?

FOUR

DAY ONE: 7:48 A.M.

As we walked to our cars in the parking lot, the slew of reporters turned their attention to us. One photographer with a long lens swiveled and pointed straight at me. I drew Whirt and Ryan into a huddle, pivoting away from him. I could sense the photographers there, hovering. I heard the faint click of the cameras. Another memory, like an old movie played at high speed.

Leaving Children's Hospital Los Angeles with my dad. At the main entrance, a huge crowd of reporters, photographers with cameras poised and ready, all waiting for me. I put my head down and squeezed my eyes shut. The doors opened and then it was like lightning, with flashes going off from everywhere, and voices speaking over each other, shouting at us.

"Emily! Emily! Over here, can you tell us about the man who took you?"

"How long were you kept in the Glendale house?"

We finally made it to the car. The reporters looked like a bunch of buzzing insects, all eyes and hands, moving on us in a swarm. Through the tinted windows, I could see their faces, pressing in, their eyes and mouths in constant motion. I put my head down and crossed my arms over my ears.

And then we were moving, disappearing into the crush of cars, taking us back toward the South Bay. There was traffic and smog and a red ocean of taillights as we crawled from one freeway to the next, making the long drive out to Palos Verdes...

"Agent Ray? What'd we huddle up for?" Ryan asked, glancing over at the crowd of reporters.

"Instinct," I replied. "I keep my face out of photos so there's not the 'former kidnapping victim turned FBI agent' thing. We control the narrative; we don't want them making up their own stories."

"I told you she was the perfect Fed for this case," Whirt said with a big grin.

A young woman with a press pass bolted under the yellow police tape and made a dash toward us. As an officer moved to stop her, Whirt waved him off and leaned into me.

"She's a junior reporter for the *Daily Breeze* and the Palos Verdes *Peninsula News*. Her name's Larissa Cinque, she's graduating from USC this year. She's a smart kid, a hustler," he said, with a fondness that may have been paternal; I certainly hoped it was given his wedding ring and the fact that she was young enough to be his daughter.

"Thanks, Detective Whirt, I appreciate it," Larissa said before turning to me. "Special Agent Ray, I'm Larissa Cinque, I work for the *Daily Breeze*—"

I shook her hand, interrupting her. "I know, Detective Whirt just told me who you are. We're having a press conference this afternoon, I have no comment at this time," I said, pressing my remote key fob to signal the end of the conversation.

"Has your own personal experience with kidnapping influenced your ideas about this case or your decision to go into this type of work?"

There it was, front and center, right away. I had to admire her nerve. I had dodged this type of question so many times in my career. As I opened the car door, I said what I always did.

"My personal history has nothing to do with this case. I don't want to take any attention away from the fact that we have a little girl missing, right here and now."

She nodded, stepping back. As I shut the door to drive away, I saw Whirt chatting with her. I hoped he would stay tight-lipped at this stage, but I doubted that. As I made my way to Hawthorne Avenue for the drive up to Palos Verdes, my phone rang. It was my therapist, Lydia. I pulled over to take the call.

"Got your text, what's up?" she asked, straight to the point as usual.

My father had hired her when I returned home. She helped me fit all the pieces of my life back together when I was a traumatized teenager who'd been in fight-or-flight mode for years. With her graying blond hair and her perfectly coordinated outfits and jewelry, she always projected a sense of calm and order which gave me a safe haven to turn to. Just the sound of her voice made me feel better.

"I'm on a new case, in Palos Verdes. A little girl, abducted from a public park, while out with her nanny," I said, no need for any more elaboration.

"Oh my, that's as close to home as it gets. How're you doing?"

"I had a minor episode as I was approaching the crime scene. A flashback to being in the van with Tibbs. And a couple of other uncomfortable moments. But there's a detective on this case who worked my abduction years ago and he keeps wanting to talk about it."

"Kind of difficult to compartmentalize it if someone keeps dragging it up again."

"The similarities in the case are weird. I'm still trying to make sense of some of them. I'm on my way to meet the family now."

"Okay, Emily, I know you're genius at keeping these things separate, but this one will be hard. When the anxiety comes on, step back and take that time for yourself."

"I'll probably need to talk to you more often. Antonio was all over me about it this morning."

"Good. Make sure you don't spend too many nights away from home. You need to ground yourself in your safe environment. And remember, you're not that little girl any longer. Tibbs can't get you. He's been dead for years and now it's just shadows, okay?"

"I know. I'll turn on the light, like you used to say."

"That's right. You are the light. You control it."

I smiled silently. That had been my mantra in so many difficult moments.

"I should go, the team is arriving at the house now," I said.

"I'm always here, Emily," she replied, the warmth and reassurance in her voice coming through the phone like a much-needed hug.

Once I pulled into the quiet streets of my old neighborhood, it was like entering a bubble. Palos Verdes meant money, privilege, security. The streets were empty, just a few early morning joggers were out. All sense of peace ended as soon as I turned onto Via La Verde and saw the throng of news vans and reporters gathered outside the Vance home. I pulled into the driveway and found a spot amid the police vehicles. The house was newer, a big Mediterranean model perched on a bluff over-looking the ocean. As I stepped out of my car, I was greeted by a tall, thin man in his forties, dressed casually in jeans with a crease pressed into them, pale blue polo shirt and a navy-colored sweater. His hair was short and dyed a reddish brown, that flat, one-tone color that is never natural.

He reached out to grasp my hand. "Hello, I'm Michael Moran, I am the house manager for Louis and Melanie. I take care of everything here at the residence. If you need anything from me, don't hesitate to ask."

His smile looked as if it had been welded in place. I shook his hand and introduced myself. His eyes were dark, almost black, and they swept back and forth at all the activity in the courtyard. He was discombobulated; this was his domain, now filled with unfamiliar faces and people. He led me inside to meet Louis and Melanie Vance.

Inside, everything was oversized, from large, European-style oil paintings to statues of classical figures. It was the kind of art sold in warehouses for people who thought it gave them class. From the foyer, I could glimpse the kitchen, all marble and stainless steel, with two women moving about. One was in a pale blue uniform identifying her as the live-in housekeeper, Patricia Muñoz. The other woman was younger, with a red pixie haircut, nervously scrolling through her phone. I recog-nized her from the photos that Ryan had sent over. She was the nanny, Elsie McBride.

Moran led me to the living room which was cordoned off from the hallway with a powder blue velvet rope, the kind seen outside of nightclubs. This room was for show, much like every-thing else. There were no toys scattered about, no Barbie Dream Houses or scooters upended against the wall. Every-thing here was in its proper place, except the one thing that mattered the most: Josie Vance.

Louis and Melanie were seated on a large velvet couch, both

wearing ragged expressions; they clearly had not slept. Louis rose to greet me. Moran, silent as a statue, stood off to the side.

"Agent Ray? The detectives told us you'd be leading the investigation. I'm Louis Vance." He shook my hand firmly, met my gaze directly.

He was in his early forties, an attractive man who had the fleshy, flushed look of someone who might drink regularly. Middle-aged girth was creeping up on him, but he hid it in a burgundy Ferragamo sweater over lounge pants. His wife, Melanie, sat clutching a cup of coffee as if it were the only thing keeping her from falling over. She reached out to grasp my hand and held on.

"Thank you for coming, we don't know what to do, what to think..." Her voice broke and only a strangled whimper came out. She wore her long blond hair in a loose ponytail. Her green eyes had an odd, unfocused quality and I suspected that she had taken some kind of sedative to cope.

"Thank you for inviting us into the case. I know this is the hardest thing any parent can go through and we're all sensitive to the stress you're both feeling. We're a very experienced team with substantial resources and we will not rest until we find Josie. The first thing, I'm going to need the logins for all your social media and bank accounts, all email as well. Do you have a VPN here at the house?"

Louis nodded as Moran tapped rapidly on his cell phone.

"I have all the logins you need, should I send them to your email?" Michael asked.

"Yes, please. We'll get our data analysts on that immediately. I also need to get some information from both of you about Josie. Is there someone in your social or family circle that she would've willingly walked away with?"

Melanie shook her head. "It's just us... and the house staff..."

"How about other families from school? Any parents she might know and trust?"

"There's a few. She isn't allowed to go to sleepovers, but they have playdates. We gave the cops their information already. They said they talked to them yesterday," Louis said, his impatience obvious.

"I know it seems redundant, but we double- and triple-check everything that was done before we join a case, Mr. Vance. Are there any neighbors in the area that you've had any issues with? Anyone who's exhibited problematic behavior?" I asked.

"Lou had a disagreement with a couple a few doors down, about their dogs..."

Louis waved her remark off. "Those were the ones with the Cane Corsos. Big dangerous dogs like that, just walking loose! So, I called animal control. There are leash laws."

"Did it escalate?" I asked.

"No. They were mad but that was it. And then they moved, to Belize, I think."

"We'll follow up with the neighbors and school families once the whole team arrives," I said. "And we'll conduct another door-to-door."

Whirt and Ryan rolled in with Starbucks cups. Must've been a line at the drive-thru.

"So, you all have a lot more to bring to the party, right? I mean, you're the Feds," Louis asked bluntly. "I just don't understand how a little girl goes missing like this. I mean, we pay the nanny a ton of money to watch her, and this happens. We were sure she must have just wandered off or something. But not this!"

"We have a large team of agents who specialize in these cases. Elsie is the first person I plan to interview. Special Agent John Grice will be here in a moment, the other agents are setting up our command center. We'll interview everyone and we'll polygraph as well."

"You're not going to polygraph us, are you? You can't think we had anything to do with this," Louis said, indignantly.

I've learned over the years that the wealthier the parents of an abducted child are, the more they bristle at the idea they could be considered suspects. As if their affluence removed them from the stain of suspicion and we should just take their word for it.

"Polygraphing the family and members of the household is standard procedure," I explained.

"But the whole idea is ridiculous!" Louis said, a fine spray of spittle flying from his lips. I was glad to be standing several feet away.

"Don't worry, Mr. Vance. Like Special Agent Ray said, it is just standard procedure. No one thinks you had anything to do with this," Whirt said.

I shot Whirt a glance; he gave me a vague, embarrassed smile and looked down at his shoes. He was a veteran cop, he knew better than to sugarcoat standard procedure, even with a wealthy, prominent family. Melanie had been sitting quietly, seemingly in her own world, when she suddenly blurted out, "Detective Whirt told us you were abducted when you were a child? Close to Josie's age? Is that right?"

"Yes, I was, and I returned home safely," I said calmly. I knew what they needed to hear.

"And the guy who took you, it wasn't ransom or anything? He was just a random nut?"

"That's right."

"Do you think that's what's happened? They told us they thought it would be ransom, but we haven't heard anything at all. We're ready to give them whatever they want but there's been no contact—" Louis rambled on before Melanie interrupted.

"I mean, was it... horrible? It makes me sick thinking of what Josie is dealing with, she's only seven... Oh my God!" She started to hyperventilate. Moran handed her a glass of water and a small white tablet.

Before I could ask, he said, "Ativan. The last one was five hours ago."

I wasn't about to tell Melanie Vance the truth about my life with James Tibbs. No need to mention the darkened bunker he had built below his house, the restraints bolted to the wall to keep me from moving freely, the erratic and terrifying behavior that ruled my days and nights for years.

"It was difficult and at times scary. But children are resilient and stronger than we think. And I'm sure Detective Whirt told you, those cases are quite rare." I tried to sound reassuring.

I saw John Grice arrive and signaled for him to wait for me in the foyer. As I excused myself, I heard Whirt placating Louis. John looked as if he had been cast in a movie as an FBI agent. Tall and athletic with a military-style haircut and a well-tailored gray suit, he was as straight an arrow as I had ever met. We were also vastly different in our world view; he was an Evangelical Christian with very conservative ideas about everything. I secretly suspected that he thought a woman should not be the head of anything, anywhere, let alone the FBI CARD team. He had three homeschooled kids and a pretty, stay-at-home wife; they lived in Simi Valley, in a new development where every house was like a cookie cutter copy of the next. We worked well together, when he wasn't angling for my job.

"I just met the parents; they're both wrecked. Their distress seems sincere."

I looked back at Melanie and Louis who sat side by side in silence, clutching each other's hands.

I continued, "The mom is medicated. He's got diverse business dealings; we have to dig deep into that area. It was organized. There's nothing at the crime scene and nobody saw anything."

"So, the offender's done it before?" John concluded.

"I think so. If he's an amateur, then he's incredibly lucky. And I don't believe in this kind of luck. C'mon, I'll introduce you."

We returned to the living room, they exchanged greetings, and I saw immediately that Louis felt more confident with a male agent. Grice picked up on it also and immediately kicked into his "just-between-us-man-to-man" act that I had seen so many times when he thought he could turn the advantage his way. It didn't matter to me; whoever got the best information was my priority. I took Ryan in tow when Moran offered to show us the way to the guest house that would be our command center, proudly pointing out the features of the property.

"There are three guest houses—this path here leads to the Sparrow's Nest, that's the name of the one you will be using. There are several fruit trees, plums, figs, citrus as well as a koi pond."

His commentary struck me as odd; a child was missing, and he sounded like a real estate agent making a sale. I made a mental note; possible red flag.

At the Sparrow's Nest, we found the rest of the team setting up. I began putting up photos on the whiteboard: Josie, her parents, household staff, everyone in her orbit, so we had all of their faces right in front of us. I arranged them in a specific order, one inch apart with a two-inch margin between rows. I arranged my work area in the same way. Laptop, multicolored Post-it notes, two yellow legal pads to the right of it. A pencil caddy with six mechanical pencils and six Hughes gel stylus pens, all blue ink. A new ChapStick and bottle of chamomile eye drops from Mexico that Dolores picked up for me. Everyone knew not to move or mess with my workspace.

I introduced Ryan who filled everyone in on the steps taken so far. Along with a handful of county sheriffs and Redondo Beach police, we had fifteen Federal agents in all: Grice, Diaz and I who specialized in crimes against children; two data analysts that could hack any server; field agents; liaisons with the National Center for Missing and Exploited Children; forensic technicians; agents to record, track and analyze any phone calls from the kidnappers; and a polygraph expert. A profiler from the Behavioral Analysis Unit was waiting for the word from us once we had a better idea of what we were dealing with.

"Okay, Detective Ryan has given you the overview of what's happened so far. We need to triple-check locals who are on the sex offender registry, anyone with a past conviction or charge for crimes against children, against the national database. We'll revisit the interviews with park employees and visitors. Grice and I will get statements from the family and staff here and as soon as we are done, Paul will conduct the polygraphs. Marty and Lila, I need you to pull anything you can from Josie's bedroom and bathroom for her DNA. Mr. Moran, has anyone been in her bedroom since she went missing?"

"The housekeeper, Miss Muñoz, dusts and vacuums daily and of course Mrs. Vance has been in there."

I would have preferred if her room had been sealed. We still didn't know enough about the family to give them free rein, even in their own home. But clearly Whirt and the local police had been careful in how they dealt with the Vances. Grice was dispatched to handle Louis' interview as well as the house-keeper and gardening staff. I would take Melanie, Moran and Elsie but first, I needed to see Josie's room.

I climbed the winding stairway and saw a big glittery "J" on the door. It was a little girl's dream room, with a big bay window that looked out to the ocean and neatly organized shelves of toys and books. There was a cloud effect on the ceiling, all fluffy Poly-Fil strung through with lights to make it look like the sky. But what really caught my attention were the balloons. There were four of them, in varying states of helium fill, beginning to sink towards the floor. All characters from popular children's movies and cartoons.

Helium balloons, trapped in the trees at the park...

I slid open the closet door, ran my finger along the color-matched outfits hanging there, in perfect order, all her little shoes lined up. So different from the jumble of clothes in my own girls' bedroom. I caught my reflection in a large mirror. I saw myself, at fifteen, returning to a room very much like this one.

When my dad took me up to my bedroom, I started to cry. I wasn't happy, not the way I thought I would feel. I felt sick to my stomach. My dad showed me how they had kept all my clothes, even though they wouldn't fit now. I looked at all those small dresses, those little jackets and stuffed animals. Why were they still here? I was not that little girl. I was damaged and broken and struggling to put one foot in front of the other, even if I was physically safe from Tibbs. He still cast a long shadow over my life that day.

I asked if I could be by myself for a little while. I walked slowly around the room, picking up things, looking in drawers. Someone had bought a lot of new clothes for me, in fancy paper bags with handles. There was a new computer. I sat on the bed and took a deep breath. I was alive. My mother, Andrea, had died of cancer while I was with Tibbs. There was so much sorrow and loss in this big house. I was the miracle that could make everybody happy again. I stood up and looked at my reflection in the mirror.

I slapped myself and said my name, "Emily."

I slapped myself again. "Emily."

I did it again and again. My cheeks were red, my eyes stung and watered.

I kept slapping my face until welts started to rise. I couldn't have that. I undressed, turned on the shower and stepped into the warm spray. I breathed in the steam and calmed down. I could do this. I could fix everything for everybody...

I closed my eyes and took three deep breaths. When I looked again, I saw a thirty-eight-year-old woman staring back at me. Fair skin, some newer lines around my eyes, blond hair pulled up in a sensible twist. A dark blue suit and a starched white blouse, all grown up. But now I'd had three flashbacks since arriving on the case. Deep breaths, again.

You are not that powerless child any longer...

Turn on the light...

I bumped into our forensic techs, Marty Landon and Lila Scroff, on the stairway to Josie's room. Now that I'd seen the balloons in Josie's room, the ones I'd seen in the park could be connected to her disappearance.

"As soon as you finish, go back to the crime scene at the park, take one of the sheriffs with you and retrieve the balloons that are stuck in the trees right next to the area where they found Josie's bracelet. Get them down and send them to the lab immediately. It's just a hunch. And run this through as well," I said, handing them the evidence bag with the Little Golden Book inside.

I texted Whirt asking him to check to see if anyone had a birthday party scheduled at the park that day. Tables must be reserved through the local Parks and Recreation office; they would have a record. Then I met Elsie McBride in the library, a pentagon-shaped room with floor-to-ceiling bookcases. Each was filled with matching leather-bound volumes that appeared to come from Easton Press, where you can order the classics, as a kind of décor that also makes you look well educated. Elsie was fidgety, seated back in a deep leather sofa that made her appear smaller and younger than she was. Her feet barely scraped the Persian rug on the floor.

"First off, was there a birthday party of any kind in the park that day? Anyone with balloons?" I asked.

"No, the weather was getting crappy, it was gonna rain. I didn't see anyone with balloons but it's funny you ask 'cause Josie loves balloons. We pick up new ones every few days at the 99 Cents Only store down in Redondo."

"And why did you go all the way to Veterans Park?"

"We went to play on the ship, that's Josie's favorite jungle gym. She was playing and then she... was gone," she said, her eyes glued to her shoes.

"Malaga Cove Park is here in PV and with the threat of rain and the time of day, why wouldn't you stay closer to home?"

Now Elsie wrapped her arms around her rib cage and tucked her head into her chest.

"I didn't say anything to Louis and Mel, I know they'll fire me! But I have a boyfriend, David Follis, he's a dog walker. We meet at Veterans Park every Saturday 'cause that's where he takes his clients' dogs and Josie likes that park." She started to cry.

"I know this is hard, Elsie. Does David perhaps have something to do with this?" I prodded her gently.

"God, no! But I was talking to him in the grassy area. I must've looked away and I... didn't see her leave the playground area." She was sobbing as she tried to get her words out. "It's my fault, whatever happens to her! I think I'm going to throw up!"

She bolted into the adjacent bathroom, and I heard loud retching mixed with gulps of air and continued crying. Human frailty was so often at the center of tragedy. Elsie was a young woman who'd wanted to meet her boyfriend, they chatted, and she got distracted for a moment. But a moment was all it took. When she returned, she was pale, and her eyes swollen.

"I meet David there every Saturday he has clients near the park. I was showing him something on my phone and when I looked up, she was gone. We went immediately to look for her, I was sure she was on the jungle gym or climbing the slide. But she had just disappeared. It happened so fast. And then I called Louis and Mel and they called the police."

"And you didn't mention David to the police?"

"I didn't want him dragged into it and I didn't want to let them know that I was meeting him when I was working. It's my fault, they're going to blame me."

"And you go to the same park every Saturday afternoon, at the same time?"

"Between three and four p.m. That's when David is scheduled to take out the French bulldogs."

"How long have you been keeping this schedule?"

"About three and a half months, maybe four."

"And how long have you been getting balloons? You know, picking up fresh ones?"

"Since she watched *Coco* last year. I took her to the 99 Cents Only store, it was like a big adventure for her." She wiped at her tear-stained face. "Lou and Mel would never take her to a place like that. We went every week to get new balloons there. It was like a little guilty pleasure for her."

Several months of meeting in the same park at the same time. Even longer picking up helium balloons regularly, from the same store. It would have been quite easy for someone to follow them and learn these routines. I probed deeper into her relationship with the family, and she drew a picture of a little girl who had everything money could buy but parents who left the heavy lifting of childcare to the hired help.

Elsie got her up in the morning, had breakfast with her

and took her to school. Elsie picked her up and learned which girls she ate lunch with, what boy chased her around the playground, which yard monitors were tough. I sensed that Elsie's connection to the little girl was strong and genuine. She was going to live with the consequences of Josie's disappearance for a very long time. I got the contact information on David Follis and sent it to the other agents to follow up. As she stood to go, she stopped and turned in the doorway.

"You're going to find her, aren't you?"

I knew better than to make promises I wasn't sure I could keep and said, "We'll do our very best and we have a lot of resources. We'll know something soon, I'm sure."

She nodded and gave me a weak smile before closing the door behind her.

Moran entered a few moments later, holding a manila envelope. He chose a straight-backed chair to sit in.

"How long have you been with the Vance family?"

"I've been here for ten years. I handle everything related to the house, the staff, I organize all repairs and upkeep as well as coordinating the master calendar. I help with entertaining, caterers, florists, all of it. I've worked for several celebrities and high-profile clients," he said, handing me the manila folder which contained a list of his previous employers. I recognized some of the names. We were already running a detailed background check on him, like everyone else who worked for the family.

"And in your capacity as the house manager, I assume you are privy to a lot of the personal dynamics within the family." I paused a moment. "I know you've signed an NDA and it goes against everything you normally do here. But this isn't a normal situation. Can you tell me more about Louis and Melanie? What are they like as parents?" I kept my voice gentle as I looked him directly in the eyes.

"I've never spoken to the FBI before..." he said, his voice trailing off.

"Did you notice anything unusual, any tensions or disagreements over Josie, that type of thing?" I asked.

He cleared his throat nervously. "Well, they're both very busy with individual activities. Louis is a workaholic, and he golfs most weekends at the Rolling Hills Country Club. Melanie spends a lot of time on her charity work and her yoga classes..."

"Any indiscretions? Marital tensions?" I asked softly.

He pursed his thin lips, looked out the window, then said quietly, "Mr. Vance has been known to have a few... liaisons with women in his office. With... er ... quite young women, specifically. Mrs. Vance is aware of these infidelities and isn't terribly bothered by them. She is quite close to her yoga instructor, Mr. Jan Moerk. He owns the yoga studio. He's very... popular with the ladies in the area."

He flashed me a pained, anxious smile and clasped his hands together in his lap. His face had a sheen of sweat rising, along with a blush of embarrassment.

"I appreciate your candor, Mr. Moran, I know this can be uncomfortable. So, the domestic situation seems settled, from what you've described. No threat of separation or divorce or custody issues?" I asked.

"Oh, heavens no! Mr. and Mrs. Vance would never divorce or separate. There's too much money involved and then, of course, the scandal would be completely unacceptable. It's as you said, it's settled. And they both adore Josie. She's the glue that holds everything together."

"And what kind of relationship do you have with Josie?"

His expression tightened and his eyes suddenly filled with tears. "She's just an angel. The sweetest little girl. Even with all their money, she never acts spoiled or selfish. One day I was on my way to my niece's birthday and she heard me say that I'd forgotten to get a gift so she went to her room and gave me her new American Girl doll. It was still in the box..." His voice faltered. "It just makes me ill to think of what's happened to her."

I waited a moment, as he composed himself.

"And you? I mean, your personal life? I'm sure your schedule is very demanding. But any significant relationships with people who might be familiar with the Vance family?"

"I don't have time for a lot of outside friendships. I'm pretty much on call twenty-four seven and there's always something to be done here. I do have a long-distance relationship. I'm seeing a woman from Kazakhstan."

"That's pretty far away. How did you meet?"

"I went on one of those trips, where an agency arranges for you to meet eligible women who want a serious relationship. They go to the Philippines, Kazakhstan, Colombia. You meet women who are marriage-minded, not the type you meet in L.A., you know, the gold diggers and the wannabe actresses, all looking for a sugar daddy. Been there, done that."

I felt sorry for him. He was an odd bird, but I sensed that was it. He'd found his comfort zone; it takes a certain kind of person to orbit around a wealthy, demanding couple like Melanie and Louis Vance and be satisfied. His girlfriend's name was Zauresh Abdulov. I sent it to the team for another background check. There were connections all through that region of the world related to child trafficking. It wouldn't be the first time someone like Moran had been used to get to a target.

As Moran left the library, Grice stuck his head in to give me an update. The housekeeper and gardening staff didn't have anything significant to aid the investigation. Louis Vance admitted to his affairs, and we were running checks on all the women he'd been involved with.

He'd also had financial dealings with Russian entities and if he got mixed up with the wrong people, this could be payback for a deal gone sour. I was beginning to think that Josie's abduction might be part of something bigger.

"What time do you want to do the press conference?" Grice asked.

"By one p.m. We should arrange another air search and engage the community, get volunteers to canvass the neighborhood. See who shows up."

At that moment, Ryan ran in excitedly.

"The mail just arrived. There is a suspicious envelope, a bogus return address. It might be something."

Grice and I hurried to the Sparrow's Nest. One of our agents, Nick Diaz, had the day's mail in a large plastic bag.

"It feels like it contains something besides a letter. The return address is made up, there is no 2465 Main Street or Joeville, California. We're doing a mail trace right now," Diaz said handing me the bag.

I slipped on a pair of plastic gloves, pulled out the manila envelope and squeezed it. There was something inside, something pliable. I knew what it was before opening it. It was a small, pink stretchy bracelet. A pair to the one found on the walkway to the park.

Without running it through the lab, I knew it was Josie's. There was a folded piece of paper as well, standard letter size. It was a drawing, done with crayon, crude and childish. My hands trembled as I unfolded it, as if my brain registered the image before my eyes did. A little girl stood in front of a house, with a window, all simple straight lines. She was wearing a pink T-shirt with a tulip on it and pink leggings. She was holding balloons. It had arrived at the Vance home, mailed the same day that Josie went missing.

It was a power play. It was a taunt. I recognized the house in the drawing.

FIVE

DAY ONE: 10:47 A.M.

I stared at the drawing for several minutes in silence, not wanting to believe what I was looking at. I sent a quick text to our field agents and drew in a deep breath before I spoke.

"First off, this was mailed the day Josie went missing, so our guy obviously knows the family address, he's been stalking them."

Stephanie Leedom, one of our data analysts added, "It was processed at a post office in Victorville. On Greentree Boulevard. We're pulling the surveillance footage from the cameras inside, in hopes that it was dropped in a box at that location. We should have it within the hour. And if we can see anyone clearly, I'll send it over to FACE so they can run it."

FACE was the Facial Analysis, Comparison, and Evaluation Services Unit at the FBI. They ran facial recognition on captured images and photos related to open investigations and counterterrorism. They matched those to photos on government databases to identify potential suspects. I knew if there were any viable images, Stephanie would be able to find them.

She was a computer genius who had entered college at fifteen and graduated three years later. Brilliant, but lacking in the social skills of her peers, she preferred to sit at a computer screen, finding the things that people worked very hard to keep hidden. Prior to being recruited by the FBI, she had worked at a very discreet but powerful company that provided computer surveillance and protection to politicians and celebrities. Now twenty-six, she wore a conservative dark suit and pumps, but she still looked like she was playing dress-up with her mother's wardrobe.

"Victorville? That's the middle of nowhere. What is there in Victorville?" Ryan asked.

"Right-wing militias, trailer parks and meth labs," Grice responded.

"And a Black Bear Diner. Also, a drive-thru Krispy Kreme," Whirt added, living up to every stereotype of police dietary habits.

Victorville was a world away from Palos Verdes, both in distance and socioeconomics. If our kidnapper mailed the package from Victorville the day he took Josie, he had covered a lot of ground in a twenty-four-hour period.

"Clearly this drawing is of Josie. The clothing matches what she was wearing when she went missing. So, he's letting us know that he has her," I said.

"Yeah, and those balloons in the trees didn't come from a party. There was nothing scheduled that day. The head of Parks and Recreation just confirmed it," Whirt said, looking up from his phone.

"You think he lured her out of the park with balloons?" Diaz asked.

"Based on what Elsie McBride told us and now this drawing, I think that's probable," I said.

"If this was a targeted abduction, do you think it's a professional job? A group?" Ryan asked.

"I don't think a criminal organization would play this kind of game. It's too risky. I doubt there will be any trace evidence on the letter and then there are the specifics of the drawing," I said.

I was venturing into waters I did not want to enter. The house in the drawing was where James Tibbs held me captive. Same brick facade, same narrow flowerbed on the walkway. It was on a quiet street in Glendale, northeast of Los Angeles. Once a conservative, white semi-suburb, it had been an Armenian enclave for decades now, with strong ties to the Armenian and Russian mobs. James Tibbs had no connection to either. His parents had left him the house when they died and after a troubled youth, he became more and more disturbed with no one to supervise him.

"The house in the drawing is the house where I was held captive by Tibbs. I saw it immediately," I said as calmly as I could, scanning the room. I could sense their disbelief and shock, as well as a flicker of doubt.

"How did you see the outside? If you were, you know, held captive inside?" Ryan asked, clearly uncomfortable but curious.

"He would take me out occasionally in the middle of the night to run in the foothills."

"How did he let you run? Wasn't he afraid you'd escape?"

I paused for a beat before answering.

"He would put a dog collar on me and attach a Flexi-leash to it so I couldn't get away," I said, evenly, feeling the weight of the silence that followed.

Finally, Grice spoke. "That is a very common style of architecture here in California. Do you think it could just be a coincidence?"

His question made sense, but it was also the thing I dreaded the most. That my colleagues would think I was reading into it, that I was bringing my own past trauma to bear in a situation where it was unwarranted.

"The address is the same. It's the same house number of the Tibbs' home."

The house was in the background of the drawing, the little girl was up front and center. But in dark-colored crayon, the faint numbers 1571 were visible. Just barely. But they were there. Whirt leaned in closely to look at it.

"I'll be damned," he whispered.

"Should we send someone out to check on that house? I mean, just in case?" Ryan asked.

"Already done," I replied, tersely. "Two of our field agents are on their way to Glendale now."

"It was burned to the ground. Tibbs did it, to destroy any evidence. And he did a damn good job, there was nothing left," Whirt said.

"The house built on that lot belongs to an older couple, the Beglarians. I doubt Josie's kidnapper has any connection to them," I said.

"How do you know? About the couple, I mean?" Diaz asked.

"Because I keep track of things related to that part of my life."

"If he had a connection to them, he'd be steering us right to him," Ryan said. "So, he's using it as a provocation?"

"A copycat?" Grice suggested.

"Maybe." I shrugged.

"In that case, we need to arrange security for your family. Your two girls could be targeted next," Grice said.

I felt as if I'd had the wind knocked out of me. He was right. My daughters were at risk. How had this suddenly spun so far out of my control?

"Could we please keep them undercover until I have a chance to speak to my husband? I don't want him to come home from work to an obvious police presence with no idea why," I asked.

"I'll handle it, discreetly," Diaz said, stepping away.

"It's been over twenty years and all the evidence is in the

LAPD archives. How would a copycat get access?" Whirt asked.

"There were a few books published about the case and a lot of media coverage that could be found online," Grice offered.

I had seen all the magazines and tabloids at the time, and I knew about a couple of self-published true crime books by amateur sleuths. The Vance case had taken a sharp swerve into territory I never expected just a few hours ago. I felt nauseous again.

"Do we think he's still in this area?" Ryan asked; the postmark from Victorville had widened our search area considerably.

"He could've had an accomplice, maybe never even set foot in Victorville. If this guy is playing with us, there will be more messages from him. Stephanie, see what you can get from the 99 Cents Only store in Redondo Beach, on Ruby Ave. Who they get their helium balloons from, possible lot numbers, any sales records for the day she was taken," I said.

"On it," she said without looking away from her screen.

Her counterpart, Izzy Doqui, was deep in a search of bank records and Louis Vance's Russian business contacts. He was a soft-spoken African American man in his forties who wore a Mr. Rogers-style cardigan every day and always had a full coffee mug perched at his left elbow. He moved through the world quietly; his manner belied his mental and emotional fortitude. His area of expertise was the dark web. If there was dirty money being moved, illegal drugs or human trafficking, he would find them. He was one of the backbones of our team. I knew better than to ask him how it was going; when he had something he'd let us know.

Our media liaison began making calls to arrange the press conference, Grice set to organizing the ground and air searches immediately. I checked in with Jeff Edmonson, our unit chief, and updated him. I made several copies of the drawing, then sent the original off to the lab. I also copied in the criminal profiler from the Behavioral Analysis Unit, Justine Reyes. We needed to figure out everything we could about the person who took Josie and sent the drawing. But if he was a James Tibbs copycat, I knew more about him than anyone should.

SIX

DAY ONE: 12:37 P.M.

"What do you think it means? If they have Josie, why haven't they contacted us? Why play these mind games if they want money?" Louis asked when I told them about the package. Melanie looked sick, like she might start heaving at any moment.

"A certain type of offender likes to toy with the victim's family, but it's better for us when they do. They eventually leave a clue that helps us find them. We're getting some kind of communication and that's a good thing," I tried to reassure them.

"But why not just ask for what they want? It must be money if they targeted Josie. When are we talking to the press? To get this out there?" Louis pushed on, wanting to take action, as if it were a business deal stalled in negotiation.

Melanie spoke quietly, almost to herself. "I can't stand it that whoever it was knows our address, was watching Josie and knew her schedule. We had no idea, and they were out there, watching and waiting!"

I sat beside her and took her hand; she squeezed hard, crushing my fingers together.

"I know it is just a small step, but we will know a great deal more very soon. We've moved the press conference up and we'll do it within the next hour," I said before excusing myself.

The forensic techs had retrieved the balloons from the park and sent them to the lab. Both Louis and Melanie had passed their polygraphs and had solid alibis, so they were eliminated as suspects. Melanie's yoga instructor had been in Copenhagen for the past month. We were still waiting for complete information on the women Louis had had affairs with, but their involvement seemed unlikely. All were low-level office employees and so far, none of the affairs had been more than a few fleeting hook-ups.

Grice had arranged the ground and air searches; they would take place right after the press conference. Our media liaison had prepped Melanie and Louis—she would do most of the talking, using the distraught mother to appeal to the kidnapper. Louis would back her up as the strong, stoic father. The chiefs of police for both Redondo Beach and Palos Verdes had arrived to show a unified front. Grice and I led the group out to the gates of the house where the media were assembled.

As we approached the microphone, Grice leaned in and whispered, "Do you want me to handle this, Emily? I know the similarities to your case are a lot to deal with."

"No, I'm fine, John. This is my job," I said, with a discernible edge.

Grice nodded and backed off.

The reporters began shouting questions as I stepped up to the microphone.

"I'm Special Agent Emily Ray with the FBI CARD team; this is my colleague Special Agent John Grice. We are working with local law enforcement on the disappearance of Josie Vance. She went missing from Veterans Park in Redondo Beach on April twenty-second at approximately 4:30 in the afternoon. We are asking anyone who has not yet spoken to the police to come forward if you have any information. Josie is seven years old, with honey-blond shoulder-length hair. She has blue eyes and was last seen wearing pink leggings, a pink T-shirt with a tulip design on it and pair of silver, light-up sneakers," I said, calmly.

I had given a version of this speech so many times, holding a hungry group of reporters at bay.

"Is there any indication of who might have taken her? Or how she went missing?" shouted a reporter named Jess Almanzan from the *Los Angeles Times*. I was familiar with a lot of the faces in the crowd.

"As I said, we have a lot of evidence to go through, but we are confident we will know more within the next few hours."

"Has there been a ransom demand?" asked an on-air reporter from KTLA. I saw Larissa Cinque trying to hold her own, being pushed aside by older, more experienced journalists.

"Not as of yet."

"Do you think you were brought into this case since it bears a resemblance to your own kidnapping years ago?"

I recognized the person asking. It was Belle Zerlin, a bottom-feeder from the local Fox News, always looking for the most sensational angle, regardless of relevance.

"Not at all. I am the supervisory agent in charge of this CARD team on every case that we handle."

I nodded to Larissa Cinque who had her hand up like a kid in school.

"Have the family been cleared of any suspicion?" she asked.

Before I could answer, Louis stepped up and grabbed the microphone.

"I want to be very clear, my wife and I had absolutely nothing to do with our daughter's disappearance. We endured being polygraphed and interviewed by the police and the FBI as if we were criminals!" he said angrily, then continued, "We are offering a reward of ten million dollars for Josie's safe return, no questions asked. We just want our daughter back. We are ready to pay whatever it takes."

Before anyone could toss out any more questions at him, I took the microphone, and Grice guided him back to his spot next to Melanie. He started to protest, but Grice's firm grasp on his shoulder stopped him.

"The family are not considered suspects and Mrs. Vance would like to say a few words," I said, offering the microphone to Melanie, hoping she would seem more sympathetic than Louis had.

"We just want to say to Josie, if she can see this, that we love you very much and we are waiting for you to come home. If someone has her, please let her come back to us. She is the most important thing in our lives," she said, speaking very slowly.

The Ativan had kicked in, she seemed unfocused and distracted. We needed to get both parents away from the press immediately. They were hurting their own case in the court of public opinion and the internet would explode with criticism. Louis came across as an entitled jerk who thought money could solve everything, Melanie seemed like the wealthy housewife deep into her pharmaceuticals. The offer of ten million dollars with no questions asked would trigger a glut of calls from people who had nothing to do with the case, hoping for a cash windfall. I cut the press conference short. We had nothing concrete to tell them and the fewer questions the better. Back inside the house, Louis was pacing.

"Why did you guys cut me off? I wanted them to know more about the reward. It will draw the kidnappers out!" he spat.

I took a moment to check myself before answering. "No, it will not. It'll make every nutcase who thinks they can bluff their way into a fortune call our phone lines with false information. And we will have to check out every 'tip' that comes in, drawing time, energy and manpower from this investigation. We have a protocol that we follow, and you need to get on board with that, Mr. Vance."

"Why can't you let them do their jobs, Lou? This isn't about you. You can't fix this just by writing a check or strong-arming people. Now you've made things worse..." Melanie's voice broke off as tears overcame her.

"I'm sorry, I don't know what to do, I just don't know," Louis replied, his voice breathless and full of panic as he stormed out of the room, with Moran in close pursuit.

I sensed a breakdown was coming and he was too proud to have any of us witness it. I felt for him. Mothers are expected to fall apart if their children go missing, fathers have the special burden of trying to remain strong in the face of abject terror. I signaled for Grice to follow him and try to ease the situation.

We needed the grid search to yield something, anything we could work with. I would go up in the helicopter; I had grown up in the area and knew the layout of Redondo and PV. While driving to Torrance Memorial Hospital to use their helipad, I called Antonio.

"Hey, Em. How's the case?"

"Did the girls get to school okay?"

"Yeah, they were excited, they're making kites in class today."

"Kites? We can take them to Hahamongna Park to fly them, maybe this weekend. So, there were no issues or anything?"

"Issues? Like what?" he asked.

"Nothing. I just worry when I'm away from home on a case," I said.

"How's it going?" he asked again. He knew me so well; he sensed something was up.

"Okay. Not a lot to work with. But the decision was made to have a protective detail at our house," I said, trying to sound as calm as possible.

"We're having a security detail? At our home? What's going on?" he asked, alarmed.

I paused, knowing this would trigger a conversation about my work with CARD and the emotional toll of it.

"The kidnapper sent a message, with a drawing that has a reference to my kidnapping. So, we think it might be a copycat and to be extra safe, we're having security for the time being."

A longer pause. Then, "Okay. I'll tell Dolores so she knows when she gets them from school. I'll also let the school office know. But how are we going to explain it to the girls? If there are FBI agents on the property?" he asked, anxiously.

"They'll be stationed outside. And I'll figure out a way to explain it that's not scary. I've asked Diaz to make sure they're very low-key, not to make it obvious."

"Good. *I* find it kind of scary, to be honest. How're you doing with this?"

"Okay. A few flashbacks, nothing major."

"I have to get back to the lab, we'll talk later. Are you coming home tonight?"

"No, I'm going to have to stay out here. I'll be working late, and it will just be easier. I'll book a room at Terranea," referring to the resort in Palos Verdes.

"I figured as much. I'm taking the girls to an outdoor movie tonight over at the high school. I guess we're going to have some people tailing us?"

"Yes, but no one will know. The bureau's good at this type of thing," I said.

"So, I'll just keep an eye out for guys who look like Mormons in blue suits with brown shoes," he said with a small laugh.

"I'll make this okay. I promise," I said.

"I know you will. Better safe than sorry, right?" he reassured me.

"How was the rover?" I asked.

"Just a few small glitches but it should be operational within a few months," he said casually as if designing space rovers was as easy as mowing the lawn.

"Can you send me a video of the test?"

"Sure, I'll do it now," he said, and I could hear the smile in his voice.

We hung up with a promise to talk later, before bed. This was the first time there had been any kind of a threat to me or my family. I had always felt so safe behind the firewall of the FBI and the power it projected.

I arrived at Torrance Municipal Airport, next to the hospital. The helicopter was waiting. As we ascended, I looked out the window at the familiar streets below. I had to spot something that had been missed. Failure was not a possibility I could consider.

SEVEN

DAY ONE: 4:41 P.M.

By late afternoon, my optimism was flagging. The helicopter search was a dead end. No suspicious bundles hidden behind dumpsters in alleyways. No abandoned cars in gullies or ravines. Moran's girlfriend turned out to be nothing more than a pretty girl who was desperate to marry an American with money and get the hell out of Kazakhstan. One possible lead came from a woman who called in and said she and her granddaughter may have seen Josie at the park. I would meet with her on my way to the hotel.

The only thing we learned from the balloons was that they came from China, the distributor was in downtown L.A. and that batch had been sent to several 99 Cents Only Stores and numerous street vendors who were spread out over Los Angeles and the South Bay. No one at the Redondo Beach 99 Cents Only store remembered someone buying helium balloons the day Josie went missing, and their security cameras confirmed it. Which meant our kidnapper could have bought them anywhere.

As I catalogued my notes, Izzy Doqui approached me.

"Find anything, Iz?"

"No. Vance's business dealings have been above board. He works with some shady players, but nothing jumps out as a deal gone bad. And Josie's not turning up on any of the child trafficking sites on the dark web. I dug real deep but there's not even a whisper of her," he said.

"So, what's bothering you?" I could tell he was unsettled.

"It just doesn't fit, there's something not right. Something we're missing."

I felt the same thing, a gnawing discomfort, a sixth sense that we were not seeing something right in front of us. The team would be heading home in a few hours but that didn't mean our work would stop. Each of us would continue, catching a few hours of sleep when we could. Diaz would stay on at the command center with two Redondo PD detectives. Two of our agents, Paulson and Mills, would stay to monitor the wiretaps on the Vance home, in case a call came through in the middle of the night.

I stood at the picture window in the Sparrow's Nest, looking out at the ocean as the sun went down, painting the sky in vibrant orange and pink. As a kid, I remembered thinking that the sunsets at the beach looked like the swirling colors of ice cream push-ups that we would buy from the truck that came by regularly, its off-key, tinkling music like a siren song to all the kids in the neighborhood.

I knew Melanie and Louis were facing down a special kind of terror, another night of not knowing where their daughter was. When the sun is up, high in the sky, hope is easier to hold onto. But nightfall is different. That hope extinguished a little more with each passing minute, as the colors of the sky turn to deep purple and the darkness moves in. Josie was out there, alone and afraid. I knew that feeling, I remembered the fear that I would never escape that darkness.

I stepped into the memory that had haunted my dreams for the first few years after my captivity; it had been my nighttime companion, staking out its territory even with the sleeping pills and anti-anxiety medications that Lydia had prescribed me.

It was late at night. When I heard his footsteps descending, I pretended to be asleep. He sat in silence next to me for a moment and then he carefully took my wrists and unlocked them from the metal cuffs that restrained me. I didn't move. He was crying, whimpering quietly. Then he left. I heard the van start up and pull out. I stayed there, immobile for several minutes, afraid that it was a trap. Then I smelled the smoke.

I sat up and rubbed my wrists, ran my hands over my close-cropped, patchy hair. I knew I had to get out, this might be my only chance. I stood up on wobbly legs.

I crouched, scurrying toward the staircase to the bunker. He had left the hatch to the bedroom above open. The heavy bookcase that usually blocked it had been moved aside. Once I was in the main house, I saw my reflection in a mirror. I looked like a blond scarecrow, a crazy child-demon from a horror film. The smoke was coming from somewhere down the long hallway, near the front of the house. As I hurried toward the front door, I saw the crackling fire churning and growing. I passed the doorways to the other rooms, the curtains and cardboard boxes were going up in flames. I smelled gasoline. The house was burning.

I couldn't see the front door; it was cloaked in smoke that mush-roomed out from the living room. I ran toward the back of the house; the heat from the flames grew stronger. As I passed a bedroom stacked with boxes, I saw one window with no security bars. I climbed over those boxes, kicking them aside. I made it to the window. I shoved it open and climbed out; the fire surged like a Chinese dragon and roared down the hallway. I was outside, in the cool evening air.

I was free.

The neighbors were asleep, no one had yet noticed the house, smoldering and about to erupt. I hurried along a tall hedge and into a narrow alleyway. I ran on broken concrete and gravel and shattered glass, but I didn't care. I was free and I was running as far as I could from the hell I had lived in for so long. I heard the sirens of approaching fire engines in the distance. And then a loud booming sound—I knew it had to be the house exploding. Smoke rose in big, billowing clouds, I heard more sirens from a different direction.

The sky was as black as obsidian with a smattering of faint stars. I looked around the quiet neighborhood, the modest houses with the porch lights on, the cars parked peacefully in the driveways. Who would have suspected that a child was held captive for years behind one of those doors? A car cruised by and seemed to slow down, then turned into a driveway. I felt exposed out on the street alone. I ran toward the foothills, where the pavement ended, and the county fire roads began. I kept running until I was lost, surrounded by scrubby bushes and droopy willow trees, boulders and fallen logs.

All that night, I heard the packs of coyotes howling and yipping as they chased down prey. I smelled the wild sage and felt the damp of the marine layer settle over me in the early morning hours. Somewhere in that dark night I made a decision that would change everything...

I shut my eyes and my mind against the recollection. I snapped the rubber band on my wrist, to bring me back to the present. The sky was darker now, the cover of night fell heavy here at the ocean's edge.

Agent Justine Reyes of the BAU arrived within the hour

and assembled our team. As usual, she was impeccably dressed, her black hair in a high, slicked-down ponytail, dark brown eyes behind tortoiseshell glasses. I had worked with Reyes before, on a kidnapping in Scottsdale, Arizona when six-year-old Jumila Robinson had been snatched from her aunt's front yard in broad daylight. After several days, we had the worst possible outcome; Jumila's body was found in a ravine at a nearby state park. Reyes had young daughters also—she and I had bonded over that harrowing case.

Reyes cleared her throat after making her introductions and spoke in her unflappable, slightly nasal voice. "We are dealing with a highly organized offender; he's been very good at evading surveillance and leaving no trace evidence whatsoever. This could mean that he has experience in law enforcement and, at the very least, this isn't his first abduction. He knows what we'll be looking for and he's left us no clues at the crime scene, which takes skill, knowledge and preparation."

I felt a slight shift in the room; no one ever wants to think that it could be one of us.

She continued. "The message and drawing sent to the family is a provocation, directed at the FBI and specifically at Agent Ray. How this perp got access to information on a case from twenty years ago raises the possibility that it's someone with access to the LAPD archives or someone very adept at searching for information online. Again, highly organized, this was a planned abduction. He had to have been stalking the family and the fact that there has not been a quick ransom request means that it might well be about something else."

"Like what?" asked Ryan.

"Payback, revenge, resentment. He clearly wants to show us that he has the upper hand, hence the taunt of sending Josie's bracelet. He has some issue with law enforcement and perhaps with Emily specifically. We need to review all of her previous cases to see if there could be some link to someone who has a grudge against her. A family member of an individual who has been incarcerated or died while in prison, perhaps an accomplice or perpetrator that was not apprehended. Or someone recently released."

"Do you think he wants attention?" Ryan asked.

"Yes. With this kind of perp, who sends messages, risks being caught, there is an element of power. And ego. He wants credit, he wants recognition that he does not get in his everyday life."

She shot me a sympathetic glance as she went on, "We can't ignore the fact that Josie Vance is very similar in many ways to Agent Ray as a child. She lives in the same neighborhood, comes from a wealthy family, is an only daughter. Josie could well be a substitute or stand-in for you, Emily. This guy could fancy himself the keeper of the flame, so to speak, carrying on Tibbs' legacy, continuing his 'work.' Which means he has also been doing his research on your background and life."

She was right; I just hated hearing her say it out loud. Suddenly it was becoming all about me.

"Is it safe for Emily to stay on this investigation?" Grice asked.

"It is imperative that Emily stay front and center on this case, especially if he's a Tibbs copycat with some personal agenda. She's the bait, so to speak, to keep him reaching out. We need him to make a mistake."

"There's something else," I said. "The book that was found in the parking lot was a favorite of mine as a child. Tibbs had a copy of it at the Glendale house. At one point, I colored one of the bears in the book with a blue crayon. The book we found has a blue bear on that page as well."

"Could it be a coincidence?" Grice asked.

"The same book, the same page, the same color? I don't think so. It's intentional," I said.

The room was silent for a few beats. I glanced at the others, knowing this information was revealing more of my own dark history. I never wanted the team to know the details of my time with Tibbs. I needed them to see me as competent and in charge, not a helpless child or a traumatized adult.

"So, what kind of guy are we looking for?" Whirt asked.

"He's in his thirties or even forties, old enough to be patient and play the long game. Most likely a guy who doesn't attract a lot of attention from anyone. He has a menial job, possibly on disability. He lives alone or perhaps with an elderly parent. He feels stuck, has grandiose ideas of his talents and capabilities and blames others for his lack of success and/or recognition. He has dysfunctional relationships with women and targets children since they are easier to control."

"Race?" asked Ryan.

"Most likely white because he didn't attract any attention being with a little white girl when he took her. I don't think it's his first abduction, so we need to look into disappearances of young girls and teens in the South Bay and perhaps greater L.A. County. He could prey upon kids who have run away or have no strong parental supervision—the easy targets."

"How does the profile change if he's one of us? In law enforcement?" Ryan asked.

"Then we're dealing with someone with a specialized skill set. He could be someone who aspired to join the FBI and didn't make it. He could work in any area of law enforcement, maybe felt he didn't get the accolades or opportunities he deserved. He could have a grudge against women in positions of power."

"What about the Victorville angle?" Ryan asked.

"I think he's familiar with that area. He chose Josie specifically, perhaps because of the similarities to Emily, so he may have come out here just to get his target. Tibbs lived in Glendale, miles from Palos Verdes. We have to consider that a copycat may be taking that same page from the Tibbs playbook."

"So, we need to expand to the Victorville area and do a door-to-door in the neighborhoods adjacent to the post office that stamped the package. And check all the CCTV footage available," I said.

"Yes. Same with running checks on sex offenders out there, crimes against children, convictions or arrests. The fact that we've turned up nothing here in PV and adjacent areas might mean that he grabbed Josie and jumped on the freeway immediately, like Tibbs did with you," Reyes said.

My mind was racing, and I steadied myself before speaking. "I ordered up digital copies of the case files from my kidnapping. Stephanie has pulled up all the media coverage so she'll be forwarding that to everyone so you can all get familiar with it as we move forward. Let's reach out to the Victorville and Hesperia police departments to help us liaise with those neighborhoods, and we need to cross reference with the Center for Missing and Exploited Children to see if we can find anyone who might have been an earlier victim of this guy."

"Sorry this one hits so close to home," Reyes said as everyone filed out and she packed up her laptop.

"Thanks. It's very weird," I replied.

"What kind of sick creep tries to copy a crime from twenty years ago?" she asked.

Someone stuck in the past. Someone who knew my weakest point and how to use it. This case had become personal in the worst way.

EIGHT

DAY ONE: 7:27 P.M.

I arranged to meet the grandmother from Veterans Park before checking into the Terranea Resort. Her name was Marilyn Lenic. The address was for a vintage bungalow close to the Redondo Beach Pier. Most of the older homes had been leveled to build new condos and apartment buildings but every few blocks, one of the original houses had managed to escape developers. Marilyn Lenic's house was whitewashed with a pretty garden and a wraparound porch. There were geraniums hanging in pots and a hand-painted sign that read "Life is Better at the Beach." Not today, it wasn't.

I knocked on the door and a moment later it was opened by a woman in her sixties with her gray hair pulled back into a long braid. She wore a loose-fitting dress with an East Indian print, long dangly earrings.

"You must be Agent Ray from the FBI, come on in. I'm Marilyn and that's my granddaughter, Molly Lenic," she said, pointing to a little girl playing with Play-Doh at the dining room table.

The house smelled of incense, and bouquets of dried herbs hung from the window overlooking a small yard.

"I wanted to follow up with you on what Molly saw at the park?" I asked, not wanting to linger or make small talk. I had a long night of work ahead of me.

"Yes. Molly, can you come here for a minute?"

The little girl came over, still kneading a ball of bright green Play-Doh. "You want to know about the man in the park, right? That's what my grandma said." Her eyes darted nervously from Marilyn to me.

"That's right. I'm just curious about what you saw," I said, sounding as casual as I could.

"I was on the slide, up at the top, and I saw a man talking to the girl from the news. They were by the tall bushes, near the parking lot. He had balloons with him, and I think she wanted one," Molly said.

My pulse quickened. We had a witness; the tall slide gave Molly a vantage point to see what was not easily visible from the ground.

"Why do you think she wanted a balloon?" I asked.

"Because I saw him hand one to her as I started down the slide."

"Did you see them again? Did they get in a car?"

She shook her head, anxiously. "I went back up to the top of the slide, but they were both gone."

"Did you see what he looked like, at all?" I trod lightly.

"No. He wore a baseball cap like my dad does and a mask like we had to for COVID," she said.

"Do you remember if he was tall or short? Fat or skinny? Maybe what he was wearing?" I pushed a bit harder.

"He wasn't fat, he was about my dad's size. I don't remember what he was wearing," she said, squeezing the ball of Play-Doh.

"Was he alone or did he have any friends with him?" I asked.

"He was by himself and then they were both gone. Did he take that little girl?"

She looked scared, as if she had done something bad. I reached out and patted her arm to reassure her.

"We think he might have, and we're going to bring her back to her mom and dad. You've been a big help to us today, Molly. Thank you so much," I said with a smile.

"I have to use the bathroom," she said before sprinting down the hallway.

"Her dad is about five foot ten, medium build. I'm sorry we can't help you more," Marilyn apologized.

"Thank you for calling, every bit of information is useful. If Molly remembers anything else, please call me directly," I said, handing her my card.

Marilyn grasped my hand suddenly and held it tightly. "She is okay, she's still alive. I can feel it. She's somewhere, isolated. There are birds, a lot of birds... I'm psychic," she explained with a knowing smile.

This was just what I needed after a long day of work. An eccentric grandmother who believed she was psychic. But we had a witness who saw Josie and gave us a basic description of the presumed kidnapper. We had something to work with. I texted the information to the rest of the team.

On my way to the hotel, I wolfed down Dolores' tuna sandwiches. I arrived at the Terranea Resort, with my folders of files and an overnight bag. I had booked a room with an ocean view and now I opened the windows to let the cool, salty breeze in. I felt my tension level drop. Being near the sea always had that effect on me.

A hot shower helped rinse off the lingering frustrations of the day. I needed to clear my head in solitude. I wrapped myself in the fluffy white cotton bathrobe and settled in to review the case files on my own abduction. It was the last place I thought I would end up when the day started. The first file I opened had the press release from the day after I was taken.

The Palos Verdes Palmetto, April 12, 1992

Police are conducting a widespread search for the seven-year-old daughter of real estate investor/developer Michael Ray and his wife, Andrea. Their daughter, Emily Ray, is believed to have been abducted from the Malaga Cove playground while in the company of her nanny. Emily Ray is forty-four inches tall with shoulder-length blond hair and blue eyes. She was last seen wearing a yellow sundress, white sandals and carrying a monkey backpack. The Ray family has offered a multimillion-dollar reward for any information leading to her safe return. Ray's company, Cali Ventura Homes, has been behind the rapid spread of luxury-planned communities in Ventura, Thousand Oaks and Calabasas, California. Mr. Ray is also a controlling partner in a number of international investment companies. Contact the Redondo Beach or Palos Verdes Police Departments with any information.

A lifetime ago. Michael and Andrea Ray. She died while I was in captivity. She was like a character in a book to me, someone perfect and always there. But she was gone, and I remember crying about it at the time, but everything moved so fast after that. Returning home. Therapy. Private tutoring. The attempt to put me back together again, like Humpty Dumpty.

The case files contained nothing related to Tibbs; the detectives had no idea who he was until I escaped and told them. I combed through the press coverage following my reappearance. Magazine articles and newspaper stories about Emily Ray, the miracle child who came home. The *Los Angeles Times* ran a driver's license photo of Tibbs and now I stared at his dirty-blond, flat-top haircut and blunt features. He had a prominent forehead and two forceps scars on either side, telltale signs that a doctor had to help him out of the birth canal. He was in his mid-twenties in the photo. I felt strangely calm, looking at the faded newsprint photo of the monster who defined my childhood.

He was dead. He held no power any longer. But someone had found this nutcase fascinating enough to emulate him, to copy his brazen abduction of a child. Several of the articles contained information about the house where I was held, one ran photos of the quiet suburban street with images of it before he burned it down. Stephanie had included a handful of true crime websites that contained even more details, like the fact that my head had been shaved and there was a secret bunker built below the house. There was a glut of them to review. I hoped one would have some mention of *The Little Red Caboose* book so I could make that piece fit into a logical explanation. Otherwise, it was like something from *The Twilight Zone*.

There was a self-published true crime book about my case, written by a woman named Morgan St. Cloud. It was titled *Gone in an Instant: The Abduction of Emily Ray*. Stephanie had downloaded it on the flash drive. It was a tabloid-driven mash-up of my story. As I skimmed through it, I realized that St. Cloud had a lot of specific details that were not in other press coverage. Like the fact that I went to the morgue to identify Tibbs. Did she have a source and if so, who was it?

I ran a background check on her. Morgan St. Cloud was a pen name, her real name was Brenda Coombs. She lived in Lomita, quite close to Redondo Beach. She had to be in her fifties by now. One thing was clear: information on my case wasn't hard to find for Josie's kidnapper. The big question was why make contact directed at me? What could he possibly want?

I opened the video my husband sent me of his rover test. It looked like the mechanical creature in the animated movie,

WALL-E, with a lot of metal arms and a chassis with thick-treaded tires. It rolled with ease over the rocky terrain of the arroyo in Hahamongna Watershed Park next to JPL. As if on cue, my phone rang. It was Antonio.

"How's the hotel?" he asked.

"Great, like always. I just watched the rover video, pretty impressive," I said.

"Kind of cool, huh?"

"That's an understatement, Rocket Man. How're the girls? Did things go well at the movie?"

"Yeah, it was fun. The security guys were invisible, pretty much, and they're outside now."

"It's just a precaution. The kidnapper would have to be crazy to try and get to us," I said.

"Of course he's crazy, he took a little girl. But with the security system and Moose and everything, I agree. It'd be hard getting in here and now, we're all on high alert."

"How's Dolores taking it?"

"Please, she's like Ironman! She didn't bat an eye, she just grabbed the crowbar from the garage and made a pot of coffee for them."

I smiled at the thought of tiny, fierce Dolores, ready to defend everyone.

"I'm sorry for this. I didn't expect it to have anything to do with me," I said.

"Em, every one of these cases has everything to do with you," he said gently.

"I know. I'll be ready one day, I promise. I'll move on and leave it behind."

"When? How much longer are you going to put yourself through this?"

I remained silent. How could I describe the way I felt when another child had been taken by a predator? It wasn't rational, it wasn't just a job for me.

Then, as if he were reading my mind, he said quietly, "You can't save all of them, Emily."

"Once Josie is found, we'll have a serious talk about it. I'll take a leave from the bureau, and we'll regroup, okay? Nothing bad will happen to any of us," I assured him and myself. "This is just a mind game from a twisted fuck who wants to get under my skin."

"Em, I trust you and I know you'll do what's right. It's not just about safety, I worry about the toll it takes—"

He was interrupted by the sound of someone grabbing the phone and a moment later I was on FaceTime with my daughters.

"Mommy! We stole the phone from Daddy!" Juliana shrieked with a laugh.

"I didn't eat all my dinner, just the cheese and potatoes," Eliza said seriously.

"That's okay, honey," I said, shifting to my best happy mommy voice, putting on a big smile.

"We saw a movie on a big screen outside!" Juli said.

"And they made s'mores but they were gross," Eliza added.

"I wish I'd been there with you. I'm having to stay at work tonight, but I'll be back tomorrow. I want you to be extra careful and listen to what Daddy and Dolores tell you, okay? I'm working on a big case, and we have to take special precautions until it's over."

"Can we have bodyguards? Like BTS?" Eliza asked.

I looked questioningly at Antonio; he shrugged in bewilderment. BTS was very big in our house; my girls knew every detail about the Korean boy band.

"Would you like bodyguards? Like BTS?" I asked.

"Yeah! A guy like Mr. Lee, he's always with the members when they go out," Juli said, excitedly.

Antonio and I shared a smile; we were worried about the

security detail scaring them and now they wanted bodyguards like Mr. Lee. Suddenly, I was the cool mom.

"All right, I'll arrange that. They'll be outside the gates in the morning," I said.

"You rock, Mommy!" Eliza said and they burst into giggles. I saw Dolores enter with a plate of cookies and they bolted toward her. And just like that, with their six-year-old magic powers, they had diffused the guilt that had been weighing on me.

Antonio took the phone back. "It's the internet, Em. They're light years ahead of us."

"Look, if there's a way to make this fun for them, I'm all for it."

"Yeah, you and BTS. Okay, we've got to do baths and then story time. So, call me later, okay?"

"Will do."

"Love you."

"Love you more," I said, hanging up.

I went to the window. The ocean was jet black, the tide like a metronome, rolling in and out. My precious daughters were safe and warm, as all children should be after dark. What was Josie Vance doing right now? Away from her home, her pink bedroom with her stuffies and her cloud ceiling?

I read through a series of cases that I had worked, setting aside those that deserved a second review, to see if there could be a link to Josie's kidnapper. None of them jumped out. I felt the restlessness creeping over my body. The twitchy, anxious energy that had to be worked off. I changed into my workout clothes and laced up my running shoes.

I had to get out, to get away from the walls of the room and the files on the desk. I had to get away from my own thoughts and memories, from where this case was taking me. I ran out the front doors of the hotel into the damp, dark night.

NINE

DAY ONE: 9:18 P.M.

The streets of Palos Verdes were quiet. With few streetlights and no nightlife to speak of, I was alone, running along Palos Verdes Drive toward the Point Vicente Lighthouse. The homes along this stretch of highway were behind tall gates and long driveways, the only lights came from the houses above on the next tier of streets.

There were no sidewalks in PV, no McDonald's or Jack in the Box, no chain stores, apart from a Starbucks. Most of the people out during the day were white-haired, Republican retirees or wealthy moms pushing strollers in walking groups, decked out in hundred-dollar Lululemon leggings and the ubiquitous coffee frappé. But at this hour, they were all safely behind the locked gates of their homes.

I made it to Point Vicente Park and Interpretive Center, where the parking lot was empty. The park sat above a rugged hillside that led to a rocky beach. The grass was dotted with trees whose windswept limbs looked like arms reaching for an embrace. A car cruised slowly by and then pulled into the lot and cut its headlights.

Instinctively, I brushed my hand over my Glock, snapping

my holster open. Most likely they were just teenagers, looking for a quiet place to make out. Even though I was an adult now, I felt the fear creeping up on me. Once you have been someone's prey, it never leaves you. I knew how Josie's kidnapper must have driven these same streets, watching and waiting, like the car idling a few yards from me in the darkness. He had to be long gone by now. But what if he were still here, closer to home? What if he liked the game? What if he liked watching?

After a few moments, the car pulled out onto the paved street and disappeared. The chill of the sea air began seeping into my body. A hot shower would be perfect before diving back into work. Multiple daily showers were also part of my OCD. Standing in the warm water in a dark bathroom was oddly relaxing and delivered the emotional reset that I needed. I trotted back to the resort and as I crossed the lobby, a voice called out to me.

"Agent Ray!"

It was Larissa Cinque, seated at the bar. She must have been waiting for me. She approached, holding a tall glass of what appeared to be Coca-Cola.

"A soft drink, I assume? Whirt said you're still in college," I asked.

"Yes, it's Coke but I am legal drinking age. Turned twenty-one three months ago. I don't drink when I'm working," she replied.

"That makes two of us," I said. As much as I wanted to treat her with the usual suspicion that I reserved for the press, she was a nice kid. Clearly, she was putting in the extra effort to get a story and I liked her gumption.

"Detective Whirt mentioned that there were some significant developments today that have changed the course of the investigation. Are you willing to discuss those with me?"

I knew he wouldn't be able to keep his mouth shut, especially with a smart, pretty girl poking around for information.

She was just doing her job; he was a motormouth who probably thrived on the attention.

"No, I can't. Detective Whirt should have been more circumspect."

"I promised I wouldn't write about it yet, but he said there was communication with the kidnapper." She pushed a bit further.

Even worse, Whirt had leaked a major development. He might well have told her we suspected a Tibbs copycat. I had to gauge how much she knew.

"I'll level with you if you'll level with me. Exactly what has Whirt told you?"

"Just that there was a letter, a package from the kidnapper."

"Nothing else?" I asked, pointedly. I had no time for games.

"Nothing," she said, earnestly.

I sighed. "Yes, we had a communication from the kidnapper. We don't know exactly what it means yet, we don't know if he wants public recognition—"

"Like the Zodiac or the BTK killer," she interrupted me.

"Right. So, I would appreciate it if you don't run with that information just yet. I'll keep you in the loop, but I need your cooperation. Sometimes a leaked story can put a victim in danger," I cautioned her.

"Definitely. I'll wait until you give me the go-ahead. Also, do you think at any point you might be willing to discuss your own history as it relates to this case?"

She was smart and she knew she had leverage now. I had to offer her something to keep her from running with the information Whirt had given her.

"Perhaps. Once the case is solved, not before. When Josie is home safely and we have a positive outcome, I will consider it," I said.

"Okay. You have a deal!" she said, and I stepped into the

elevator. As the doors closed, I saw her practically skipping with excitement out to the parking lot.

I had just made a tentative agreement to discuss my past with a young reporter. Nothing about this case was unfolding as I had planned. I stripped down and stepped into the marble shower. The warm water hit my lower back, relaxing the muscles that had started tightening up after my run. I would call Lydia for a mental health check-in before resuming work. My phone rang loudly; I reached out to retrieve it from the bathroom counter. It was Diaz calling from the Vance home.

"Diaz? What's up?" I asked, turning the water off and wrapping myself in a fresh towel.

"We got a call from someone claiming to have Josie. The voice was electronically distorted. It came from an address here in Palos Verdes, over in the Rolling Hills area," he said.

"Did they speak to Louis or Melanie?" I asked.

"Yeah, they did great. Paulson and Mills were right there, coaching them, and they stuck to the script."

"I'll be right over. We will need backup from Redondo and Palos Verdes PD as well as a full SWAT team. Get someone outside the residence immediately to see if anyone comes or goes," I said.

"I'm on it," Diaz said.

"We're moving on this. I'll be there in ten minutes."

Closer to home, closer to home...

I pulled my wet hair back into a claw clip, threw a black cashmere sweater over a T-shirt and jeans and hurried out the door.

TEN

DAY ONE: 11:05 P.M.

I was at the Vance home within minutes. Along with Diaz, Paulson and Mills were present. I listened to the call several times. Grice was on his way from a nearby hotel.

"We have the little girl, she's safe but you need to pay two million dollars for her return. We will call back to let you know when and where to drop the money..."

"The voice distortion is weird, don't you think?" I asked.

"I agree. It's not a TruTone or Provox," Paulson replied.

"And he sounds like he's saying lines from a cop show on TV, you know? Very stilted," Mills added.

"The distortion bothers me. He also sounds hesitant when demanding two million, which is low, given the family. What do you think, Diaz?" I asked.

"There could be any number of reasons for the crappy voice distortion. Maybe he picked up a cheap one from some guy selling them out of his trunk, you know? No paper trail, no Amazon order. And maybe two million seems like a lot to him," Diaz said.

"But he must know they offered ten million. He's done his

homework. It just doesn't fit. I don't like things that don't fit," I said, half to myself.

"What do you want to do?"

"We have to hit the house, of course. It just bugs me, that's all."

"Criminals usually have a fuck-up at some point, maybe this is his," Diaz mused.

Izzy came into the room with a printout. "The house belongs to Janice and Keith Frank. They've lived there since 2012. It's held in a family trust. He's a real estate broker, she runs one of those pyramid scheme skin-care companies called Manon. They have no criminal records. They flew out of LAX on Sunday, their passports were stamped in Barcelona the following day."

Janice and Keith Frank didn't fit any part of the profile, but someone obviously had access to their house, possibly illegally. Maybe that had something to do with the other details that weren't quite right. Stephanie had prepared a grid of the neighborhood so we could plan our approach. Izzy handed me a detailed printout of the building plans that he had pulled up from the public records so we could see the layout of the rooms and possible exits. The agents stationed outside the Frank house reported no activity, a few lights on and a Toyota Highlander in the driveway.

Grice arrived and stuck his head in the doorway. "SWAT came in just behind me," he said.

A moment later we were conferring with Jared Stillman, the head of the South Bay SWAT team. He spread out the map of the area and the building plans for the house.

"We can come in through the front door, see what's going on. There are a lot of big first-floor windows, we can secure them ahead of time to prevent anyone escaping. Once we get in and clear it, your team can follow us," Stillman said. "And we can stage it in one of these open space areas."

Palos Verdes looked like a big nature reserve with houses on it; there were large swathes of open land and paths down to the beach and tidepools. We had a lot of options to set up our operation away from prying neighborhood eyes. While Stillman got his team up to speed, I stepped out onto the terrace to call Lydia.

"How's it going?" she asked.

"Moving. But it's a mind fuck, I have to say," I replied.

"What's going on?"

"A few flashbacks. And there's a link to me. The kidnapper sent a drawing of a little girl, standing in front of the house where Tibbs kept me." I didn't tell her about the book or the blue bear. She would've insisted I step away from the case when I knew very well that I couldn't. I didn't have the mental space for that conversation while waiting on SWAT.

"*What?* So, it's personal and directed at you?"

"I've been revisiting the files on my case, going over everything. It's just hard."

"When are you going home? I don't want you staying isolated, getting into that obsessive zone," she cautioned.

"Definitely going home tomorrow. Today was just a long, demanding day and right now we are waiting for SWAT."

"Okay, I want you to do some box breathing, just to help reset your nervous system. The four-two-six model, find a quiet spot and take that time for you."

We hung up and I remained on the terrace, facing the ocean. The mist off the waves rose up, carried on the wind. I remembered so many nights when I was a teenager and I would step out onto the balcony off my bedroom just to breathe in the damp, salty air. I inhaled for four counts, held my breath for two and then exhaled for a slow count of six. Hold for two. This was a box breathing pattern I had practiced for years. I repeated it, over and over, and felt my body relax. All I had to do now was wait.

An hour later, we were ready. Grice and I drove together.

"What do you think? I can tell you're bothered by something," he asked.

"I just don't like the details that don't fit. Clearly, we have to go in, but something just doesn't seem right. Maybe I'm overthinking," I sighed.

"Well, this is turning out to be pretty close to home for you. If you need some space, I've got your back," he offered.

I nodded silently. Maybe he thought I could take a nice, low-stress desk job in the Westwood offices of the FBI while he took over CARD. I wasn't going to give him that opportunity.

When we arrived at the staging area, the wind was picking up and it was noticeably colder than it had been earlier. Diaz arrived a few minutes after we did. Without a word, we all pulled on our bulletproof vests. We didn't need to talk; we had been in this situation many times. Tonight, we would find Josie and bring her home.

I kept repeating that mantra in my head as I checked my firearm, and we waited for the full SWAT team to assemble. Whirt paced anxiously, chain-smoking his Camel cigarettes while Ryan cracked his knuckles loudly. Stillman and his team arrived, and we followed as they made their way to the Frank house. They fanned out silently around the property, like a bunch of ninjas in a video game. Grice, Diaz and I hung outside the front door with Stillman, waiting for the go-ahead to announce our presence.

The wind whipped the eucalyptus branches, their sharp scent swirling around us. Stillman gave us the signal and two of his team hit the door with the ram. It sounded like a high-speed car crash, followed by the shouts of SWAT entering. In other parts of the house, they threw flash-bangs to disorient the inhabitants. They swarmed into the house, and we waited for Stillman's go-ahead.

I adjusted the grip on my gun, impatient to get inside. The

smell from the flash-bangs drifted out the door but there had been no exchange of gunfire.

Then we heard Stillman over the walkie-talkie: "All clear!"

I raced in but hadn't advanced past the foyer when he approached, furious.

"It's some fucking teenagers!" He spat the words out.

I brushed past him into the dining room to find four terrified high schoolers seated at the table in varying states of distress. Two girls were crying, and one boy was hyperventilating, his head buried in his arms. The other boy scanned the room nervously, completely shocked to see SWAT officers in full regalia surrounding him, and the FBI with guns drawn.

"Who are you?" I asked, holstering my gun.

"I'm Leo Frank... I live here," he stammered.

Diaz entered. "No sign of Josie, no sign that she's been here, ever," he said, shaking his head. Grice was right behind him, holding a small device that looked like a bullhorn.

"It's a voice distorter, the kind you win at the county fair," he said, setting it in front of me on the table. It was cheaply made, mass produced in China, no doubt. It had a series of buttons on the handle. I picked it up and spoke into it, my voice morphed into an almost unrecognizable babble.

"Did you make some phone calls earlier, Leo? You and your friends thought it would be funny? Act like the bad guys, like you had Josie Vance?"

"We were just joking around, and we thought we might get some of that reward money," Leo replied, his voice rising like a nervous piglet. One of the girls began to cry harder.

"You think this is a joke to her family? Her parents spoke to you on the phone, hoping they would get their child back tonight. You were *joking*?"

"We didn't think it would be like this, I mean, the fucking SWAT team broke the front door!" he whined.

"Of course they did!" I shouted. "You said you had a

missing child! What the hell is wrong with all of you?" I slammed my hand on the table. It made a loud slapping sound and the girls flinched.

Leo cowered, the boy with his head down looked up briefly through teary eyes and asked, "What happens now?"

"Now, you get charged with interfering with a federal investigation. Since you're minors, you'll be charged as juveniles, but you will go before a judge, and it will be on your record. Your parents will be contacted tonight," I said.

One of the girls wailed, "But that will ruin my chances of getting into Stanford! I can't have a charge on my record!"

"You all should have thought of that before you made that call. Consequences are a bitch."

"But you can't call my parents, they're in Spain on their second honeymoon. They'll kill me!" Leo moaned.

I stared at them for a beat, my heart thumping in my chest. These clueless kids, with no idea how the real world worked, were blubbering about getting in trouble and their college admissions while a little girl's life was at risk. I knew kids like this from high school, who never faced a single difficulty or dark moment without their parents stepping in to fix everything for them. They never knew fear or desperation or helplessness. I felt sick with anger.

"I can't... I just can't... Grice, will you handle them? I need to talk to the parents..." I said, rising to leave the room before I exploded.

I was on the edge, brought to that precipice by the events of the day. Diaz was on the phone with Leo's groggy parents in Spain, explaining to them that they had to return immediately. I heard loud protestations on the other end of the line and Diaz handed the phone to me.

"Are you the parent of Leo Frank?" I asked.

"Yeah, I'm his dad. What the hell is going on? Who are you? You can't just bust into my house!" Keith Frank shouted.

"I am Special Agent Emily Ray with the FBI Child Abduction Rapid Deployment team and yes, we can bust into your house when your son and his friends make a prank call pretending they have a kidnapped child."

"You better have a warrant!' he warned.

"I don't need one when a child is in imminent danger," I snapped back at him.

"My lawyer is Joseph Weiner. I'm calling him right now!"

"Go ahead. Your son is going to need him. Leo's being arrested and charged tonight. He will go before a judge in the next few days so I think you better come back to the United States, Mr. Frank. He is a minor and you are responsible for him," I said.

"You're kidding! You can't do this!" he protested.

"Sir, we are the FBI. We can do it and we are. And you may be financially responsible for the deployment of the local SWAT team that came out here in full force to respond to your son's actions," I said, before handing the phone back to Diaz.

I hoped they busted Leo's ass for it. But they wouldn't. They'd hire him a good lawyer and play the wealthy white kid card about how he'd never been in trouble before and this was a youthful lapse in judgment. It would be the same for all of them but at least tonight, I hoped they were shaking with fear. I didn't realize I was still holding the cheap voice recorder and in a moment of fury I threw it against the wall, shattering the handle and splitting it. I heard Grice's voice behind me.

"You okay, Emily?"

I took a deep breath before turning to face him. I couldn't let any more emotion show, I had already shown too much.

"I'm fine, John. Just really angry and thinking of the family."

"I can handle updating the Vances. You should get back to the hotel and get some rest," he offered.

"That'd be good, thank you," I replied, grateful for the

chance to get away by myself. I waited while the terrified teenagers were put into Redondo Beach police patrol cars to be driven to the station.

Back at the hotel, I swiped the key in the door and stepped into my room. I lay down on the bed and stared at the ceiling for a moment before closing my eyes.

Everything was quiet, too quiet. I lay still in the back, my hands and feet tied, my mouth covered, waiting. Tibbs came to pull me from the van.

I blinked. We were in a garage and through the window, I could see that the sky was dark. Tibbs grabbed my arm roughly and led me across a small yard to the back door of a house. There were neighbors next door, I could see a light on. I pulled back as we approached the door. Tibbs' fingers dug into the soft flesh on the inside of my arm and he had a hand at my back to steady me. I couldn't run, I could only hobble, and with my hands bound, how would I manipulate the chain-link fence and gate that had a fat padlock on it? My only chance was to go along and try to appease him, whatever that meant. He pushed me through the door and into the house. The floor inside was painted red. The whole place looked like old people had lived there for a long time. Newspapers were piled up in the corners of the rooms and cardboard boxes along the walls. Most of the windows had metal security bars on them. Everything smelled musty and slightly sour, a lot of medication bottles sat on a side table.

He led me down a hallway, past a couple of bedrooms and a bathroom and into a room that had a large heavy bookcase against one wall. It looked too heavy to move but he pushed it aside. Behind it there was a trapdoor that pulled out from the wall...

I bolted upright in the king-sized bed, unsure of where I was for a moment. The clock read 3:45 a.m. I stood and stretched. I needed to sleep but I knew I wouldn't. I opened the files on my own abduction again. There was one piece of evidence I had never been able to look at —Tibbs' confession. It was found when he plunged to his death in the van over a steep hillside and burned down to nothing more than a blackened pile of rot.

My hands trembled as I pulled it from the case files. It was time to read the monster's last message.

ELEVEN

DAY TWO: 4:02 A.M.

I unfolded the creased paper, stiff from years of storage. I had always avoided reading his final message; once he was dead, I wanted him to stay that way. Holding his confession in my hands brought Tibbs closer to me, as if he were seated in the chair across the room.

it wasnt suposed to be this way i never ment to hurt anyone but i did. theres somthing insid me I cant control any more what I do now... emily was a perfec doll but she gru up and now I am lost in the piichers in my head I hear to many people taking at me not leting me sleep... I cant get away from it... i cant do it anymor... i cant live this way...

And that was it. Just rambling babble as he prepared to drive his van off a cliff. It was found in a knapsack next to where the car had plunged over the low railing. Why had he let me go? Lydia and the police had surmised that keeping a teenager captive was harder than keeping a small child. Or something had triggered such a dramatic shift. Something startling and sudden.

In those weeks after I escaped, before they found his van, how many nights and days had I lost in a fog of fear that he would somehow reappear? I scanned the investigation notes; it had been years since I had reviewed them. I flipped through the crime scene photos. Tibbs had burned the house down to rubble and ashes but the springs on the mattresses in the bunker remained. Same with the iron chains bolted to the wall, the metal hinges of the shelves that held our clothes and books. *The Little Red Caboose* was gone. And in the bathroom, just the porcelain tub...

I had been home almost a month when the detectives came by the house. I could hear their voices in the foyer downstairs.

My dad stuck his head in my room and said, "Emily, the detectives are here; they want to speak with you."

I followed him down the big staircase and found the two detectives that had been on my case from the beginning. I had spoken to them many times at the hospital and afterward. I trusted them.

Brandy Schultz, a tall athletic woman with a blond bob, spoke first. "The police in San Bernardino found a van registered to Tibbs. It was burning at the bottom of a ravine up in the mountains. When search and rescue got there, they found a body and a note. We think it's Tibbs, but we need to see if you can identify anything from the remains."

A body? He was dead?

"You want me to see if it's really him?"

"If you can, it would be a big help," Schultz said.

"I'll do it," I said quickly.

"Are you sure, sweetheart? It might be traumatic," Michael said.

I needed to see with my own eyes, whatever was left of him. The idea of him being out there terrified me and I knew that other little girls would never be safe if he had just moved to a new place. If he were dead, it would be over.

"I'll do it," I said. "When?"

"Can you meet us at the San Bernardino County morgue tomorrow? Around noon?" Herman asked.

And the next day, we were driving out to San Bernardino; it seemed like we were traveling to the other end of the earth. My dad chatted nervously.

"They're pretty sure it's him. They don't know if he had already killed himself before the car went off the highway and into the ravine or if it happened on impact."

He'd killed himself. I knew why. I didn't remember walking into the morgue but suddenly I was in a long white hallway with tile on the walls and floor. The coroner came out, her name was Dr. Gamble and she looked like a ferret. Everything was so sterile and cold; the sharp smell of chemicals filled the air.

"You ready for this, Emily?" Brandy asked.

I nodded. I was ready.

"Right this way," Dr. Gamble said, moving toward a wall filled with metal doors. As she opened it, I realized it was a refrigerated *drawer, large enough for a human body. She slid the body out on its steel pallet.*

"You give us the word," Brandy said, placing a steadying hand on my shoulder.

I nodded. Dr. Gamble pulled the sheet back and there was just a charred frame of a human being. Just bones and ashes and a few tufts of his dirty-blond hair. And a gold skull necklace he always wore was there with the remains. It was him.

"Yes, it's him, that's his necklace," I whispered.

My head felt light, and I backed away from the body. I turned and rushed out into the hallway. I didn't make it very far and I threw up in a trashcan. Once my stomach stopped doing somersaults, I raced to the bathroom and splashed cold water on my face.

He was gone, forever. A monstrous weight was lifted off me. He could never return to hurt me in any way. All I had to do was keep moving forward, I would stop feeling like I was walking on a high tightrope with no net...

I closed my eyes. I hadn't thought of that day in years. But there were weeks and months afterward when the memory of it would push its way into my consciousness, like a dark, sticky substance oozing up through concrete. I pulled back the covers and slid between the cool, clean sheets. I thought of my daughters, their smiling faces, their sweet bubble-bath scent as they stepped out of the tub every night, getting ready for bed. The comforting feel of their soft pajamas. Putting my attention on happy, sensory experiences helped break the grip of old, toxic memories. I listened to the waves breaking outside and at some point, I fell asleep.

Early the next morning, I was on my way back to the Sparrow's Nest. I had slept two hours and my brain felt like crumpled tinfoil. Reviewing my own case files the night before had confirmed that Whirt was right about one thing: Tibbs was wholly unremarkable in every way, and I couldn't fathom how someone would want to copy him. A high school drop-out, moving from one low-paying job to another, kept afloat by disturbed parents. He was an angry, maladjusted nutcase. His only success in life was in kidnapping children. But perhaps that was it, the copycat wanted to be another master manipulator, going out on his own terms, just like Tibbs did.

I arrived at the Vance home as the sun was coming up. Diaz was crashed on a leather couch. The rest of the team arrived over the next hour. Everyone had spent a sleepless night, mentally sifting through every detail of the case. Izzy arrived with his ever-present coffee cup, sporting a fresh cardigan.

"I checked the dark web every hour last night—nothing. Whoever has her isn't a trafficker, that's my opinion," he said as he set up his three laptops on an open desk.

Stephanie hung her suit jacket on the back of her chair as she settled in. "I pulled up information on a range of missing girls in the area, ages seven to fourteen. That's how old you were when Tibbs took you, right?"

"Yeah," I said.

"There are a few of them who could fit. I red-flagged them for you. Also, only two of the guys you put away were released from prison. One died three years ago of a drug overdose, the other one found religion and runs an outreach for ex-cons out in Nebraska," she said.

Grice arrived, freshly showered, looking like he stepped out of a brochure for the Latter-Day Saints.

"So, who's up for going to Victorville with me today? Got a lot of ground to cover," he said.

Whirt rolled in, McDonald's coffee in hand. He looked awful; his pallor was gray with dark circles under his eyes.

"Okay, Diaz, you go out and talk to the street vendors in the area, see if anyone remembers selling balloons to a guy in a ball cap on or around the twenty-second. Grice, if you and Whirt cover Victorville, Ryan and I can go talk to the families of the other missing girls."

"I'm ready when you are," Ryan said to me, taking a final slurp of his Starbucks cold brew. Whirt gave him the side-eye.

"You know, this coffee is better than that shit you're drinking," he said, brandishing his McDonald's cup.

"In your dreams, Grandpa," Ryan said with a laugh.

"Really, that crap is bitter. And burned. Mickey D's upgraded their coffee. For those of us who don't want to pay ten bucks a cup," Whirt said.

"It's not just the coffee, man. It's the whole experience. The egg bites, the cake pops," Ryan said with a flourish.

"Oh, fuck me," Whirt said, tossing his empty paper cup into the trash like an NBA pro, which elicited a few cheers from the group. Two of our agents and two sheriffs stayed at the Sparrow's Nest while the rest of us fanned out to start the day's work.

As we drove, I leafed through the list of missing girls in the area. Stacy Rennfort, Cassidy Godoy, Sierra Smith, Simran Velasquez, Deborah Kilby. Several were teenagers by now. A couple of the younger girls had been taken on the run by the non-custodial parent, some had just disappeared. They had never been found, dead or alive. Time moves on. Cases go cold. Other investigations take on more urgency. Sex trafficking had exploded in the U.S. in the last decade, so many girls fell into that black hole and just vanished. I braced myself as we pulled up to the first house on the list, the family of Stacey Rennfort, taken at ten years old. Ryan knocked on the door.

A woman in her forties opened it, Mary Louise Rennfort. She had the faded look of something left too long on the clothesline, color drained away by the sun. Five years of waiting for her daughter to return.

"You're from the police, right? You want to talk about Stacey?" Mary Louise asked as she ushered us inside.

"We're investigating the abduction of a little girl from Palos Verdes and we wanted to ask you about Stacey's disappearance," I said gently.

We weren't there with any information about Stacey. I knew that's what this mother desperately hoped for, and we didn't have it. I felt like a fraud.

"You mean the little Vance girl? I saw it on the news last night. She was in a park, right? My Stacey was taken on her way home from school. It was the first time I'd let her walk; she was supposed to be with a group of friends, but they went without her..." She tailed off and then began the story she had no doubt replayed hundreds of times in her head.

She recounted every detail. Stacey left school at 2:45. She walked the route down Hawthorne Boulevard from her elementary school. She was seen walking past a Mobil gas station at 3:10 p.m. and then she disappeared.

Ryan leaned in, his voice calm and reassuring. "I know this is hard for you and we appreciate your meeting with us. Is there anything else that you can remember about that day or the weeks leading up to it? Had Stacey mentioned anything out of the ordinary, any change in her habits or behavior?"

Mary Louise reflected for a moment and said, "She said a man in a sedan had pulled up near the apartment a few weeks earlier. She was playing with some of the other kids, and he was, you know... touching himself and looking at the kids through the window of the car. She got scared and ran away. I told the police about it back then, so I didn't think any more of it. She was a little nervous to go near that street for a few days. The cops told me it was nothing to do with her going missing."

There was nothing in her story that jumped out as being similar to Josie's abduction, other than the fact that she disappeared with no witnesses. We said our goodbyes.

Back at the car, I handed Ryan the keys and said, "You did really well back there."

Ryan smiled briefly and said, "I have a younger sister. I don't think I could handle these cases all the time like you do."

"Hell, some days I don't think I can either," I replied.

"But you do, right?"

"Yeah, I do," I said quietly as we headed to the next house on the list.

We had covered about half with no major updates when we got a call from Diaz.

"We found a guy, a street vendor who sells those Mexican popsicles, he remembers selling balloons to a guy in El Segundo who matches the description. Same height, white guy, ball cap, face mask. The day Josie was taken, around ten in the morning," he said excitedly.

"Where's he at?"

"We're with him now at Plaza Segundo, talking to the other vendors. Then we're taking him back to the Redondo PD to get him with the sketch artist. His name is Procopio Valdez. He's pretty nervous about talking to us, he's undocumented."

"Reassure him there will be no consequences with immigration of any kind. Great work, this is just what we need," I said, slapping the dashboard in satisfaction.

A witness who had interacted with our suspect. An upclose description, a police sketch to release which would generate a flood of information. Someone knew him, had seen him. It was just a matter of time.

TWELVE
DAY TWO: 10:42 A.M.

I knew we had a good hour before Mr. Valdez would be at the Redondo Police Department, so Ryan and I finished with the families of other missing girls; two of them were promising. Deborah Kilby and Simran Velasquez had both disappeared from crowded public places, both near the pier and Veterans Park. They warranted a deep dive; I texted Stephanie and Izzy to get them started on it.

We were close to where Brenda Coombs lived. The self-published book she had written about my abduction was the worst kind of true crime non-fiction, filled with grammatical errors and crazy assumptions, but if Josie's kidnapper was obsessed with my case, he may well have read it. I needed to speak to her.

We drove into a rundown part of Lomita, with older Craftsman houses now covered with cheap stucco. Brenda Coombs' house fit right in with overgrown, half-dead wisteria vines pulling on the rain gutters and piles of newspapers on the porch. I rapped on the door briskly. From deep inside the house we heard a voice call out, "I'm coming! I'm coming!"

A moment later, the front door was yanked open by a

woman in her late fifties with an inch of gray roots pushing past her dyed red hair. She was heavyset, wearing a stained sweatshirt and khaki shorts that looked as if she hadn't changed them in a week. A glimpse past her into the house revealed a hoarder's paradise.

"Yeah, what do you want?" she asked.

Ryan took the lead. "I'm Detective Ryan and this is Special Agent Ray with the FBI. We would like to talk to you about your book, *Gone in an Instant*."

Her eyes grew wide, and she slid her glasses down her prominent ski nose to peer at me.

"You said Special Agent Ray? Emily Ray?" Her voice rose in excitement.

"Yes, ma'am, that's me," I said with a smile that I hoped seemed sincere.

She pulled the door wide and ushered us in. "Oh, come in, come in! Excuse the mess, I sell a lot of stuff on eBay, OfferUp. You gotta make a living somehow! Let's go to the kitchen, where we can sit down."

She led us through a house so crowded with junk that there was just a narrow path to follow. The kitchen was not much better but there was a clear spot at the Formica-topped table.

"I don't have company much these days. Would you like some coffee?" she asked. The Mr. Coffee glass carafe on the counter was stained brown and half-filled with a muddy-looking liquid.

"No thank you. We just had Starbucks," I lied.

She settled into her chair and stared at us with eager fascination. "So, what do you want to know? I can't believe you're really here!"

Ryan and I sat down on wobbly chairs that looked like they'd been left outside too long.

"We are investigating some missing children in the South

Bay, and I wanted to speak to you about your book and how you accessed your information about my abduction," I said.

"You're working on the Josie Vance case, right? I saw it on the news and yesterday's press conference. It's a lot like your case, isn't it?" She moved to the coffee maker and poured herself a cup. "You don't mind if I indulge, do you? I drink about six cups a day to keep going!"

When her back was turned Ryan shot me a disgusted look and I shrugged as she turned back to us with a big smile. There was a cloudy film on her coffee as she poured half the container of sugar into it.

"That's it, right? It's Josie Vance?" she asked.

Ryan responded smoothly, "We are working that case as well as several others. Our main interest here is how you got the details for your book? Some of the key information you included wasn't released to the public."

She took a loud slurp of her coffee and winked. "Oh yes. I had an inside source. Someone who let me in on some of the juicier details!"

"Can you tell us who it was?" I prodded.

"Oh, no. I can't reveal my journalistic sources," she said, with a self-important wave of her hand.

Ryan was about to push but I spoke up. "Oh yeah, I get that. We all have our sources. I've always been impressed at how you knew so much. Like, when I went to identify the body at the morgue. Nobody knew that."

"I know. Same with the location of the van. It was on Highway 330, below that town called Running Springs. Very remote area. I drove up there to see it years ago. Want one?" she said, holding out a box of donuts at us. I could tell they were days old and rock hard.

Ryan reached for one gingerly. "Don't mind if I do."

He was taking one for the team, doing his part to loosen her up. I watched him bite into the donut; he looked as if he was chewing Fix-All.

"You really drove all the way up there? I drove up there once when I was in college just to see it. It would be very easy to go off the road."

"Oh yes, that's true. It's a lovely drive if you can take the curves. Ed had warned me to go during the day since it's quite treacherous at night," Coombs said, chewing loudly with her mouth open.

"Do you mean Ed Whirt?" I asked.

She slapped the table and laughed. "I said it, didn't I? I guess it doesn't matter after all these years. Whirt was the one who gave me the inside information. He was a young buck back then. I don't mind telling you that he really filled the old bathtub, if you know what I mean."

I stared at her blankly. "No, I don't know what you mean."

"You know, we had a little thing. A fling, I guess," she said, with a faint blush.

I hid my surprise and nodded. I didn't even want to imagine him filling her bathtub.

"So, did he just feed you information or did he show you any evidence?" I asked casually.

"Oh no, he never showed me anything. He just gave me little tidbits of information. It was his first big case, and he was just in the background. He did want a piece of the profits, though. We both thought it would be a bestseller but that didn't happen," she said with a sigh.

"Did he ever mention anything about a children's book? Anything found at the Glendale house, perhaps?" I asked.

"A book? No, nothing like that. He said everything was just ashes when they went through it. Obviously, Tibbs didn't want anything left behind," she replied.

"Have you and Detective Whirt continued to share information about my case or any others?"

"No, we drifted apart years ago. I'm really only interested in the kidnapping cases but maybe if there were a serial killer or something that would make a good book."

Ryan and I exchanged a look and stood up. We had what we needed. Brenda Coombs chattered non-stop as she accompanied us to the door.

"Oh, I followed every detail of your case, for years. All the time you were missing, I kept on it. I wasn't a Janey-Come-Lately who just got interested when you showed up later. Can I get a selfie before you go?"

"It's against FBI policy but thank you for your help," I demurred.

"Thank you so much for your time, Mrs. Coombs," Ryan said, extending his hand.

"That's Miss Coombs to you. Never married but still hopeful!" she said with a laugh.

As we made our way across the untidy yard, she shouted from the doorway, "If you need more help with your case, just let me know! I'm quite a sleuth. I watch Investigation Discovery every night!"

Back in the car, I handed Ryan a bottle of water, "Just to get that donut down."

He laughed and said, "It wasn't that bad, lemon-filled. She's a nut, huh?"

"I could have told you that before we met her. But it is interesting that Whirt was the source," I said.

"Do we say anything to him about it? See how he reacts?" he asked. "I hate to say it, but what if he's... off? You know, enough to set something like this up? Like those movies where the fire chief is the arsonist?"

"Do you seriously think Whirt could be involved somehow?"

"You're the expert. What do you think?"

I waited before answering. Stranger things had happened.

Sometimes cops go bad. They stalk women who reject them. They prey on teenagers and drive across the country to abduct them. Whirt didn't seem to have the dark streak in his character that would make him commit a copycat crime like Tibbs'. But I had only known him for a day and a half. Detectives have a lot of unsavory contacts: criminal sources, informants, guys who want some quid pro quo down the line. It wouldn't be hard to find someone to do it.

"Okay, if we suppose it is him. On the plus side, he's the local detective in Palos Verdes. Knows the area, the families. It's a very insular community, he's part of it, an insider," I said.

"And it would be way easy for him to find out the Vance family routine. Everything our guy did was lined up perfectly. The power outage, a ton of cops at the classic car parade on Hawthorne the time of day when people are leaving the park. Whirt knows how all of it goes down," Ryan added.

"Motive?" I asked.

"He wants to go out with a bang—recognition for solving a heavy case like this. He was a rookie cop on your case, now he can be the big dog. And he can work with you on it," he said, echoing my thoughts.

"But on the downside, he's a career cop. He seems like a straight arrow, very old-school. You have to be really bent sideways to do something like this. It's a huge risk," I said.

"He's not that straight—he gave Brenda Coombs information from your case, had a thing with her. And wanted a piece of any profits. Kind of shady, if you ask me."

"Let's keep this under wraps. I'll tell Grice but no one else. We have time, we can swing by his house on the way back. Just have a chat with his wife. It will all seem very routine," I said.

"Without telling him?" Ryan asked, cautiously.

"Right," I said.

Whirt lived on Anza Avenue in Torrance, a wide street with a grassy divider. The lawn was neatly tended, it even had a couple of ceramic gnomes nestled in with the plants. I knocked and a few moments later, a woman in white capris and a sleeveless silk top opened the door.

"Mrs. Whirt?" I asked.

"Yes. Is Ed all right? Has he been hurt?"

"He's fine, we just saw him at the station. My name is Emily Ray, I'm the FBI agent in charge of the case he's working on, and this is Detective Ryan."

"Oh, yes. It's all he talks about. You can call me Ellen," she said as she ushered us inside. "I'm heating some water for coffee or tea if you'd like a cup."

"We're fine, thank you," I said. "I know Ed worked on my case years ago and that it was important for him—"

Mrs. Whirt interrupted with a laugh. "Important? It was the biggest case of his life. I feel like I know you. When the little Vance girl was taken, he wanted to call you in immediately, but they waited a day, which Ed was just furious about," she said.

"You mean he wanted to call in the FBI, not me specifically, right?"

"No, you specifically. He knows you're the head of the CARD team here in Southern California. He knows everything about you. Come with me," she said, leading us down a narrow hallway lined with family photos.

She opened a door and stood aside for me and Ryan to enter. It was a small bedroom; the walls were covered with cork bulletin boards with newspaper clippings and photos from my abduction. Photos of my dad at the press conference announcing my return. Photos of me, hiding my face in the backseat of my dad's car while photographers chased us. Photos of me as an adult from other investigations with the FBI. There were images from the police files, documents and evidence from the investigation. And on a whiteboard, the timeline of Josie Vance's case juxtaposed with the timeline of my case. There was a photo of Josie next to a photo of me at the same age; both photos that were given to the press when the cases broke. It was eerie. I looked to Ryan, whose eyes darted back and forth, taking all of it in.

"Ed is obsessed with your case, he always was. When you came back it was the greatest day of his career. He's followed your whole life, even when you were in college at UCLA and everything," Ellen said, proudly.

"Wow, this is... impressive," I said.

The kettle in the kitchen began to whistle.

"Oh, let me get that..." Ellen said, excusing herself.

Once she was out of earshot, Ryan said, "This is some weird shit."

I nodded. It was unnerving and now the possibility that Whirt could have staged the Josie Vance abduction didn't seem so far-fetched. The whole room spoke of someone who had lost perspective, a strange kind of obsession. Ryan snapped a few quick photos of the room with his phone, and we headed back up the hallway to the kitchen.

"How do we get out of here?" Ryan whispered.

As we entered the kitchen, Ellen was setting out three mugs with tea bags.

"Please don't put yourself out. We must get back. We have a press conference coming up. I just wanted to see if Ed had any copies of the book, *Gone in an Instant*, that Morgan St. Cloud wrote about my case? I gather Ed was a source for some of the material."

Ellen's face fell when I mentioned Morgan St. Cloud, aka Brenda Coombs.

"He worked with that woman for a while. We do have a few copies of it in the hall closet," she said. Her voice had become an expressionless monotone. Clearly Brenda Coombs was a sore subject. I guessed Ellen knew about the affair. She went to the coat closet and reached far into a back shelf, pulling out a cardboard box. She handed it to Ryan.

"These are the copies we have left. You can take them all, as far as I'm concerned," she said.

"Thank you so much for your time, Ellen. It was a pleasure meeting you," I said as we stood in the doorway.

"I'm glad to finally get rid of those things," she said with a disdainful toss of her head.

Once we were in the car, Ryan sat back and shook his head.

"Whirt is a weird case. He knows you're the head of CARD. He knows you'll be called in; he knows it will kick up all kinds of old shit. He gets to be center stage with the person he has obsessed about for years. Nothing back there reassured me that he's clean," he said.

"Me neither," I said quietly as we began the drive to Redondo Beach.

THIRTEEN
DAY TWO: 1:23 P.M.

When we arrived at the Redondo station we were shown into a room where Diaz was seated next to an older, heavyset Mexican man, Procopio Valdez. The sketch artist had almost finished the drawing of the man who bought balloons. Diaz introduced me and Ryan to Mr. Valdez, who took off his ball cap and held it nervously in his hands.

"Thanks for coming forward, Mr. Valdez. It's a great help to us," I said, shaking his hand. "How did you see this man in the plaza? Did he have a car?"

"No, he came to my *carrito* by walking. I sell candies and *paletas*, also balloons and toys for the kids. He was a *gringo*, maybe thirty-five years or more. With a *cachucha*, a hat for baseball."

"What time was this?" I asked.

"Maybe 10:30 in the morning. He had on a COVID mask and a backpack," Valdez said.

"Get Stephanie to pull all the camera footage from Plaza Segundo and the surrounding area and send it here to Ryan's email," I told Diaz.

"Do you remember what balloons he bought from you that day?"

"I remember that he bought a *Frozen* balloon, because it was the only one I had. And some of the other Disney ones," Valdez explained.

He confirmed the sketch, and it would be released to every police department in Southern California within the hour. We would show it at the afternoon press conference. The drawing looked like any number of unremarkable white males but at least it was something.

A young officer brought Mr. Valdez a coffee while we waited for the camera footage to arrive and load onto the Redondo PD server. I received a call from Grice, out in the badlands of Victorville.

"Any news?" I asked.

"Nothing related to our case. No one at the post office remembers a lone guy dropping anything in a box. There were people coming in and out all day."

"How about the door-to-door?"

"*Nada.* The people out here really don't want to talk to law enforcement."

"Okay. We just finished with the popsicle vendor. You got the police sketch I sent, right?"

"Yeah, got it right here on my phone. We're swinging by the post office again to see if it triggers anyone's memory."

I received the text that the video footage had arrived. We pulled up chairs around Ryan's desk and he fired up his computer. I scrolled through the footage until we found Mr. Valdez with his pushcart. A number of people made purchases from him, several with children in tow. Then a man approached, wearing a ball cap pulled down low. He was compact and lean, with a slight shuffle to his gait. We couldn't see his face; he entered the frame only visible from the back. But he matched the height and body type of the man Molly had described at the park. He bought three balloons from Mr. Valdez. I zoomed in on them; they were the same ones we found in the trees at the park.

"Mr. Valdez, could you take a look at this, please?" I asked.

He joined us at the computer screen and pointed to the man in the ball cap.

"Yes, that's him!" he confirmed.

"Okay, let's see where he goes," Ryan said.

But our suspect never turned back to face the camera. He walked away from the pushcart, into the crowd of shoppers. He went down an exterior stairway and disappeared. I quickly scrolled through the footage from the other cameras at the plaza, but he never reappeared.

"Shit! What happened to him?" Ryan shouted in frustration.

"He could have taken a pedestrian exit off the stairwell. He could have left a waiting car outside of the camera's view. Whatever it was, he's very careful. And he knows exactly what he's doing and what the camera is seeing," I said, trying to hide my dismay.

We offered Mr. Valdez a ride home and assured him that his name would be kept out of the press. Diaz stayed at the station to bring the Redondo police up to speed on the case while Ryan and I headed back to prepare for the press conference.

At the Sparrow's Nest, Stephanie and Izzy were pulling up information on the cases of Simran Velasquez and Deborah Kilby. The exhibitionist who had exposed himself to Stacey Rennfort had been arrested later that day outside a middle school in Playa Vista. His name was Joshua Selbo. He had a string of similar offenses in the intervening years leading up to Josie's abduction, but he died a year earlier of COVID. I found Louis in his office, attempting to work.

"Updates?" he asked brusquely.

"Yes, a few. There is a witness who sold balloons to our suspect the day Josie was taken. We have some images of him and a police sketch. We'll be putting it out at the press conference."

"Let me see it."

I pulled a copy of the drawing and handed it to him. He looked at it closely and shook his head.

"I've never seen this guy before," he muttered.

Our media liaison signaled me it was time to deal with the press. A larger group of reporters had gathered outside, along with the regulars.

"We are looking for a person of interest who was seen at Veterans Park, talking with Josie Vance on the day she disappeared. He is a white male, between thirty and forty years old. He was wearing blue jeans, a light-colored T-shirt, a baseball hat and a paper face mask, the kind that was used during the COVID-19 pandemic. His hair is close-cropped. If anyone recognizes this man or has any information, please contact the FBI directly," I said, holding up the sketch as it was distributed among the reporters.

"Is there any reason to think Josie's disappearance could be tied to Vance Media International?" asked Haley Nettles, a crime reporter from the *Santa Monica Sun.*

"Not at this point. We have looked into Vance Media and have found no connection to anything related to Josie."

"Can you explain the police action that took place last night involving Redondo Beach SWAT?" Belle Zerlin of Fox News shouted, her grating tone sounding like squealing brakes on a car.

"We had a phone call and ransom demand that turned out to be false, but we had to investigate in the event that it had been real," I said.

"Can you comment on the other cases of missing girls that you are reviewing? Is there a link between those cases and Josie

Vance?" Larissa Cinque shouted out her question, holding her own.

"We are looking at several cases from the past few years to see if any have similarities, but we cannot elaborate on those. The main focus at this point is identifying the man in this police sketch," I said, wrapping it up.

They kept shouting questions after me as I headed back into the house. The rest of the day, I reviewed all the CCTV footage from the greater Redondo Beach area to see if anyone matching our suspect was caught on camera. Unfortunately, I was unable to read all the license plates and the ones I was able to run through the DMV came back registered to men who didn't fit the profile at all. Still, I sent two deputy sheriffs out to interview them.

I flagged the others and printed the images to add to our whiteboard. None of them were wearing a baseball cap or a face mask. Our guy could easily have taken side streets to avoid any CCTV footage. He was organized, way too organized. I always felt that Tibbs took me on impulse. He saw a chance and acted on it. This guy was a different kind of predator.

Lila Scroff called me from the lab with an update on *The Little Red Caboose.*

"No touch DNA, fingerprints or other trace evidence. It's about ten years old, at most. It looked older because of the wear and tear but it's never been out of print so it could've been bought last week," she said.

I still had no idea how the book fit into the narrative of Josie's kidnapping. Maybe it was just a strange coincidence. But that didn't explain the blue bear. I shook the uncertainty off; I couldn't let myself spiral down a rabbit hole, trying to make sense of something that had no logical explanation.

I went through the case files for Simran Velasquez and Deborah Kilby. Simran disappeared from a fourth of July celebration on the Redondo Pier. Several witnesses had seen a lone male in the vicinity, but the police never found him or interviewed him.

Over four hundred thousand children go missing each year. Some have been taken by a parent or relative, some kicked out of the family home. Some run away from a bad domestic situation, and some are abducted. They are out there, vulnerable, and dependent on adults, for better or worse. I knew the likelihood was that Simran Velasquez had either been trafficked or killed or perhaps both. Once a child-trafficking victim gets older, they don't let her go. They dispose of her because she knows too much, has seen too many faces.

Just as I was finishing my dive into the Simran Velasquez case, Grice and Whirt returned. I signaled for Grice to meet me outside to speak privately.

"What up?" Grice asked when we were alone on the terrace.

"I spoke to the woman who wrote that true crime book about my case. Her inside source was Whirt—they had an affair, both thought they would make some big bucks with the book," I said.

Grice's expression soured. "Completely unethical. He could have jeopardized the investigation."

"There's that. Then Ryan and I went to talk to his wife, to see if she had any copies of the book, since he was the link. She showed us a room at their house..."

I went on to describe the bizarre back bedroom at Whirt's house. I showed him the photos Ryan had taken.

Grice shook his head, stared at his shoes for a beat, then asked, "What do you want to do? He could have conceived the whole thing, you know? Solve a copycat of the case that defined his whole career."

"I know. But if we're wrong, we could destroy what's left of it and his reputation. He's an odd guy but a lot of detectives are."

"I think we should speak to his chief and take him off the case while we check him out."

"Let's give it the next twenty-four hours before we make that call. And keep this between us—Ryan knows but he'll keep quiet about it."

We went back inside. I still had to go through the Deborah Kilby file. She was last seen in the company of an unrelated woman at a street fair adjacent to the Redondo Pier. Her mom had stepped away to buy a funnel cake and when she returned Deborah was gone. The woman seen with her claimed to have taken her to a lost-and-found booth.

One of the booth workers, a twenty-something guy named Pete Hainly, came under suspicion. He had been working the booth when Deborah went missing but insisted that he had no recollection of her. He had priors—an assault charge against his twelve-year-old stepsister with allegations of sexually inappropriate behavior—but their parents had declined to pursue charges. The detectives on the case thought that Hainly was good for the Kilby disappearance, but they did not find a single connection to the young girl.

Where was Pete Hainly now? I found his photo. He bore a resemblance to our suspect, taking into account the age progression. He had served a few years in prison for unrelated assault and burglary charges. I did a background search and found his address hadn't changed, he was still living in his parents' house. It wasn't too far away, just at the edge of Redondo Beach.

I was on my way to revisit Josie's room when I saw the mailman arrive. He pushed his way past the reporters and was cleared to enter the driveway. In his hands, he held another small manila envelope, just like the last one. I knew it was from the kidnapper; I dreaded the discovery of what it contained. I froze as he handed it off to Moran, who dutifully headed to the Sparrow's Nest to deliver it. I met up with him at the doorway and took the envelope. This time it was postmarked from

Hesperia which was another forgettable small city next to Victorville.

I slid the letter opener along the edge of the envelope and pulled out a thin piece of paper, a second drawing. Same house, same walkway. Only this time there were two little girls in front. Two little girls who looked almost identical, even with the limitations of a crudely done drawing. Both were blond. This time there was no balloon. My heart stopped. My vision blurred. And then I fainted.

FOURTEEN
DAY TWO: 4:10 P.M.

I came to a few minutes later, laid out on a couch with a bag of ice cubes on my forehead. I had hit the edge of a chair on the way down and could sense a swelling coming up. Diaz, Grice and the others were standing around me. I sat up gingerly, Ryan put his hand on my shoulder to steady me.

"Do you want us to call the paramedics, Agent Ray?" he asked.

"No, I'm fine. I didn't eat this morning," I lied. "It was probably just low blood sugar."

Grice handed me a glass of water. "Do you think you should take the rest of the day off? You need to have that knot looked at. You're going to get a pretty big bruise."

"No, I just need to eat something. Do we have any protein bars here or some other snack?"

Stephanie grabbed a Kind Bar and a package of peanut butter crackers from the kitchen area and handed them to me. "Here. These are the good protein bars, not the crappy Clif Bars."

"I love Clif Bars," said Whirt.

"Hey, Boomer," Ryan replied, and everyone laughed, breaking the tension.

I swallowed the crackers and washed them down with a big swig of water.

"You sure you're not preggers?" Whirt asked, with his usual lack of tact. "My wife fainted all the time when she was pregnant with Eddie Jr."

"You named your kid after yourself?" Ryan asked.

"Yeah, back in ancient times we gave kids real first names, like Ed and John. We didn't name them Apricot or Gravity, imagine that?" Whirt answered with a snide smile.

"No, I'm not pregnant, Whirt," I said, rising to my feet.

I had gathered my wits and was ready to proceed. I picked up the new drawing, my stomach tightening.

"So, what do we make of this?" I floated the question to the group.

"Either he has another girl, or he plans to take one. It could also be a threat against your daughters, Emily. They're twins and the drawing is of two girls who look the same," Grice said with ominous concern, shaking his head.

I just stared at him for a beat, my mind pushing back against his words. A direct threat against my girls. I felt a visceral, maternal rage boiling up inside me at the suggestion. But I took a deep breath and collected myself. I knew what the drawings meant. First one girl, then two outside the same house. It was not about my daughters. This was a story from long ago and only I knew how it ended.

"I'm checking to see if there have been any reports of a missing child in the area," Stephanie said, her fingers tapping away on her laptop.

"Check from here to Santa Barbara and the Inland Empire. This guy moves around," I said.

"Can we put this out to the public?" Ryan asked.

"We could cause widespread panic or some vigilante bullshit. This is a message. There might be a potential victim, or this could be a girl he has already taken. I don't think it's related to my daughters. These little girls are clearly blond, my girls have brown hair. And it started with one girl, who was obviously Josie, and now there's a second girl," I said.

"So, this could be any one of the missing girls we know about or a different one that's off the radar?" Ryan asked.

I nodded, my eyes scanning the drawing. Two little blond girls, hand in hand.

"In this drawing, there's nothing specific about the clothing, just stick figures. There's no way to match any details to the missing girls we're looking into," I said.

"I think we have to look at this as a provocation. The probability that he has taken another girl is high. Why else would he send this? To alert us so we could potentially stop him?" Grice said.

"Maybe it's a taunt, to see if we are able to before he does it?" Diaz said.

"Maybe he wants us to cause panic? And we look like fools if nothing happens?" Whirt said.

"There are no reports of a missing child in the South Bay, I'm still waiting for the other areas," Stephanie said.

"This guy is all about playing mind games. And power," I said. "He might have taken another child. But he wants a reaction from us that fits a bigger plan. The Tibbs house is clearly another link between my case and Josie's. This is something different. There's something else that he wants."

"I think he wants us to overreact," Grice said.

"Maybe it's another girl from back in the day when Tibbs took you? Maybe Tibbs had other victims that this guy knows about? Did he ever bring any other girls to the Glendale house?" Whirt asked.

I shook my head. "No, he didn't. I think Josie is still alive. I know we have no proof of life but he seems to be more interested in playing a game. If he were an impulsive child murderer, he wouldn't be doing any of this," I said.

"Maybe we put this out to the public, just to see if anyone recognizes the drawing style?" Diaz asked.

"We can consider releasing it if we don't get any solid leads with the police sketch, but I think we will," Grice added.

I needed to get out, to get away from the team. I needed time by myself and the growing lump on my forehead was a perfect excuse.

"I think you're right, John. I'm going to have this bump checked out and work from home for the evening. Will you handle the update with Melanie and Louis? I'll be reachable at all hours, as usual," I said.

"Certainly," Grice replied, happy to step into the top job, as ever.

I gathered my laptop and other files, feeling suddenly paranoid. Once I pulled away from the Vance house, I drove around the winding streets of Palos Verdes, with no destination, no direction at all. Just driving, to keep moving.

When I'd seen the drawing of the two girls, it was as if a hand had reached up from some buried, long-forgotten place and gripped my shoulder. Suddenly, my breath started to come fast and shallow, I was on the verge of hyperventilating. I pulled the car to a stop at the lookout above Lunada Bay and got out. I leaned on the hood and bent over. The knot on my head throbbed. I counted as I took deep, slow breaths.

Four counts. Hold for two. Six counts to exhale. Hold. Repeat.

I had lied to Whirt. I had lied to the team. I had lied to everyone. This time, the memory didn't come as a flashback or a panic attack. It didn't come as a dream that I bolted out of in the middle of the night. This time, I let it in.

Tibbs opened the hidden door and pushed me in front of him down narrow, cement stairs and into a room that was some kind of underground bunker.

The walls were covered with thick soundproofing. No windows, a table and a couple of chairs, a small bathroom with a sink and toilet, separated from the rest of the room by a plastic curtain, a mattress on the floor. The only light in the room came from the screen of a TV that was on in the corner.

And then I saw her: a girl, about my age. Skinny, with big hollow blue eyes and dirty blond hair pulled back into a ponytail, sitting on the mattress with a metal cuff around her wrist and her ankle, attached to the wall with a chain. A thick piece of duct tape with cotton padding was over her mouth. I felt like I was going to throw up. It was a scene from a nightmare. Who was this girl and how long had she been here?

He had another set of restraints ready for me and deftly guided me onto the bed and attached them. She and I looked at each other in silence, gagged and chained. Helpless. What I saw in her eyes that day, I will never forget. It was my own future.

Tibbs *had* taken another girl. The forgotten girl.

I shut my eyes, refocused my mind. I snapped the rubber band on my wrist, hard. Survival requires fortitude, the ability to forget and move on. To compartmentalize. I was a master at that, I had to be. I had made my choices years ago, the night I ran from a burning house into uncertain and terrifying darkness.

Only I knew about the other girl. Tibbs had taken that to his death. I headed toward the freeway to begin the long trek home. The miles and miles of multiple freeways spread out, connecting and converging into tangled knots as cars slowed to a crawl. Coming from the South Bay through downtown was always a deadly commute but I welcomed the time alone. I couldn't wait to slip into the safe cocoon of my family, to see my daughters and their sweet smiles. To reaffirm that the world made sense. My phone rang, I saw Ryan's number.

"What's up?"

"Grice removed Whirt from the case. He spoke to the chief at the Redondo PD, and they pulled Whirt while we check him out," he said.

"What the hell? He can't make that decision unilaterally,

he's not the head of this investigation. I told him to wait twenty-four hours before we moved on it!"

"Well, he acted on it. Not too long after you left. Whirt was super pissed, he just blew up and stormed off. The house guy, Moran, saw the whole thing and was asking questions. It's a fucking mess!"

It was a power play by Grice, who didn't wait long for me to be off-site to make a move. I wondered if he had spoken to Powers and Edmonson at the FBI offices.

"Thanks for the update, I'm calling Grice and then Whirt," I said, hanging up.

I was stuck in a sea of red taillights. I speed-dialed Grice and got his voicemail. I tried again. No answer. I dialed Whirt and got the same.

"Whirt, it's Emily Ray. Ryan just told me what happened. It's my fault. We talked to Brenda Coombs and she told us about you being her source. It raised some doubts, but Grice made this call on his own. I will fix this," I said.

Everything about this case was going wrong and now I was losing control of the whole thing. Grice had done an end run around me and I didn't know how bad the damage was yet. We had sullied a career detective's reputation with no solid proof. We were no closer to finding Josie Vance, aside from a basic police sketch, a worthless video and some cryptic drawings.

I banged my palms against the steering wheel in frustration. I turned the music up and screamed at the top of my lungs, just to get it out. I sensed Josie was not the end game. Our guy had a wider target and it included me, in some way. I had to think way outside the box since nothing inside the box was making any sense.

I dialed Grice again and still no answer. I ran my fingers over the knot on my head which was sore and tender to the touch and was already a deep shade of purple. I was heading out of downtown L.A. when Grice finally called back.

"What happened with Whirt?" I asked.

"After the issues you raised, I felt it was best to have him taken off the case," he replied evenly, as if he were telling me what he ate for lunch.

"We agreed to wait on this decision."

"Emily, you're not yourself on this case and with good reason. I get it."

"It's not your call to make, I am the supervisory agent."

"And you're on edge, you fainted and got injured when the newest piece of evidence arrived. What is going on?" he asked.

I was silent. He was right.

"Did you clear this with Edmonson and Powers?" I wanted to know how far up the FBI chain of command he had gone.

"Yes, I filled them in. We don't have jurisdiction over Whirt so I spoke to his chief about our concerns."

"And?"

"Chief Drayson thought it would be best for him to step back, especially since this case seems to have some link to yours and Whirt acted unethically at that time by giving information to that Coombs woman," he explained.

"I'll deal with Whirt and I'll speak to Drayson as well. I would've preferred if you had waited until we made a decision together."

"I get that, but I had to do what I felt was best for the investigation," he replied.

He was jockeying for position, but I couldn't waste time or attention on internal power dynamics.

"I'm almost home let's check back in later," I said, curtly.

We hung up and I had another hour of driving before I reached home. It was late afternoon when I pulled onto my street, the canopy of trees filtering out the sun. I saw an unmarked vehicle parked outside our gate and I nodded to the agents inside. The electric gates opened, and I drove in, feeling the full weight of safety and security close around me. I walked in the house to find Dolores and the girls watching *The Owl House*.

"Mommy!" they shrieked, running to grasp onto my legs, almost knocking me over. I scooped them into my arms and for a split second, I forgot everything else. This was all that mattered, these little squirming creatures, talking over each other.

"Dolores said we can have pizza as long as we have a salad, too," Juliana said.

"And we made sugar cookies at school today. I brought mine home!" Eliza said, running into the kitchen and returning a moment later with some scrunched-up, gloppy discs decorated with smeared icing.

"They look great!" I said, popping one into my mouth. They were quite good; I grabbed another as I moved to lock my Glock into the safe in the laundry room.

"What happened to your head, *mija*?" Dolores asked.

"I tripped and fell at work. I hit my head on a chair," I explained, and the twins hurried to get the first aid ice packs from the freezer.

"Put this on it, Mommy. And take some ibuprofen," Eliza ordered.

As Juli put the second ice pack on my neck, I pulled away.

"Too cold!" I shrieked.

"You need it back here also," she said, pressing the pack against my shoulders.

"Thank you, doctor," I said.

"I am going to be a doctor," she said as if this were common knowledge. Last week she was going to be a bike mechanic.

"I'm going to be a doctor, too. The kind that helps babies," Eliza said.

Antonio entered, fresh from a run on the treadmill. He scooped Eliza up and turned her upside down.

"A doctor who treats babies or delivers babies?' he asked as she squealed with joy.

"A doctor who gives them shots!"

Dolores put a kettle of water on the stove. "I'm going to make you some salvia tea, Emily. It's good for bruises. Toño, look at her head, she slipped!"

He walked over to me, planted a kiss on my lips and checked out the bump. He ran his forefinger over it, and I flinched.

"We should go to Urgent Care, just to be sure you don't have a concussion," he said, worry etched across his face.

"No, not now. I just got home. We're having pizza and salad and sugar cookies! Don't ruin my fun!" I said, putting on a bright smile. "Later, I promise. I need to take a quick shower, wash off the day! And I want to fly kites!" I headed for the stairway before anyone could protest, stripped off my clothes and stepped into the warm water splashing over me from the giant showerhead. Then I wrapped myself in a large fluffy bath towel and dried off.

After I'd slipped into a soft pair of sweatpants and a T-shirt, I grabbed a comfy cashmere cardigan from the closet and headed downstairs. Juliana and Eliza had their kites ready on the kitchen counter.

Dolores was chopping vegetables for the salad and ushered me towards the back door. "Go outside with the kites for a few minutes, I have to put the pizza in the oven."

Antonio and I carried the kites outside to the front yard, the twins bouncing along behind us.

"It would be better at the park," Eliza said.

"I know, sweetie, but we're going to have dinner soon. Here will work just fine," I said. Our front yard was huge, they had more than enough room to fly.

We helped them gain momentum to catch the breeze, running back and forth for a few failed tries. Finally, they had them in the air.

"We did it!" Juliana shouted, as her kite crashed into a tall magnolia tree. Antonio and I worked to dislodge it. He gave me a boost to climb into the fat branches, where I wedged myself, struggling to reach the kite.

"Don't slip, that's all we need today!" he cautioned me.

"I've got a good grip, I can almost reach the tail..." I said, falling an inch or two short.

"How about if I try?" he suggested.

"You're too big! The branch might break and then we'd both be banged-up," I said with a laugh.

"You're almost there, Mommy!' Juliana said, excitedly.

I made one big lunge upward and grabbed the tail of the kite, gently pulling it toward me until it was free.

"Success!' I shouted, as I climbed down.

When we turned back, I saw Eliza's kite on the grass. She was nowhere to be seen.

"Where's Liza?" I asked.

Antonio scanned the yard. "Eliza!" he called out. No response.

"Liza!?" I shouted. "Where are you, honey?"

The yard was still, silent; the breeze swaying the flowers in their neat, orderly beds.

I felt panic rising; where did she go? The yard was fenced, there were agents outside the front gate. I ran to the house and flung open the door. "Dolores! Is Liza with you?"

"No, *mija*. She didn't come inside," she said, maneuvering a large pizza into the oven.

I grabbed my phone from the counter and pulled up my home security app, but the video footage was slow to load; I ran back out to the front yard. Antonio was looking behind the row of hedges near the garages. Juliana was searching in the tree-house we had built into a tall jacaranda tree. There was no sign of Eliza.

"Where is she?" I cried, terror overtaking my reason. Was he here? I was sure they were safe, but the copycat had been waiting, hiding right here in my sanctuary and he had taken my daughter. Antonio had gone around to the backyard, and I bolted to the path on the other side of the house. A moment later, he returned, carrying Eliza who held a large crystalized pink rock.

"Look, Mommy! I found this in the back, it's called rose quartz!" she said, proudly.

"Where did you go?" I shouted and then immediately regretted my outburst. Her tiny face contorted, and tears of confusion welled up in her eyes. I grabbed her and held her close.

"I'm sorry, baby. Mommy's sorry for raising her voice. You didn't do anything wrong, I just got scared when I couldn't see you," I said, trying to steady my breathing and squash the panic that had consumed me.

"I found this rock by the stables, and I wanted to show you," she cried into my shoulder.

Antonio shot me a pointed look and wrapped all of us in his arms, leading us toward the house.

"Okay, my girls. It's all over now, everyone is safe and sound. Eliza just went exploring without telling us. You have to let us know if you go to the back of the property, okay? You can't go alone."

"I thought it was okay because the bodyguard was back there," Eliza said, her voice quivering.

"Where?" I asked.

"By the fence—to the creek," she said, pointing towards the far end of the property.

"You all get ready for dinner, I'll be there in a minute," I said, sprinting to the front gate to check on the security detail. I found both agents, Johnson and Adeff, in a sedan, parked next to my gate. They rolled down the window as I approached.

"Do you have someone at the back edge of the property? Near the creek?"

"No, Agent Ray. We're just here in front. Was there a problem?" Adeff asked.

"My daughter said she saw someone back there; she thought it was one of you."

"We'll go check it out. And we'll split up and make sure someone is always in the back as well," Johnson assured me.

I walked back to the house. My heartbeat had returned to normal, but the rush of sudden adrenaline left me exhausted. Who did Eliza see behind our property? I put it out of my mind, determined not to let it ruin my precious time at home.

I helped Antonio pull a large cheese pizza from the oven; it smelled heavenly. The fresh dough, melted cheese and tomato sauce were perfect comfort food. Antonio pulled a bottle of Daou Cabernet from the wine fridge and uncorked it. I got a glass from the cupboard and slid it toward him.

"You're having a glass? While you're on a case?" he asked, surprised.

"Yes, please," I replied, grabbing a piece of pizza, dripping with hot cheese.

Dolores had made a blueberry cheesecake for dessert and brewed decaffeinated *café de olla*, with cinnamon sticks and star anise. The wine was excellent, from a vineyard in Paso Robles, near where we got married at Los Olivos. The evening was perfect.

After we cleaned up the kitchen, I took advantage of being home early enough to give the girls their bubble bath. Listening to their high-pitched voices bounce off the bathroom tile was heavenly. I didn't care if they got soap on the floor or splashed water on me. Bathtime with my girls was a luxury. Afterward, Antonio and I carried them to their room to tuck them in.

"Mommy, are you looking for the girl who went missing at the beach?" Juli asked, buttoning a cardigan on her Jellycat bunny.

"How did you know that?" Antonio asked.

"Kids at school. They know that Mommy works for the FBI," Eliza said, attempting to put her hair into a ponytail, to no avail. Antonio took over, expertly securing it with a scrunchie.

"Jacob Smith said you're looking for the little girl," Juli added.

"Is he in your class?" I asked. I had never heard of Jacob Smith.

Juliana rolled her eyes, to let me know how supremely lame I was. "No, Mom. He's *old*! He's in fourth grade. We go to the Kids Club with him."

They went to an afterschool program with older kids from their elementary school. Back in kindergarten they gave me a very detailed and accurate explanation of where babies come from. A fifth grader named Brady told them. Life moved a lot faster these days.

"Are you going to find her?" Juliana asked, folding her hand into mine.

"Yes, I am. Now you need to go to sleep!" I said, kissing her forehead.

We closed the door to their room, leaving the Elmo night-light on. Antonio slipped his arm around my waist as we padded along the hall to the stairway. I leaned into him, feeling the warmth of his body. At six feet, he was a nice, cozy fit for my five-foot-four frame.

"What did the agent outside say?" he whispered into the top of my head.

"They didn't have anyone back there. But they will from now on. Who do you think it could've been?" I asked.

"Anyone. People hike back there, they walk dogs. But we'll keep the girls away from that area from now on. So, tell me. I know this case is a tougher one than usual," he said.

"The perpetrator is very savvy and organized. We have a six-year-old witness who saw him with Josie adjacent to the park, a popsicle vendor who sold him balloons, and a police sketch and two drawings."

"I saw the sketch was released to the press. More than one drawing?"

"Yes, a second one came but we can't figure out what it means," I said, casually. There was no way I could begin to even talk about the two girls in the drawing and what it meant. It was my secret, even from him.

In the kitchen, he refilled my wine glass halfway and we settled into the big sofa.

"How're the adjustments to the rover going?" I asked, changing the topic.

"Good. I'm working on the rocker-bogie and how it attaches to the chassis. We have to make some changes to the differential."

The rocker-bogie is the system that functions like feet or wheels on the rover, allowing it to pivot and remain stable while navigating other planetary surfaces. I loved Antonio's work, and I enjoyed being part of it, even just by extension as the spouse. He leaned in to look at the bump on my head again.

"This must hurt like hell. You tripped and hit your head on what, exactly?"

"A chair," I said flatly, feeling like an idiot. I didn't tell him I fainted.

"I still think I should take you to Urgent Care. Just to be sure you don't have a concussion," he said.

"I don't want to go, I'm fine. What if we have to wait hours?" I protested.

"Then we won't stay. But I'd feel better if they checked you out. I won't make you give up your whole evening at home," he said, rising.

I knew there was no way I would get out of it. Antonio was a caretaker, always protective of me. I sighed and stepped into a pair of sneakers I had left by the fireplace.

"Okay, we'll go. But we leave if it's packed!" I insisted.

"In La Cañada? Everyone's about eighty and asleep by seven p.m.!" he laughed.

He told Dolores we were leaving as I slipped on a light jacket. Moose thought he was going for an evening walk and accompanied us to the door. I gave him a kiss on his muzzle.

"You'll go out when we get back, big boy," I said, patting his ears.

We took Antonio's car, a black Range Rover, and pulled down the long driveway. We both watched as the electric gate closed behind us. We pulled up next to the sedan parked outside our gate. Johnson rolled down the window.

"Just running her over to Urgent Care," Antonio said.

"Stay and keep an eye on the house. We'll be back soon," I said.

"Will do, Agent Ray. Adeff is out back. The fellow who was there earlier was a neighbor of yours, he was looking for his cat who escaped. He checked out," Johnson said, before rolling up the tinted windows.

"It's like something from *Men in Black*," Antonio muttered as we pulled onto the quiet streets of our little city. The local Urgent Care was on Foothill where La Cañada meets up with Montrose, another quaint community in the northeast part of the city. Antonio was right, there was only one person and no wait. We saw a doctor right away and she grilled me on the symptoms of concussion. No pressure in my head? No dizziness or confusion? No vomiting or nausea? Again, I didn't mention the fainting. She told me to take Advil and drink plenty of water. We were back in the car within an hour.

"We really didn't need to go," I chided him.

"Yes, we did because now I feel better and I can relax," he said, sliding his hand along my thigh. I took his hand in mine and traced my forefinger along the inside of his palm.

He glanced over at me and said, "What are you doing, Agent Ray?"

I smiled and said, "Nothing. Nothing at all."

"We'll be home in ten minutes," he said.

We had turned down a quiet street en route to our house. It was secluded, most of the homes had tall, stone walls around the perimeters of their properties.

"Pull over and park for a minute," I said.

He complied and turned to me. "Okay—"

I cut him off, leaning over and pulling him into a kiss across the console of the car. I felt his hands in my hair and on the small of my back. He kissed me deeply, his tongue pushing through my open lips. I guided his hands under my T-shirt and felt his palms encircle my breasts.

"Honey, we're just around the corner from home," he whispered.

"I don't want to go home, I want to do it here, like when we were young," I said, my heart pounding.

He chuckled. "Like that time we visited my mom in San Diego? In my Chevy Blazer?"

"Just like that." I climbed into the backseat of the Range Rover.

"We could get caught," he said, following me. "What would we tell the cops?"

"That we're two married people who felt like having sex in a car," I said, reaching to undo the zipper of his jeans. "Remember how exciting it was back then? Just to reach under clothes and touch bare skin? To free just enough of ourselves to do it?" I whispered, as he ran his fingers along my back and tugged my sweatpants down.

I felt myself getting wet and grabbed his hand and slid it into me so he would feel it, too. His breath quickened and he pulled me on top of him, my legs straddling his waist. He wiggled out of his jeans and I felt him up against me, hard. I ran my thumb along the small bead of semen at the head of his penis and he moaned, his eyes closed, his head back against the car seat. I lifted myself up so he could enter me and with a thrust of his hips, I felt him inside me.

He grasped my waist and rocked me against him. The windows of the car were steamed over, and I was breathing hard and fast. I felt feral. All the fear and frustration of the past two days coursing up through my body and into every push and pull against his flesh. I came suddenly, unexpectedly, and I felt myself grip him deeper into my body. And then he let out a low, throaty groan and I felt him release inside me. We were both sweating, our hair wet, our clothes plastered against our skin.

I rolled off him and leaned back against the clammy leather of the seat. A security light on the wall of the house suddenly came on, illuminating our fogged-up windows.

"Okay, ADT Security will be here in a few minutes," he said.

We slid our clothes back into place and climbed into the front seats, giggling like two kids.

He started the engine and said, "You know, I really like you. Can I have your phone number?"

I laughed. "You just like that I'm willing to go all the way in the backseat of the car."

He smiled and took my hand. We drove in contented silence for a few blocks until we reached home. The house was quiet, Moose padded across the floor to greet us when we came in. Upstairs, we stopped by Dolores' room where she was watching a *telenovela* in Spanish.

"*Y que pasó?*" she asked, snuggled up on her love seat, wrapped in a super plushy Mexican blanket.

"No concussion. The doctor just told me to take Advil," I said.

"I left a pot of tea for you on the kitchen counter. And some *conchas* if you want a midnight snack. And there's a *niño envuelto* for you, Toño."

He moved to give her a kiss. *Niño envuelto* was his favorite, a Mexican jelly roll from a bakery in Eagle Rock that Dolores visited each day.

"*Gracias*, Tia. I'm off to bed. C'mon," he said, grabbing my hand.

"Goodnight, Dolores. Thank you for everything."

We checked in on the girls who were fast asleep.

"You ready for bed? I'm just going to take a quick rinse off," Antonio said, stripping down to shower.

"Yeah, I'll take Moose out to do his business. Then I'll rinse off, too."

Moose wagged his tail and followed me down the stairs and across the den to the back door. I turned the alarm off, and we stepped out into the cool, slightly damp air. The backyard was deep and lush, the paver lights illuminating the pathways among the flower beds. Moose went to the far corner of the yard, near the gate to the stable area. I would put a new padlock on it tomorrow.

I sat in a lawn chair and closed my eyes. I could see the second drawing as if it were in front of me. Two girls who looked the same, hand in hand. Only Tibbs and I knew the truth about the other girl. And I was the only one of us still alive.

Wasn't I?

One thought kept running through my mind, no matter how much I tried to outpace it.

He's still alive, he's coming for me...

Back inside, I pulled my small gun case from under the bed and unlocked it, checking the bullets in my Smith and Wesson .38 revolver. I slipped it quietly into the drawer of the bedside table.

Just in case.

SIXTEEN

The morning came too quickly, and I was on the treadmill getting my workout in by 4:30. By six I had put the .38 back in lockup, kissed my family goodbye and was on the road back to Palos Verdes. It would take over an hour, so I dialed Whirt's number.

"Agent Ray? I got your message," he said. His voice sounded thick and strange.

"I'm sorry, Whirt. Grice moved on this without my knowledge," I explained.

"You and Ryan came to my fucking house to talk to Ellen? What the hell?" His words were slurred; I realized he was drunk, at 6:30 in the morning.

"I'm sorry, Whirt. Brenda Coombs revealed some information that was concerning, and it raised questions in my mind about your veracity in all this."

"My 'veracity'? Fuck all the fancy talk, Emily. Do you really think I could've done this type of thing?"

"I'll speak to your chief today and fix this, I promise," I said.

"Forget it. I handed in my resignation today. My pension is

secure, I don't need this shit. Fuck you all," he said and then hung up.

Ninety minutes later, I pulled up outside the Vance home to find the press had not dispersed. Inside, Grice had not yet arrived. Diaz and Stephanie had pulled an all-nighter to go over the information that was coming in from the release of the police sketch.

"We've got a lot to work today, Emily. We've had tons of calls from people who think they recognize the guy," Diaz said, drinking a thick green smoothie in a plastic bottle.

"Is that good?" I asked.

"No, it tastes like a plant from the yard. But it's supposed to be healthy. I don't always get those five servings of veggies a day," he replied.

"Where do you usually eat?"

"Del Taco," he said.

"Oh, hell..." I replied with a weak laugh.

I sifted through the information that was coming in. I categorized it all and compiled lists for the agents and sheriffs to work off, making sure every tip would be checked out. I knew some would be completely crazy, but we had to do it. Izzy arrived and called me over as he set up his laptop.

"I was on the dark web until about three this morning and there is a new child being auctioned from one of the sites offshore. It could be Josie, based on the description," he said.

My stomach dropped. This was the worst-case scenario. One of the most unsavory parts of the job is coming across illegal trafficking sites on the dark web, where kids are taken, often drugged and then sold to the highest bidder. Two out of three children abducted for sex in the United States are trafficked online. Kids and teens are sold to pedophiles in Saudi Arabia, the Philippines, and other far-flung destinations. We had informants overseas, and with good intel, we could catch some of them. But these groups are like the Hydra; we cut off one head and three more spring up. They are almost impossible to trace to a specific location.

"Let me know when you have more information and get Dana Linderman from Missing and Exploited Children involved," I said, praying silently that it wouldn't be Josie.

I reviewed the video footage from Plaza Segundo again, but they erased their tapes every ten days and the guy with the balloons hadn't shown up on any previous footage.

"We're fanning out today to follow up on the tips that have been called in with the release of the police sketch. We have a lot of ground to cover. I've drawn up contact lists for each of you to work off. Ryan and I will go check out Pete Hainly, the guy from the Deborah Kilby case. And then we'll start on the calls reacted to the sketch."

I could sense their despair at how little progress we had made. And the possibility of Josie being on a trafficking site knocked the wind out of everyone.

"Don't get discouraged, it's probably not her if it's coming from a foreign server. We need to stay in high prey drive to push through," I encouraged them.

I heard shrill, angry voices. I went to the door and saw Louis and Melanie approaching, mid-argument.

"I was just coming over to give you both an update," I said.

"What the hell is going on? Moran said he heard that detective, the older one, yelling last night and then he left!" Louis barked at me.

"Detective Whirt was taken off the case by his chief," I replied, calmly.

"So, what? You guys are just falling apart now? You haven't found my daughter, you're hemorrhaging people from the case! How are you going to find Josie with this kind of shit?" he shouted.

I saw Diaz and Landry at the window, checking out the ruckus.

"We are far from falling apart, Mr. Vance. We are all doing a lot of work that isn't obvious or even appropriate to share with you."

"Why haven't you found her yet? I think I should bring in a private investigator or maybe we need to put it out on social media, get all those crime fanatics involved. They help solve cases, right?" Louis ranted.

"At this point bringing in outside people will make our job a lot harder, if not impossible. We have a perpetrator who has a bigger plan. I have every reason to believe that Josie is still alive, and we will find her. The more he contacts us, the closer we get to him," I said confidently.

At that moment, Izzy came to the door and stuck his head out. "Emily, I need you to come in to look at something."

"What is it?" Louis started to push past me, but I stopped him, with a hand on his arm. If Josie was on a child trafficking site, the last thing we needed was for her parents to see it.

"This is internal FBI work, Mr. Vance. I know it's very hard to wait and all you want is to see Josie walk through the front door. We are working around the clock to find her and either Agent Grice or I will keep you updated. Please, try to stay calm," I said, releasing his arm and gently turning him back toward the house. I watched until he had disappeared inside.

We gathered around Izzy's laptop to view the video. I prayed silently it would not be Josie. It was shot with a cellphone, and it showed a child approximately seven or eight years old sitting in a wooden chair, holding a beat-up stuffed animal. She looked as if she had been drugged.

"She looks a little too tall," Izzy said, hopeful.

"And the facial features don't match," Diaz added, letting out a sigh of relief.

I leaned in to look more closely at the child. She was skinny, her hair was pale blond and brittle. She had dark circles under her eyes. It wasn't Josie Vance. But it was someone's daughter. A man's voice spoke off camera in Russian, giving the auction details. I turned away; it made me sick to see it. The child was most likely from Eastern Europe; she may have been abducted or sold by her own family, which happened sometimes to people living in desperate circumstances. There were so many children trafficked and we could save barely any of them. The knowledge of it weighed on me every single day.

"It's not her," I said, quietly.

"I'll keep on it. I'll go through other channels," Izzy said, with his quiet resolve.

He didn't say what we were all thinking; that if Josie were trafficked, a lot of press coverage would make her a high risk. Her value as a commodity to traffickers would go down and they could dump her off somewhere, maybe alive but probably not. They get rid of unusable merchandise with a hotshot, a lethal injection of heroin and cocaine; that was the usual fate of girls who had no value any longer.

I signaled to Ryan. "We're going to check out Pete Hainly, from the Kilby case."

He grabbed his Starbucks cup, and we headed out to the car.

"How's your head today?" he asked, entering the GPS information to Hainly's house into his phone.

"Sore. But better. My husband made me go to Urgent Care last night. No concussion."

"Your hubs is a scientist, right?"

"A rocket scientist, actually. He works at JPL. How about you? Married?"

"Not yet. Maybe in a few years," he said with a small grin.

"What's that little smile about?" I asked.

"Oh, well, I'd get married now but my partner isn't ready yet."

"Does she or he work for the police department?"

He blushed and turned to me with a laugh. "How'd you know it could be a 'he'?"

"You said 'partner' instead of 'girlfriend'."

"Yeah, well, no one at work knows. Being gay in the police force is no fun."

"I'm not telling," I assured him as we turned onto Hainly's street in the cluster of jewel streets in Redondo Beach, on Beryl Avenue. The Hainly house was a holdover from the mid-sixties, with a hideous neo-mansard-style roof. The paint was peeling, the flimsy aluminum windows had newspapers over the glass. We pulled into the driveway.

Before we could get out of the car, a woman came barreling out the front door toward us. She was in her late sixties and wore a lightweight cotton nightgown with a pair of huge, dirty Pokémon slippers on her feet. She clutched a baseball bat in her hand.

"What're you doin' in here?' the woman demanded.

"We're looking for Pete Hainly. We're with the Redondo Beach Police Department and the FBI," Ryan said.

"You're cops? You're not from that Devil group in Fontana?"

I figured she was referring to the Devil's Disciples, a drug-running biker gang in the Inland Empire. The Kilby case files said Hainly had been mixed up with them in the past.

"We wanted to talk to Pete about an old case. Do you know when he'll be back?"

"You can go find him at Torrance Memorial. Something wrong with his brain, it's all swelled-up from meth!"

"We want to speak to him about the Deborah Kilby case," Ryan said.

The woman's eyes narrowed, and she tapped the bat against the cement.

"He didn't have nothing to do with that girl, never even met her!" She stepped closer to us, aggressively.

"Thank you very much, Mrs. Hainly, we'll be on our way," I said as I began backing out of the driveway. She took a sudden and random swing at the headlights, smashing one. I kept going; we didn't need this situation to escalate over a broken headlight.

Once we were safely on the street, Ryan asked, "Do you ever think it might be nice to work in an office? Same routine every day, very predictable."

"We'd both go nuts with boredom, you know it."

As I drove, Ryan called Torrance Memorial and confirmed that Hainly had been hospitalized for the past five weeks with a drug-induced brain inflammation. We were on Hawthorne Boulevard on our way back to the Sparrow's Nest when I got a call from Larissa Cinque.

"Agent Ray? This is Larissa, from the *Daily Breeze*," she said earnestly.

"Hello, Ms. Cinque, how did you get my number and how can I help you?"

"Detective Whirt gave it to me. I wanted to talk to you about some old cases. I got the idea to look into cases from back in the day when you were taken. I'm doing a two-part series on how wealth and privilege play into these cases."

Old cases, back in the day...

I felt a nervous tingle at the back of my neck. I glanced at Ryan and gripped the steering wheel tighter. "That's a disparity that's very real. Some cases get a lot more media attention than others," I said.

"So, I was looking into cases from the mid-nineties, and I found one of a girl who went missing from Redondo Beach, just a couple of years after you. It was 1995, and there was no attention given to her case. I'm going to do research on her backstory, but I pitched it to my editor, and he likes the idea. So, I'm going to go with it," she said, excitedly.

"That's a great idea for an article. What do you need me for?" I asked.

"I just wanted to send you a photo I found. She looks almost identical to you at that age. I compared her photo to the one on your missing child poster. It's kind of uncanny. Can I text it to you?" she asked.

"That's fine. Send it over," I managed to say, my heart hammering in my chest.

"Okay. Her name was Danica Hansen," she said before hanging up.

I slipped my phone into the pocket on the door of the car. My hands were clammy, and my vision shifted as if I were seeing everything through a glass of water.

"What did the kid reporter want?" Ryan asked.

"Oh, she's writing about kidnappings," I said, casually.

A moment later my phone pinged, and the two images arrived. I pulled the phone from the door pocket and glanced briefly at the photos. I recognized the picture of the poster from my case. And next to it, a washed-out photo of Danica Hansen. She and I did look almost identical. She never got a missing child poster. But I knew that already. I knew all about her, even if I hadn't heard her name in over two decades. I knew. Because twenty-three years ago, I was Danica Hansen.

SEVENTEEN

TORRANCE, CALIFORNIA, 1995

The day Emily Ray was taken, I was seven years old. If you'd looked at the second-grade class photo at Jefferson Elementary you would have seen me in the front row: skinny, blond hair, most likely wearing high-water jeans and a boy's T-shirt from the thrift store.

At the time, I probably heard about her abduction on the TV that was always blaring at my aunt Janelle's trailer. Three years later, I was taken from a park, by the same man who took her, James Tibbs. And then our stories became one.

He was a living darkness that swallowed us up. He was the part of the carnival ride where the monster's distorted shadow looms and grows huge as he approaches. But in the haunted house, you shriek and cover your eyes, waiting to burst through swinging doors into the bright sunlight. You laugh nervously with your friends and go in for another spin. But the ride didn't end that way for us. For Emily, it never ended at all.

How did he get me? By the time I was eight, I had bounced between my mother's apartment, two foster homes and my aunt Janelle's place. My mom divorced my dad when he was sent to prison again and wouldn't be out for a decade. She took up with an unemployed truck driver named Jedidiah and one day they got the brilliant idea to move to San Antonio. A new start for them, not for me. I got dropped off with Aunt Janelle at the Beach Palms Trailer Park in Torrance. They drove off, promising to come and get me once they got settled. I never saw my mother again. My aunt Janelle was a low-level con artist and occasional criminal. She didn't want me, and I didn't want to be there but I had no place else to go.

I was always out roaming around on my own. I loved going down to the water, sitting on the Redondo Beach pier and looking out at that huge expanse of ocean in front of me. Just wide-open space for me to make into whatever I wanted it to be.

I'd imagine that I had a different life, that I was a different girl. I pretended I had a big bedroom with bunk beds and matching comforters, that I made cookies after school with my pretty, smiling mom who would take me to Girl Scouts or soccer. But then I'd have to go back. I'd walk in the door and Janelle would be sprawled on the couch like a wrung-out kitchen rag, still in her faded pajamas with a bowl of microwaved nachos on the floor next to her. There were no cookies, no Girl Scouts, no soccer.

Until the day when I was ten and I got a postcard from my mom. She was coming back to get me on a Greyhound bus and I should meet her at the bus station at noon, on the following Friday. I told all my friends in school and even my teacher, Mrs. Goodwin. They had a goodbye party for me with cupcakes. But when it was time to go to the station, Janelle just laughed and refused to take me.

"You're nuts, Dani. There's no way your mom is coming across the country on a bus to get you. My girlfriends and I are giving each other manicures today. If your mom wants you, she'll call and come get you here," she shouted over the mixer that was blending a batch of margaritas. I was so angry I wanted to throw something across the room.

"You have to take me," I insisted. "What if I'm not there and I miss her?"

Janelle snorted as she laughed, as if what I was saying was the stupidest thing she had ever heard. At that moment, I hated her.

So, I went on my own. I got to the bus station at 9:30 in the morning. I waited as each bus came in and pulled out again. I waited and watched until four o'clock and I knew Janelle was right. No one was coming for me. I went to the park down by the Redondo marina. There were other kids when I arrived but after an hour or so, they all left. And that's when he found me. James Tibbs, who approached a solitary child, building a fort out of rocks and twigs.

He said he'd buy me a hotdog from the vendor in the parking lot and I was hungry, so I followed him. And then I was gone, spirited away into his van, restrained, gagged.

I thought of Janelle with her friends, drinking margaritas. She wouldn't even notice I was gone. I had told everyone that I was going with my mom to Texas. I'd had a goodbye party at school. Would anyone even know I was missing?

He took me to the Glendale house and down to the hidden bunker. To the other girl he had taken three years before me, Emily Ray. Larissa was right, we looked so much alike, we could have been twins. His parents had left him the house in Glendale when they died. After I went to the police, the newspapers went crazy, cars driving up and down that quiet little street. Everyone was asking the same thing: why didn't anyone notice anything? Because people aren't looking for evil in the windows of the house next door.

I was in that room for five years. Emily was there for eight. In that bunker, built of cement block with no windows, it was as if we didn't exist. We never went outside, except for the occasional midnight excursion to the foothills, where we could run and do jumping jacks, attached to extendable dog leashes. With duct tape over our mouths. If we were good while we were out, we'd get a long hot shower in the main bathroom of the house, not a chilly sponge bath at the miserable little sink in our room.

One day he came to our room with scissors and electric clippers and cut off all of our hair, chopping and shaving until all we had left was pale, blond fuzz. It was too dangerous; what if a strand of long blond hair caught the attention of the handyman who came now and then to fix things? We both cried when he did it.

He told us our families didn't want us anymore, they were glad he took us. He wanted us to forget who we were, to forget everything that came before him. But we didn't. Late at night, when he was gone, we would tell our stories in whispers.

"We live in a big house, right above the beach. My room is pink and white. What color is yours?"

"My room is just plain. I live with my aunt, because my mom moved to Texas..."

"My mom's named Andie. She used to be a lawyer. My dad builds houses..."

"I haven't seen my dad in a long time..."

"When we get away, we'll be together, forever. You'll live with me by the beach. I promise, Dani..."

"Together forever, like sisters..."

We'd tell each other again and again. Those stories were all we had. Over time, we knew every detail of our short lives before we were thrown together. It was as if we were the same person. I didn't know back then that one day, we would become just that.

I had been captive there for just over five years when it happened. We had been out on the hiking trails and when we got back to our room, Emily showed me an old bobby pin she had found and slipped into her shoe. She had been getting more and more withdrawn in the weeks before that.

When we were about thirteen, Tibbs started taking us into

his bedroom alone. I didn't know what it was then but now I know that he couldn't get an erection so he would just touch us. But Emily had become different since it began. All she did was sleep and cry and she barely ate at all. He'd shout at her and try to force food into her but then she'd just get sick. Those were the bad nights.

That evening, Emily flushed a huge wad of toilet paper and clogged the drain, so we had to go upstairs to the main bathroom. It was late, she was lying curled against my back, the way we always slept. I could feel her breathing.

She whispered, "I'm going to get away and leave."

"How? When are we going?"

There was a pause and then, "I'll tell you more later..."

Then she rang the little bell that Tibbs had hung by our bed to call him. He showed up bleary-eyed and sleepy a few minutes later. Emily pointed that she had to use the bathroom, and he led her up the stairs. His routine was that he'd wait outside the door for us.

The bathroom had no windows, no way to escape. Sometimes, if it was the middle of the night, he'd fall asleep in the hallway. I guess that's what she was counting on. I saw her walking away and she looked back at me once, her eyes clear blue and shiny. She smiled and disappeared up the stairway to the main house.

I stayed awake, waiting for her to come back. But she never did. Then I heard Tibbs shouting and cursing, and I knew something bad had happened. He came down the stairs to our room and I saw blood on his hands, on the cuffs of his pajamas. He was crying and shaking and slapping his forehead like a crazy person. He was yelling at me, as if I had an answer, then he bolted upstairs.

I heard his footsteps walking on the floor above me, up and down the hallways. But no sign of Emily. An hour or so later, he dragged something heavy along the floorboards overhead. Then he came for me and took me to the bathroom where he had a mop and bucket with a bottle of bleach waiting.

I saw traces of bright red blood around the drain of the bathtub and splashed on the tile wall. On the edge of the tub, I saw it. The bobby pin she had found and hidden. It was bent and twisted. She was gone, by her own small hand.

At some point in the pre-dawn hours, Tibbs drove away. I knew he was taking Emily's body somewhere. It was hours before he came back, and I feared what would come next. When he came down the stairs to our room, I pretended to be asleep.

And that was when he unlocked the metal restraints on my wrists, sniveling and weeping. Then he left. And I escaped a burning house, barefoot and barely dressed in a thin cotton nightgown. I ran and hid in the foothills of the Verdugo mountains. In the dark, I remembered my life with Janelle and my mother; it was like watching a scene through a dirt-streaked window, hazy and yellow and sad. I did not want to go back to my life, I didn't want to be me without Emily.

When the sun rose, I walked back toward the streets below. I got to the boulevard. The sun was hot; the sky was blue and cloudless. And then I saw it: a black and white police car cruising down the street. I waved and ran to the curb.

"Help, help me! Please!" I shouted as the police car slowed down. The eyes of the policeman in the passenger seat were hidden behind dark sunglasses.

"What's the problem, young lady?"

"I've escaped from a house, up the street. I was kidnapped and held there..."

The officer who spoke to me was named Moreno; I read it on his badge as he stepped out of the car.

"Okay, slow down, young lady. Tell me where you were and how you got there," he said calmly.

"I was kidnapped, years ago—"

"Who took you?" Moreno asked, cutting me off.

"A man... his house is just up the street... he set it on fire..."

"How old are you?"

"I think I'm fifteen..." I started to cry.

Officer Moreno gently steered me to the backseat of the squad car. My tears turned into a torrent, I felt a pressure pushing down on my chest and I couldn't breathe. He guided my head down between my knees.

"Take a deep breath, nice and slow. You're safe now."

I gulped the air into my lungs, the full weight of my freedom settling over me.

It was over. I could hear the approaching siren of an ambulance. A crowd had gathered outside the convenience store. Officer Moreno blocked their view of me with his solid body.

"What's your name?" he asked softly.

I looked up at him. The sun reflected off his badge, he was safe.

"My name is Emily Ray."

The next few hours were like a merry-go-round on methamphetamine. An ambulance ride to Children's Hospital. The exam by a team of doctors, a rape kit. Two detectives waiting in the hallway to speak to me.

I hadn't really considered what would happen when I said I was Emily. I just knew that she was gone, I was free, and I didn't want to go back to being me ever again. I didn't know anything about how cases are solved or investigated. But I knew more about Emily than anyone else alive and I could remember all the things she told me about her life, if I had to.

Outside, a crush of news vans, reporters, and photographers were waiting to catch a photo of the missing girl, finally found. They weren't waiting there for me, no one cared about Danica Hansen who went missing five years ago from Torrance. They wanted Emily Ray. They wanted the girl who mattered. I could be that girl. I could keep her alive. I spoke to the detectives about Tibbs but I only mentioned myself. I told them I was the only girl there. Danica Hansen ceased to exist that day.

Michael Ray had been notified and was on a flight back from China. That's when the first wave of dread hit me. Of course, he would know that I was a fraud. I wanted to run away but the return of Emily Ray was big news. I couldn't just walk out the door and disappear.

I decided that I would be asleep when he arrived. And after that first shock, I could tell the truth, and everyone would forget about it. The nurse came in with my sleeping medication. I swallowed it down, eager to escape the anxiety that I would soon be exposed. The pill began to take effect, and I fell asleep. And that was how it began. The secret that defined my whole life, like a fast-moving river that I had jumped into and now I had to stay afloat.

The sun was hanging low in the sky outside my window when I awoke. It was a big, orange ball, light diffusing off its edges. I shifted and then I saw him, seated at the side of my bed. Emily's dad, Michael Ray. He looked the way she had described him, dark, wavy hair, hazel, soft-around-the-edges eyes. He was holding my hand. His eyes filled with tears when he saw that I was awake and he whispered, "It's me, Emily. It's Daddy."

He pulled his chair closer.

He said, "I know it's been a long time that you've been gone, sweetheart. But I want you to know that we never stopped looking for you, ever. And we never stopped believing that you would come home safe."

"Where's mommy?" I asked and he took both my hands in his.

"That's one of the hard things that happened when you were gone. Mommy got sick and she fought so hard to get better, to be here for your when you came home. But her illness was just too strong for her. She's in heaven now, watching over you. And I know she's so happy that you've come back."

He was crying by then and I started crying, too. Andie was gone. He had lost her but Emily was back. I was trapped in my own lie. I saw how Emily's return was the miracle he had been praying for, how much he needed her to come home. I had been so afraid of being found out; I was only thinking of what would happen to me. I hadn't thought about how Emily's return would affect him.

I felt horrible for deceiving him, but I couldn't speak. How could I take her away from him again? It would have seemed a cruel joke to tell him the truth. Now, it wasn't just for me that I had to pretend to be Emily. I had to do it for him, too. I struggled to make my voice work, to find the right words, to find any words.

"Daddy..." My voice sounded like scratchy sandpaper. Michael Ray reached out and pulled me into a hug, his shoulders heaving with sobs of relief. We stayed there like that for a long time. I felt my body relax. I could do this. I would make it work, for him. And that was it. Later that day, I overheard the detectives and doctors talking to Michael about DNA when they thought I was asleep.

"We've already drawn her blood, we just need you to authorize the DNA test," the nurse said.

"It's not that easy and of course it's Emily, look at her. I'm not spending weeks in some DNA limbo, waiting to confirm what I already know. I'm not doing that to her or to me. She's back and that is all that matters now," Michael whispered fiercely.

I learned much later that Michael had contracted mumps as an adult and it had made him sterile. They had used an anonymous sperm donor to have Emily and Andie had been cremated after her death. Michael had spread her ashes on a bluff overlooking the ocean. There were no grandparents left alive, only an estranged, distant cousin of Andie's who suffered from schizophrenia and lived in a psychiatric facility in Arizona. Michael hadn't ever met her. The task of getting a mitochondrial DNA match would have been difficult and complicated. And as it turned out, Emily and I were both blood type O. So, there was no DNA test done. Michael believed that I was his beloved daughter because he had no reason to think that I could be anyone else.

Taking on Emily's identity was relatively easy as I knew so much from the five years we spent together. And after eight years in captivity, any lapses were to be expected. Emily Ray came back alive, case solved, happy ending.

Michael did everything right. He was so different from my real father, Glen Hansen, who had spent his life running drugs and racking up felonies like a kid in an arcade getting prize tickets. I was determined to be the best daughter Michael could ever have. I could realize all the dreams he had for Emily, I could make him whole. I could accomplish the same thing for myself. The weight of deception was the price I willingly paid.

And that was how I became a tightly wound, type-A, high achiever with OCD and buried trauma that I managed in any way that I could. Becoming Emily had given me a new chance at a different life and I lived it for both of us. The weight of that lie was my responsibility. No one knew. Not Lydia, not my husband.

Now, Danica Hansen was becoming part of the narrative and I had to ask myself the hard question: how far was I willing to go to protect the life I had built?

EIGHTEEN

I pretended to focus on the road as I drove back to the Sparrow's Nest but all I could think was that my real story, my real identity, would be splashed all over the local newspaper, with photos. The girl who had been so conveniently forgotten by everyone was now being thrust into the narrative of Josie's abduction. Two girls, who looked the same. Two girls, one alive and one dead, but I had turned the survivor into a ghost. I had to keep up the appearance of being in control with the team, even if that control was fraying dangerously.

Ryan and I got to work following up the tips that came in from the police sketch. It gave me a chance to work alone at my laptop. I ran a search on Danica Hansen. There was not much information available. Back then my mother was in Texas and had no idea I was missing until Janelle reported it several weeks later. My dad was in prison, helpless to do anything at all. A cursory investigation by the police came up with nothing. There was a brief mention of my disappearance in the *Daily Breeze* newspaper with my name spelled incorrectly and the faded photo that Larissa had sent me.

With no real pressure from my family, the case languished

and went into the cold case file. I was just one of thousands of kids who go missing every year and are never found. I knew what to expect from Larissa's article. She would try to bring Danica Hansen back to life after I had spent decades erasing her. But it wouldn't generate any new leads in a long dead case; there was nothing to find. It would not lead to my door or the discovery of my identity. I was the only one who knew the truth. I just had to keep focused and moving forward, like I had been doing my whole life.

I called Chief Drayson at the Palos Verdes PD and he confirmed that Whirt had a clean record, no hint of suspicion. I had to face the hard fact of my own miscalculation and give him the big, fat apology that he deserved. I put that happy task on my evening's to-do list.

I started working through the list of callers who had seen the sketch and thought they knew who it was. Most were way off base; people who bore grudges against ex-lovers or family members. Contentious neighbors who wanted to stir up trouble. I ruled out the people who had died or were severely incapacitated or incarcerated. Still, there were many I had to follow up with which was time-consuming, tedious work with little reward. In the afternoon, Grice and Diaz came back with a couple of promising leads.

"An elderly man, Walt Moody, thinks the guy in the sketch could be his neighbor who has an outstanding warrant for battery against a dancer from the White Rhino Gentlemen's Club, out by the airport. We're sending two deputies over later to pick him up and see if anything plays out," Grice said, sliding down into a chair, cracking his knuckles.

Diaz moved to pour himself a fresh cup of coffee. "But more interesting is a woman who has a surf shop right across from the Elks Lodge. She looked at the sketch and said she saw a guy who could be a match driving out of the alley behind her shop in an older blue sedan, the afternoon that Josie went missing. He wore a ball cap and a face mask."

"Which fits with the rest of this guy's MO," Ryan joined in.

"Why didn't she come forward sooner?" I asked. "We've put it out to the news outlets for the past few days."

"She's a pot head! Her shop reeked of weed," Grice said with disgust.

"She was kind of clueless," Diaz affirmed. "But she did get a partial license plate. She said it was an older blue sedan, maybe a Chevy Malibu or something close to it."

He handed me a piece of paper with the partial plate number which I jotted down and then gave to Stephanie.

"Steph, run this through every possible combination and then cross-check for blue sedans," I said.

"It's going to be thousands of cars," she said.

"I know. We'll eliminate as we go through them and then we can focus on the ones that could be viable," I said.

"That's a huge job. I'm on it!" she said. She relished this type of search.

"With you and Izzy working on it, Ryan and I can handle the rest. We'll narrow it down to the shortest list of people and then go talk to them."

It had been a long, tedious day of door-knocking and boots on the ground and I still had to give Melanie and Louis an update. I found Louis in his office, scrolling through true crime websites, Moran at his side, taking notes while Melanie sat on the nearby sofa.

"I think we should call some of these people in," Louis said excitedly. "They work on all kinds of cases. These two even have a reality show on Hulu!"

"I watched that show. It's called *Cold Case Hunters*," Melanie chipped in.

I looked at his screen which showed a photo of a hefty blond woman and a short man with a mullet hairstyle. They were posed in front of a courthouse building. Jemmie and Dylan Jones, online sleuths who trolled the internet to find new information that law enforcement had missed. The problem was that they rarely had all the case files or information on any given investigation; they were trying to solve a puzzle with half the pieces missing.

"I think that might make things a bit more complicated. We can't share our information with them, and they would most likely cause a lot of distraction," I replied.

"But they helped find a guy who everyone thought had drowned in Alaska. He was alive, living off the grid in a tent," Melanie said.

"She's right, and you all don't seem any closer to finding my daughter so I think we should utilize all our resources. And you could share everything with them, so they'd be on the same page," he said.

"Unless you think it'll make things worse? Maybe we should trust the FBI, Lou," Melanie said, crossing to stand behind her husband, her hand on his shoulder.

"We've been trusting them and we don't have Josie back, do we? No offense, Agent Ray, but you see the state my wife is in? She can't go on like this and neither can I. When Grice told us about those fucking kids trying to get the reward money, I almost drove over there myself!"

"We're about to give a press update and then we have a long night of work ahead of us. We have several significant leads today. Would you be willing to put a pin in the private investigator idea for now?" I asked.

He stared at me for a long beat. "Just for now."

I excused myself to prepare for the press conference. I had to get away, I could feel my equilibrium slipping. My head was throbbing, I could feel a migraine coming on and knew I needed to get out in front of it which meant getting to a dark, air-conditioned room as quickly as possible with a bag of ice at the base of my neck. I hadn't suffered from one in several years, but the shock of the Danica Hansen story had hit hard. My nerves felt raw and brittle; my brain was ricocheting wildly, trying to find a safe place to land. I motioned Grice over.

"John, why don't you handle the press conference? I'm still a little out of kilter from my fall yesterday. I think I have a migraine coming on and I need to get through this list."

"No problem, Emily. Take all the time you need," he said, giving my arm a supportive squeeze.

"I'll be staying over at the hotel if you need me," I said, packing up my laptop.

I called the Terranea Resort and booked a room for the evening. As much as I wanted to retreat to the safety of home, I couldn't face Antonio in my current state. I was descending into panic. The pounding in my head intensified. I needed to be alone to process the day's revelations. I had run from my past for twenty-three years. I had hidden my true self from everyone and now, there was no more running. The life I had built was about to implode under the weight of my deception and there was nowhere to hide.

NINETEEN
DAY THREE: 1:43 P.M.

At the hotel I asked for a bag of ice from room service, and it arrived within a few minutes. I hung up the change of work clothes I always carried in my car, then dimmed the lights and set the air conditioner to a low sixty-two degrees. I popped two Sumatriptan tablets, which I always kept in the glovebox of my car and laid myself out on the bed with the ice against the base of my neck. I called home. Dolores had taken the girls to ice skating after school and now they were in the yard planting a vegetable garden as a school project.

"I'm going to be staying out here in Palos Verdes tonight, we have a ton of work to do," I said, omitting the information about the migraine; I didn't want her worrying.

"You didn't pack anything for dinner, did you? Can you get something healthy out there?" Dolores asked. I could hear the concern in her voice.

"Don't worry, I can pick something up," I lied. Food was the last thing I wanted with a migraine.

"Make sure to get a salad. Do you want me to get the girls to come to the phone?"

"No, don't bother them. I'll call before bedtime. I'll text Toño now to let him know," I said.

"Okay, *mi guerita*. Make sure you wear a sweater when you go out. It's cold by the beach."

She was always taking care of me, so different from my own mother. I hadn't thought of Amber Hansen in years. I texted my husband and settled into my migraine routine. I put in my AirPods, set the Spotify station to meditation music and closed my eyes. I owed Whirt a call, but I put it off. The migraine forced me to lie there and just think. I couldn't escape into exercise. Any kind of screen activity made it worse so I couldn't bury myself in work or even watch some mindless television as a distraction.

I remembered things I had banished from my history: hanging out at the local gas station with grown men while my mom was out drinking; asking the neighbors for food when I hadn't eaten for several days. The kids at school making jokes about how I wore the same dirty jeans every day and my Goodwill shoes were always too big. My dad being put into a police car and disappearing from my life. Once I returned as Emily, I was able to forget about my parents quite easily. There was nothing to miss, just an illusion of who they could have been. That's a trap that a lot of traumatized kids fall into—the idea that at some point, someday, their parents will act the way they should. And if you could be good enough, smart enough, just be enough of something, they will love you. They won't act crazy; they won't be mean. I felt that way before Tibbs. But it was just an illusion, like a hologram that is always out of reach. After Tibbs, I was not interested in illusions. I had lost all of those along with my childhood.

I pictured Emily that last night, her nightgown hung on her like a shroud. When she looked back at me, her smile was so wide, it took up most of her face. Was she scared? Did she reconsider after making that first jagged cut, when the blood began? Did she think of me, alone, waiting for her to come back?

The ice pack caused a numbing effect, and I felt the pressure in my head begin to release, just a bit. But lying there, diving into the memories and the feelings I had repressed for so long, made my heart pound and my stomach turn.

I took several deep breaths and repeated a mantra in my head: *This can't hurt you now, it can't hurt you now.*

I took an inventory of all the things I had willfully erased from my memory. The gnawing sense of lack. Danger. The hollow feeling that I didn't matter to anyone. I was like an unwanted package that gets shunted from one doorstep to the next, unopened. I remembered how the feeling of safety had slowly developed, until I could relax into it and claim it as something I deserved.

And if I had told the truth all those years ago? I would have been put back into foster care. And Michael Ray would have had to endure the pain that his daughter died the cruelest of deaths, unable to endure another day of the hell we lived in. People say the truth will set you free. Would that have been the case for Michael Ray? That truth would have killed him, literally.

I would have fallen through the faulty safety net for unwanted children with no resources. The pain of that existence, so devoid of hope and opportunity, always triggered me. So, wasn't it better for everyone that I became Emily? Wasn't I able to make something good out of it, helping to bring other children back home? That was the story I had written for myself over the years. But was it really true?

Alone in that darkened hotel room, I felt how heavy that burden had been. I felt the ever-present tightness in my chest, the constant vigilance that I could never drop. I let go of the clenched control that drove me every day to succeed, to be the best at my job, my marriage and family.

My story would be out there for the world to see in Larissa's article. Maybe someone who knew me in childhood would come forward. Maybe my mother or Janelle would want to tell their side of it. It was like having a scab torn off a wound to discover that it wasn't healed after all. I couldn't pretend that Danica had simply disappeared. She was right there, inside me; she always had been. Tears welled up and I turned my face into the pillow. I cried uncontrollably, for everything. For the lies I had told for decades, for the traumas that Emily and I suffered, for the unloved, unprotected child I had been before Tibbs. It was like falling down a well to discover that there was no bottom and you will never find your way back up. Two steps from the abyss.

I fell asleep eventually, worn out from crying. When I awoke, I lay in the big king-sized bed, on top of the covers, just taking in the smell of the ocean coming in from the terrace. I had slept deeply, exhausted from the emotional upheaval. I saw several notifications on my phone, three from Antonio, two from Diaz. I called him first.

"Hey, Emily. Nothing to report. I've had migraines, don't try to work on a computer. We've got it handled until tomorrow. Have a Coke, that helps sometimes," he suggested.

He was right, Coca-Cola did help migraines for some reason. Maybe the toxic mix of chemicals worked the way it did cleaning your car battery. I called home next, Antonio answered in one ring.

"Hey, Em! Dolores told me you're staying over. I tried you a few times."

"I'm sorry. I took migraine meds and fell asleep."

"A migraine? They've come back?"

"Just today, I think," I explained.

"This is getting more serious, Em. We've got the guys outside, you're getting sick from stress."

"I can manage it," I said. Those words came out of my mouth on autopilot.

"I don't think you can. Your body's telling you it's too much," he insisted.

I hated hearing the worry in his voice, the last thing I wanted was to cause him more stress.

"Honey, I feel like crap with this headache. Can we continue with this tomorrow?" I asked.

"Yeah, when you're feeling better. The girls fell asleep early after ice skating. Do you want me to wake them so you can chat?" he asked.

"No, no. They must be exhausted. I should get back to sleep also. I just woke up and wanted to call. That medication knocks me out!"

" Try and sleep it off. Call me if you feel worse, okay?"

"I will," I assured him.

"Text me in the morning, let me know how the headache is. If it hasn't let go, you should come home early."

"I will, don't worry," I said, then added, "I love you."

I could hear the smile in his voice. "I love you more."

We hung up. I stared at the cellphone in my hand. I tried to imagine some scenario in which I told him the truth about Emily. There was no version of it that didn't end in heartbreak and misery, with me losing the most important people in my life.

TWENTY

DAY FOUR: 5:15 A.M.

By morning my headache was gone. My usual routine was to spring out of bed and start my workout. But this day, I struggled to get up. Everything felt heavy and gray.

Outside, I ran through the quiet streets; I felt the depression lift. Movement, sunlight, fresh air all helped to dispel it. With the landing of each step, I was rebuilding my emotional armor. An hour later I was pulling up to the Vance house. I ignored the cameras and news crews outside. In the Sparrow's Nest, I found Ryan, who wore the same suit as the previous day and had three empty Starbucks cups at his workspace.

"You didn't go home, Ryan?"

"Nah, I just got caught up in this list of cars that could be a match. I have a change of clothes in the car, so I'll shower here. The bathroom in this place is amazing!"

I settled in to review the previous day's work. Ryan and Diaz had eliminated several hundred possible DMV matches for the sedan that the surf shop owner saw. There were seven possible matches in the South Bay. The rest of the team had arrived and were hard at work when the morning mail came. Moran hurried in with a small white mailer.

"Another package, it just came!" he said, handing it to me.

This time from Apple Valley, another rural community adjacent to Victorville and Hesperia. Inside, there was nothing but a folded, blank piece of paper. And a single, twisted bobby pin. I kept my composure, my voice and hands steady. But I knew what it meant.

"A hairpin? This guy is whacked," Diaz said.

"I'll check with Melanie and Louis to see if Josie was wearing a pin like this when she went missing," Grice said, heading out to find them.

I held the bobby pin in my gloved hand and raised it up to the light coming in from the picture window. It was so small, so sharp.

The smell of blood was metallic and sharp. Tibbs sat in the hallway, rocking back and forth and crying. He was in full mental meltdown, but I knew I had to clean up the mess or there would be punishment. I poured bleach into the tub; the smell was so strong it made my eyes burn. I rubbed the torn rags Tibbs had given me across the surface of the tub, washing away any trace of Emily. I threw towels on the floor to absorb the water that pooled and shimmered in the light from the hallway. I wrung the heavy towels out by hand. The bobby pin fell into the tub, and I watched it swirling and circling the drain as it disappeared. I dipped the mop into a bucket of bleach and made sure to clean every corner, every crevice until there was no sign of my only friend who had taken her life in that horrible little room with the frosted glass mirror...

I knew exactly what the bobby pin meant. It was the instrument Emily used to set herself free from Tibbs and he was the only other person who knew it. Now the book with the blue bear made sense, as did the drawing of two little girls who looked alike. He was alive. All those years I thought he was gone, and I was safe. He was out there, waiting.

"What do you think, Emily?" Diaz asked.

"This one baffles me," I lied, certain that he could read the deception in my voice. I avoided eye contact, too afraid that I would break apart if someone looked directly at me.

Grice returned, shaking his head. "Melanie and Louis say Josie never used hairpins like this. I don't see how this ties in or what we're supposed to get from it."

"Maybe it's just a random thing sent by a crazy person," Ryan ventured, having showered and changed into a fresh set of clothes.

"This time it's from Apple Valley, which is right next to both Victorville and Hesperia. I think he's out there, holed up in some remote location. He's giving us a clue by using the post offices. I think we need to organize a sweep, utilizing all the local agencies we can out there," Grice said.

"Those are three spread-out communities, very rural with a lot of places to hide. It'll take a ton of coordination, and we have to have a discernible target. He could also be sending us off in the wrong direction so let's put the bobby pin aside until we have a better idea of what it means. We need to finish sorting through the DMV information and Ryan and I need to go talk to the possible matches," I said.

I grabbed the list of the seven people who had cars that matched the description. All I wanted to do was break free and find a quiet place by myself to process everything. I could feel the sweat rising between my shoulder blades, soon my face would be flushed. But I had to keep it together, stay focused and behave normally.

I slapped Ryan on the back as I moved for the door. "We're hitting it. I've got the list. The rest of you take the others. Stephanie, you and Izzy keep going through the DMV records. I hope we can have it done by this evening."

We were on our way to the car when my knees buckled, and my vision blurred. I reached out to grab Ryan's arm and he caught me as I fell hard onto the driveway. When I awoke, I was seated in the Sparrow's Nest with my feet elevated. I looked around at the team, confused.

"You fainted again, Emily," Grice said, handing me a glass of water. "I've called the paramedics, I think you need to get checked out."

"Oh God, no! I don't want to go to the ER, I have work to do," I protested and tried to stand up, but I felt woozy again and had to sit down.

"I've spoken to Chief Edmonson and SAC Powers; they both want you to take at least five days' leave and figure out what's going on. We'll manage without you," Grice said.

I gave him a hard stare and he looked away. Five days was an eternity in a CARD investigation. This fit his plans perfectly. With me sidelined, he was the supervisory agent on the team.

I didn't need to go in an ambulance to the emergency room. I had blacked out. And I knew why. It had been years since it had happened but when I first came home, I had lost consciousness several times. I blacked out and fell in the kitchen and the den of the Palos Verdes house. Michael was terrified and we met with Lydia to discuss it, after we had done every test imaginable to rule out a physical problem.

"This is a reaction to extreme stress, the complex PTSD of being held captive for so long and the adjustment of returning home. It happens when the body is overwhelmed, and it shuts down. It's a protective mechanism," she said.

The Vance case was proving to be too much for my brain circuitry to handle, even though I didn't want to face it. I could tell myself again and again that everything was fine, but clearly it wasn't. The coping mechanisms that I had built up over the years and relied on weren't working. Who was I without them?

If I wasn't the super-high achiever, the woman who could handle anything life threw at her, then what? Edmonson and Powers were right to put me on leave for a few days, but I couldn't just sit at home and do nothing, especially now that I was almost certain that Tibbs was still alive. But I needed to be sure before I took any further steps.

"Where are you taking me?" I asked the EMT who sat next to me, monitoring my blood pressure.

"Torrance Memorial. You'll go in through the ER and they may keep you overnight," he said.

"They have Wi-Fi, right?"

The wait in the ER was interminable. I texted Antonio to let him know and tried to discourage him from driving out to see me, to no avail. He was heading to the South Bay straight from work. After a series of tests including an MRI and a CAT scan, I was transferred to a room for observation overnight. I opened my laptop and logged into the guest Wi-Fi. I needed to get in touch with Dr. Gamble from the San Bernardino Coroner's Office to review their files on Tibbs and his DNA status.

DNA sequencing had gotten much more sophisticated in the past two decades and there were newer, more sensitive tests available. If I could test the DNA found at the scene of Tibbs' death, I would have a definitive answer. I did a background check and found that Gamble had retired several years earlier. She lived in Redlands, an upscale suburb in the otherwise gritty, crime-ridden county of San Bernardino. Her phone rang three times before she answered.

"Hello, Dr. Gamble? This is Special Agent Emily Ray with the FBI. I'm not sure if you remember me—"

She cut me off. "Of course I remember you, Agent Ray! I

saw on the news that you're working a case in your old neigh-borhood?"

"Yes. I have some questions about the death of James Tibbs, my kidnapper," I said, evenly, casually, as if this were a normal question on a normal day.

"Wow, that's a step back in time. What do you want to know?"

"Was my identification of his body the only way you confirmed it was him?"

"Pretty much. You may not recall but there was really very little left of him. I think we only had a few teeth but no adult dental records or DNA to check it against. He had no living relatives. He wasn't in CODIS or any other law enforcement database."

"So, the police were willing to close it with just my ID?"

There was a pause on the line, then she said, "The pressure to find Tibbs was huge and they wanted him either in jail or dead. People were scared that a child-stealing madman was out there, ready to strike again."

"So, they pushed to declare him dead and close it?"

"They didn't say it outright, but we could feel it. But I felt certain that those were his remains and it was a suicide. They were found in his car, he left a note, the body size and hair matched Tibbs. And the necklace that you said he never took off clinched it."

"Is there any chance that the physical evidence from Tibbs' suicide might still be stored somewhere? Could the BFS lab have it in their archives?"

"It was such a long time ago. They do keep some stuff from high profile cases. So does the coroner's office but I'd have to check with my former colleagues."

"Could you do that for me? I'd just like to see if there's anything left."

"I'll call today and get back to you," she said before hanging up.

As I now suspected, Tibbs was never identified with absolute certainty through DNA. If he were still alive then someone else had been in the burning van found off Highway 330. Had he really been capable of planning such a complicated scheme? And why now, after all this time, was he coming for me?

I imagined him learning that Emily Ray had returned home, knowing that it was really me. Had it infuriated him, and he'd been seething, plotting all these years to get back at me? Did he hate that I had escaped in more ways than one? That I didn't turn out to be the damaged, disturbed nutcase that he was? All of those scenarios were possible and terrifying.

A doctor came in and I closed my laptop and slid my cell phone under the thin sheet of the hospital bed.

"Ms. Ray? I'm Dr. Hoenshell. I reviewed the tests they ran in the ER and you don't seem to have anything going on physically. You're actually in very good health; your blood pressure is ninety-eight over sixty-four," he said with a smile.

"Thank you. I don't think I really have to stay here. My work colleagues called the ambulance. I had a blackout," I explained.

"Any idea why?"

"Yes. It was a PTSD episode. I'm an FBI agent, working a child abduction case and..." I took a breath before continuing, "I was a kidnapping victim in childhood." I waited for his reaction.

"Wow, that's got to be rough. Have you had these before?"

"Yes, as a teenager when I returned home. My therapist explained that it was a stress reaction."

"Do you currently take any SSRIs or any other anxiety medications?"

"I used to take Celexa, ten milligrams a day, but I stopped last year."

"Well, you seem fine but with a blackout, I have to keep you overnight. I can't risk that it'll happen again when you're driving."

"Do I have to stay a full twenty-four hours or is overnight good enough?" I asked. I had work to do and if my suspicions were accurate, I needed to be on my feet and ready for the biggest takedown of my life. Twenty-four hours in a hospital bed was not an option.

"It depends if you have another blackout episode or not. Lunch will be here soon, so I suggest you just get comfortable and rest. And I'd like to give you a mild sedative, just to calm you down."

"No, I don't need that. I have work to do," I protested.

"Work is the last thing you need to be doing, Ms. Ray. Work is what landed you in here. You need to rest, mentally as well as physically. I'll send a nurse in with something." He sighed as he shook his head at my stubbornness.

I waited until a nurse came back with a small white pill. I smiled dutifully and swallowed it down. Once I was certain she was gone, I reopened my laptop. I did a broad search for anything related to Tibbs. It had been years since I had looked into his history. I was obsessed with finding out about him after I escaped but Lydia suggested that I stop after a few months. He was dead and I had to decide how much more of my energy and focus I was willing to give to him. And at fifteen, I decided that he wouldn't get one molecule more of my mental space. But with a more sophisticated internet, I was able to find detailed information. And now I needed it.

His parents had been named Lucille and Garvey Tibbs, they had died together in a car accident in the early nineties. Lucille was a homemaker and Garvey worked as a handyman for a company called Glendale Commercial Maintenance that took care of city schools and office buildings. I found the recorded deed for the house in Glendale which had James listed with them as dual occupancy, so it transferred seamlessly to him when they died.

I ran a more advanced search and found previous addresses in Sylmar and Santa Clarita. And I uncovered an old property tax record of a cabin in Arrowbear, a town in the San Bernardino mountains. They had purchased it in the late eighties with no mortgage, so I assumed they had bought it with cash. There was no record of any other activity until a transfer of title to a Joe Lavois, a plumber from Long Beach in 2003, and he had owned it ever since. I had seen his name somewhere before, but I couldn't place it. Tibbs died back in the year 2000, a few weeks after I escaped. His body was found off one of the major highways up to the mountains, the road that leads to Running Springs. And Arrowbear.

I had never given much thought to where Tibbs had chosen to end his life. It was simply a road that was not heavily populated that suited his purposes. He was dead and gone, how could it matter? There was no record of a probate case or the county taking possession of the cabin after his death. Stephanie could figure it out, but I was on leave with no official way to ask her. I dialed Jeff Edmonson in the FBI offices to try and rectify the situation. His assistant had me on hold for several minutes before he came on the line.

"Emily! Are you okay? Grice told me you had another fainting spell." I could hear the concern in his voice.

"I'm fine, I'm in the hospital overnight but I think I can go back to the team tomorrow."

"No, both SAC Powers and I think you should take at least five days off. Grice is very worried about you."

"I appreciate that, sir, but I really think I need to return. This perpetrator is making contact that seems to be tied to me in some way and I don't want to lose that connection," I said.

"We won't make it public that you're on leave. You just won't be at the press briefings, and we'll tell them that you're in the field if anyone asks," he said in a tone that made it clear there was no need for further discussion.

We hung up and I texted Ryan and Stephanie. I had to scope them out, to see if they were willing to keep me in the loop. It was too risky to reach out to Diaz, he was an ambitious young agent who would go to Grice with any request I made for information, same with our other field agents. I needed to know what Grice was doing. Ryan replied immediately.

I'll come by at the end of the day to check in.

I was still waiting for a response from Stephanie when the sedative started to kick in. I fought it as long as I could but eventually, I slipped into sleep. When I awoke a few hours later, there were messages from Dr. Gamble and Stephanie on my phone. I called Gamble first.

"Hi, Emily, good news. The coroner's office still has some of the Tibbs material. You can contact them to get it. Ask for Brian Martin, he'll be able to help you."

"I'll give him information on where to send it for analysis, right?"

"I'm assuming the BFS lab?"

The California Department of Justice operates several Bureau of Forensic Services laboratories in the state for analyzing forensic evidence related to crimes. I wasn't planning to send the Tibbs material to BFS, but Gamble didn't need to know that.

Next, I called Stephanie who answered in one ring.

"What's up? Are you feeling better?" she asked.

"Yes, I'm fine. I have to stay here overnight but with this five-day leave imposed on me, I need to know what's going on in the case. And I may need some data analysis for a hunch I'm working on," I said.

"No problem," she whispered. "Whatever you need, just text me."

I contacted a genealogy researcher I had worked with on a previous case named Elsbeth Winter. Running a DNA sample through CODIS or NDIS—the Combined or National DNA Index Systems—only shows a match if someone has been arrested or convicted of a felony and had their DNA taken. For individuals with no criminal record, they won't give us any information. Investigative genetic genealogy—or IGG—searches through the DNA profiles of people who have submitted samples to find information on family members or ethnic background. The Golden State Killer was caught after four decades using IGG. I wanted to see if the DNA from Tibbs matched anyone in those databases.

I left a message on Elsbeth's voicemail. Once I confirmed that she could do it, I would arrange to have the sample sent over.

Just a few days ago, I had a perfect life. Now I was sitting in a hospital bed, with the certainty that the monster who had stolen my childhood was still out there and worse, he had taken another little girl.

But this time I was not a ten-year-old child. This time, he would not win.

TWENTY-TWO
DAY FOUR: 3:30 P.M.

The sedative the nurse gave me left me feeling slightly groggy the rest of the afternoon. I nibbled at the bland egg salad sandwich that was my lunch. Just before four o'clock, Elsbeth Winter returned my call.

"Special Agent Ray? So good to hear from you," she said warmly.

"Same to you. I have a DNA sample I need you to run a family search on, see if you can find any relatives. Do you have time in your schedule?"

"For you, of course. I saw that you're working on the kidnapping case in Palos Verdes?" she asked.

"Yes, but this is for an old case. I don't know how good the DNA will be or if you'll be able to pull anything from it. It's in the San Bernardino Coroner's Office. I can have it messengered to you today, if that works?"

"Perfect. I can work on it tonight."

We hung up and I immediately called Brian Martin, who answered promptly.

"Mr. Martin, this is Special Agent Emily Ray with the FBI

CARD team. I believe Dr. Gamble spoke to you earlier about some DNA material I requested?"

"Oh yeah, you want the DNA material from the James Tibbs case? I can't believe they didn't toss this out years ago."

"Dr. Gamble said that San Bernardino County is a bit overwhelmed," I said.

"Overwhelmed? Try understaffed, underfunded, mismanaged, corrupt... don't get me started! After L.A. started charging street gangs under RICO statutes, they all came out here. I've seen more dead bodies of young Latino men than you can count. Our evidence files are stacked up and backed up, we have no staff to manage them..." he rambled on.

"Could you messenger the sample to Stemma Lab Services in Huntington Beach, attention Elsbeth Winter?" I said, cutting off his litany of complaints about the dysfunction of local government.

"Sure. Do you want it done today?"

"Right away. She's waiting for it," I said.

I hung up and texted Stephanie.

> Check out the property at 727 Hookbill Road in Arrowbear, California. It was owned by Lucille and Garvey Tibbs, the parents of James Tibbs. I need to know what happened to it between 1999 and 2003, when it was transferred to Joe Lavois, from Long Beach.

Within minutes, she texted back.

> Do you mean the James Tibbs who abducted you?

> Yes. Keep this between us.

She sent back a thumbs-up emoji. At moments like this she seemed like a kid—I was sure she still played video games at home after work.

I did a basic background search on Joe Lavois. He worked for Speedy Plumbing in Long Beach and lived in the neighborhood known as Northside. He was divorced, an adult daughter lived in Oregon. He didn't seem active on social media and had a very slim digital footprint. I checked his DMV records and found he owned two cars. A work truck and a 2007 blue Nissan Sentra.

I had heard of Arrowbear; it was between the bigger communities of Lake Arrowhead and Big Bear. My father had taken me on summer vacations to Lake Arrowhead as a teenager. Arrowbear had a population of 736 people. In photos it appeared to be a rough landscape of scattered homes and cabins punctuated by large rocks, with a small lake that seemed more like a big pond. There was no commercial district or other amenities; it was close to the Snow Valley ski area, catering to locals and people too tired to drive to the superior skiing at Big Bear. Years ago, I had to interview a witness who worked at Snow Valley. I remembered the interior smelled of damp carpet and mildew.

An hour later, Stephanie called back.

"Hey, Emily, I came out to my car to call you so no one can hear me. Nothing was done with that cabin in Arrowbear after James Tibbs died."

"So, it just sat there, for three years?" I asked.

"Yep. But here's the weird thing. When the title was transferred to Joe Lavois, Lucille and Garvey were still listed as the owners. And Garvey Tibbs signed the paperwork."

I sat up and kicked the thin blanket off. "Garvey Tibbs signed it? He'd been dead for over a decade!"

"Something's not right here," she said. "Gotta go, Grice is coming to get me!"

I did a more detailed search on the area, checking crime statistics and property records. Arrowbear was one of several unincorporated mountain towns in the area that had deteriorated over the years as San Bernardino County struggled with the loss of major factories and Norton Air Force Base. Once, they were glamorous getaways for movie stars and well-heeled professionals from nearby Los Angeles and San Diego. Now, the mountain towns were dominated by short-term vacation rentals and the full-time, local communities had shifted dramatically. A lot of the residents were retired right-wing conservatives and Christian Nationalists. There were small-time criminals and con artists, and a surprising number of residents on the California sex offender registry. And of course, high rates of methamphetamine use and the black-market sale of opioids.

The property searches showed that many homes had no verifiable address listing on county maps. Some streets had even- and odd-numbered houses right next to each other. Some had one address on property tax rolls and a different one on utility accounts. In short, Arrowbear was a mess in terms of record keeping. Perhaps the cabin had never been transferred to James Tibbs when his parents died? Maybe it just sat there, in limbo, until it was signed over to Joe Lavois? I dug deeper into the property tax records and found that the taxes on the cabin had been paid regularly up to the day that Lavois took ownership. Who had been paying those taxes for three years?

Obviously, someone who knew about the cabin's existence. It was the same person who forged Garvey's signature on the transfer of title. A person who had a motive for keeping a remote cabin off the radar of the authorities. A person who didn't want to be found. A person like James Tibbs.

Next, I pulled up a generic photo of a 2007 blue Nissan Sentra to send to Ryan. The surf shop owner in Redondo Beach had seen a guy who matched our police sketch, with the ball cap, driving a blue sedan in the alley. I checked my notes against Lavois' DMV record and then I realized where I had seen his name. He was on the list of possible matches that

Stephanie had found, to the partial plate caught by the surf shop owner. He was on our list.

The Lavois–Tibbs connection was getting more interesting. I was forming a story in my head, the story of how James Tibbs could've pulled off the Josie Vance abduction. And how I had stepped right into the role he planned for me without even knowing, until now.

He fit the profile, he wasn't a first-time offender. He had successfully kidnapped and hidden two little girls for years. He would be forty-eight now, old enough to have the patience for the long game. He was our guy, he took Josie Vance. My breath caught in my throat; I was suddenly keenly aware of all the things in the room that were out of order. The long, industrial-style curtains were caught on a chair by the window. I got out of bed to straighten them, so they fell in a clean line to the floor. The sheets and blanket were bunched up and needed smoothing. The mobile tray next to the bed had torn cutlery wrappers and those small envelopes of salt and pepper tossed carelessly next to a Styrofoam cup. I scooped them all up and put them into the trash. I was pushing the wheeled carts that held the monitoring equipment into a line against the wall when Ryan arrived.

I had my back to him when I heard his voice. "What are you doing, Agent Ray?"

"Just straightening up," I said casually, sitting back onto my bed.

"I've noticed how your car looks like it just came from the showroom and your workspace is like a staged advertisement. What's up?"

"Manageable OCD, kind of like an old friend. What's going on with the case?"

If I was worried that Ryan would have any misgivings about keeping me in the loop, I was wrong. He sat down and gave me a detailed update.

"Grice is completely sold on his idea that the kidnapper is somewhere in the Hesperia–Victorville area. He's coordinating right now with the local sheriffs and police out there. He says the copycat is doing what Tibbs did with you, he's taken Josie to a far-flung area where he has contacts and feels safe."

"That's an enormous area to cover. How does he plan to narrow down the focus of the search?"

"I don't know. He said he's figuring out the details."

Ryan sounded skeptical. I closed the door to my room and pulled out my computer.

"Okay, look at this. It's a generic image of a 2007 Nissan Sentra. It belongs to a guy from Long Beach named Joe Lavois. Three of the plate numbers match what the surf shop lady saw. She needs to see this."

"Does this Joe Lavois guy match our suspect? How did you get onto him?"

"Lavois bought a house up in the mountains that used to belong to James Tibbs' parents. The guy who kidnapped me and supposedly killed himself. I suspect that we are not dealing with a copycat and that he may still be alive. And Josie Vance may be about something bigger," I said.

Ryan's eyes locked on mine for a beat. I waited. This was the moment when he might decide I had lost my mind. His response was measured, cautious.

"What makes you think that he's still alive?" he asked.

"There are details in the messages that only Tibbs and I would know. I wasn't sure about that until today. I checked with the medical examiner that handled his remains. I'm having a DNA sample sent to an IGG lab in Orange County to see if they can match it to any relative to confirm that it was really Tibbs. Or not."

Ryan stared at me again, expressionless. I braced myself, sure he had lost all confidence in me at this point.

Then he said, "And you've done all of this, from a hospital bed, after blacking out?"

"Yes."

He shook his head. "Fuck, you've got some skills! I guess it goes without saying that you're not resting here in the hospital?"

"I'll rest when I catch him and he'll never hurt another child again."

TWENTY-THREE
DAY FOUR: 6:57 P.M.

Ryan and I agreed to stay in touch on the case and I sent a photo of the Nissan to his phone. The nurse came in with my dinner which consisted of a Salisbury steak with dried-out mac and cheese. She had just left when Antonio arrived. He looked frazzled, exhausted from the long drive.

"How're you doing? Any more blackouts?" he asked, sitting on the bed, taking my hand in his.

"I feel fine. How're the girls?"

"They miss you, like always. But they both got cast in the class play about the rainforest. They play monkeys."

"And the security detail?"

"They're always there, out front and in back. We're well protected. Dolores started bringing them dinner plates covered in foil. What's going on with you?"

"It's just stress with the case. I called Edmonson to try and get back on it tomorrow, but he insisted on a five-day leave," I said.

"Well, I agree with him. You need to stay on leave."

"They said they'll let me go home tomorrow if I don't black out again."

"Okay, but you can't drive. I'll take the day off work and pick you up. The rest of the week at home will be good for you."

I smiled and squeezed his hand. We sat in silence for a moment, the big question hanging in the air between us.

Finally, he said it: "Do you think you should let Grice have this one and leave it?"

I shook my head, still holding tight to his hand. "No. The kidnapper is making contact that is directed at me so if I'm off it for good, he may go silent. That's why my five-day leave is being kept under wraps," I said.

"I'm worried, with the migraine and now this fainting spell," he said, looping a strand of my hair over my ear, running the back of his palm along my cheek.

"I'll be fine. I always am," I assured him, leaning into his touch.

"What if you're not this time?" he asked.

I shrugged and said simply, "I have to find her. I can't stop until I do."

Antonio knew when to push and when to leave something alone. He wisely chose the latter this time.

"How about getting some decent food?" he asked, smiling brightly. "This stuff looks inedible."

"Maybe those fish sandwiches from the place by the pier?" I suggested.

He gave me a quick kiss and left. While he was out getting dinner, I heard back from Elsbeth Winter.

"Hi, Emily. I ran the DNA at the lab, it's viable. You know we can't run it against Ancestry or the other commercial genealogy sites due to the restrictions," she said.

"Yeah, I know. But you can run it through GEDmatch and FamilyTreeDNA, right?" I asked.

The popular genealogy sites have strict regulations for law enforcement; we can't just run suspects through their database to find relatives; it's a violation of privacy laws.

"Yes, GEDmatch automatically opts users into law enforcement searches, they need to sign a special request to opt out. FTDNA requires you to submit a request. I'm sure the FBI has one on file, right?"

"Yes, it does. I'll get that over to you," I stalled, wondering how I was going to do that without alerting my superiors that I was still working the case. And from an angle that, most likely, they would consider insane. "But you can run GEDmatch, correct?" I continued.

"Yes, I'll do that later. I'll be up all night, working. We could skirt the warrant if we use a chromosome browser, which gives a graphical view of DNA segments shared between matches in individual chromosomes," she suggested.

"Just start with GEDmatch and we'll see if anything lines up. I'll get you the request for FTDNA," I said.

Antonio returned with the fish sandwiches and I did my best to put everything else out of my mind and live in that happy moment. We watched some silly television and he left, promising to have the girls call me before bed. The nurse came in and gave me a second sedative. I tucked the pill into my cheek and pretended to swallow it. I didn't want to be knocked out for the rest of the evening. I had put off calling Whirt for twenty-four hours, but I figured now was as good a time as any. I dialed and waited; he answered on the third ring.

"Hello, Detective, It's Emily Ray," I said.

"Yeah?"

"I was wrong and I'm sorry. We were hitting one dead end after another and Brenda Coombs created some suspicion," I explained.

"Suspicion, my ass! How could any of you think I could do something like that?"

"Look, Whirt, you know as well as I do there are cops that go off. Sometimes this kind of work can push you over the edge.

You kept bringing up my case, it was clearly a significant moment in your career—"

He cut me off. "And your BAU profiler said it could be a cop, right? Someone wanting to go out with a bang, solve the big case that he set up, right? You think I'm that crazy?"

"No, I don't. It was a question that was raised, especially after we saw that room in your house. Grice is the one who ran with it after I was gone. I told him we needed to wait before taking any action and he went ahead with your chief after I left early. It was the day I fainted."

Whirt was silent for a moment, then said, "Okay, I admit that room is kind of weird. I know, it looks like I'm an obsessive nut."

"Well, yes, it does. How did you get all those photos of me?"

"Online searches. Look, I followed your whole career. It was the biggest success story ever. So, I kept up what was going on with you," he said, sheepishly.

"Okay, but you can see why that Emily Ray shrine raised some questions?"

Now he let out an embarrassed laugh. "Yeah, I can see that. I probably would've suspected me, too. So, how's it going? I haven't seen anything in the news, except Grice at the press updates."

"I had another fainting spell and I'm off the case for five days." I sighed wearily.

"No shit! So, Grice is in charge? He must be loving that."

"So, do you think you'll go back to the PV police? Stay until your original retirement date?"

"Nah, I can get my pension now. Ellen is already making plans for some trip on one of those cruise lines. God, I hate ships! But I'm not going to upset her. You two bringing up the whole Brenda Coombs thing put me in the doghouse. Hey, did you hear that Larissa is running a story about another abduction that happened in Redondo, back when you went missing?" he asked.

"Yes, she told me," I said casually.

"It wasn't our case in PV, but I remember it. She was kind of a troubled kid, I think. We thought maybe she was a runaway."

"A runaway? She was ten years old. And what made you think she was a troubled kid?"

I could hear the edge in my voice and took a deep breath to calm down.

"I don't know. Just the family seemed pretty messed up and they weren't that concerned about it. But you know, Larissa's article might lead to something. It's in the paper today. The case has been cold for decades. She said the Redondo PD might reopen it."

We hung up, his words echoed in my head.

Larissa's article might lead to something...

Years ago, they wrote Danica Hansen off. She came from a low-income, unstable family. She must've had problems. She may have run away, no need to search very hard for her. How many kids fell between the cracks of the supposed safety net, like I did? Deemed not worthy or important enough for a full-scale investigation? I felt the bitterness bubbling up inside me.

I tried scrolling through the TV to distract myself but despite countless channels, I couldn't find anything that held my interest. I needed to build the narrative for how James Tibbs could've lived undetected for so long. He must have always had an escape plan. He would never have let himself get caught by surprise. He disappeared after setting the Glendale house on fire, then was found dead by suicide with a note, several weeks later. The case closed; he was off the hook. He went underground, perhaps in a small town where he had a foothold, a place filled with people who don't ask a lot of questions.

Long term, all he needed to do was find a job that paid him under the table and if he ever went online, to use the Wi-Fi at a public library or a McDonald's. With no cell phone contract, no permanent address, no bank account or credit cards, he would've been a ghost. But why come out of hiding now? Why risk a new abduction at this point?

I had recently received a special commendation from the Bureau and the Governor's office and even though I had declined to do any interviews with news outlets, several ran stories about it. One online site had briefly featured an unauthorized photo of me and my family, which had been taken down after a few days.

But to an obsessive, disturbed recluse it might have seemed like a stick in the eye, a reminder that Emily Ray lived a charmed life. Emily Ray, who was really someone else, someone who didn't deserve all that good fortune. It could have been the trigger.

And now, the kidnapping of a girl so similar to Emily, the cryptic messages, letting me know that he was out there, and he knew my secret. How he must have enjoyed imagining the moment when I realized he was still alive. If Josie was just his pawn in this psychological warfare, then she had a chance.

I was tired, my eyes felt like bags of sand. I had just drifted off to sleep when my cell phone rang. I grabbed it and shoved it under my pillow to stifle the noise. The screen read 1:42 a.m. It was Elsbeth Winter.

"Hi, Emily. Did I wake you?"

"Oh no," I lied, "I'm just here going over some case files."

"We were lucky and got a hit from GEDmatch. Actually, we got several."

"Immediate family members?" I asked.

"Yes, both the parents and two siblings. They are based in Highland, California. The whole family submitted their DNA. It's a clear match. This DNA belongs to a white male, between the ages of eighteen and twenty-five. He is the biological son of Frank and Eleanor Barriage and the brother of Ben and Kelly.

The siblings live in Arizona now, but the parents are still in California. This DNA is most likely for their younger son, whose name was Cody and who was reported missing over twenty years ago."

I thanked her and hung up the phone. I felt the full weight of the truth she had revealed. Cody Barriage burned to death in that van twenty-three years ago. Where was James Tibbs?

TWENTY-FOUR
DAY FIVE: 2:12 A.M.

Elsbeth texted me the contact information for the Barriage family. Highland was a town in San Bernardino County, at the foothills of Highway 330, where Tibbs' van was found. My online search found that Eleanor and Frank Barriage had lived in their house on Pearl Street since the late eighties. There was a birth certificate for Cody. He had been arrested for minor crimes, shoplifting at a Dollar Tree store, loitering in a local park after dark. In his mugshot he bore a strong resemblance to Tibbs and they were about the same age. He'd been reported missing in 2000, two weeks before Tibbs' body was found. I would pay the Barriage family a visit in the next day or two.

Getting bad news late at night was always an emotional oil slick for me. For those of us prone to late-night terrors, getting your mind stuck on something with no daylight distractions is worse than circling the drain, it's sliding down into it. You imagine the worst possible outcome of every situation. Some fortunate people fall into sleep, unbothered by irrational fears and anxieties. But I wasn't one of them.

I couldn't stay in my bed, I wanted to move, to get out. I wandered into the hallway. It was quiet, a nurse passed by and nodded. I walked the length of the corridor and back, passing patients sleeping in darkened rooms, illuminated only by blinking lights of medical equipment. I approached the nursing station and saw several copies of the *Daily Breeze* newspaper. On the third page, I saw Larissa Cinque's byline. And a photo of me as a child next to a mugshot of my mother from Texas. I quickly folded it and returned to my room. I spread the newspaper out on the bed and read my story, laid bare for everyone to see.

Danica Hansen, ten-year-old child who went missing three years after Emily Ray and so on. The story continued with basic details about my childhood. She had gotten vintage photos of the Beach Palms Trailer Park where I lived with my aunt Janelle, even a school photo from my kindergarten class. It was a two-part story. The next installment promised interviews with police and family members.

Emotionally, I felt like one of those strings of firecrackers that people set off on the fourth of July in the driveway, the kind that blow off a finger or singe an eyeball. I wished I had taken the sedative the nurse had given me earlier. I poured the contents of the waste basket onto the bed and found what was left of the small pill, partially dissolved, swallowing it down with a gulp of water. I sat in a chair by the window, looking at the nearby lights of the neighborhoods.

I wanted to tell Lydia, but I knew she would go into hyper protective mode, and I couldn't handle another person I loved pressuring me to quit the case. I knew I had to tell the team about Tibbs faking his death and he had to be put at the top of our suspect list. I weighed telling them as a group but decided to speak to Grice privately first. I should have waited to call him, but I was so agitated, I couldn't. It was too important. The clock read 2:32 a.m.

"Emily? Are you okay?" he asked, sounding groggy.

"I'm fine. I'm going home tomorrow morning," I assured him.

"Good. You need a break. What's up?"

"I've been doing some digging, and I discovered that Tibbs faked his own death, years ago. I don't think we have a copycat with Josie. I think it's him. And the messages are directed at me."

There was a long pause, then he said, "Emily, I know this case is extremely stressful for you, given all the similarities to your own abduction. But this idea is really kind of out there in the crazy zone."

"John, I had IGG testing done on his DNA from the crash site where Tibbs drove off the highway and they found his body. I contacted the coroner in San Bernardino. It links to a completely different family," I said.

"Okay, Tibbs' DNA was badly degraded at the time they found his remains. What are the chances that this sample is even accurate? And even if he did fake his death, why on earth would he risk getting caught now?"

He fired off these questions at me in quick succession, determined to shut me down. Before I could even begin to answer, he continued, "You're on leave from this case—that came down from the SAC. I know that's hard for you, but you must step back, Emily. Everything you've been doing is out of line. We're going in a completely different direction. I can't have the team pulled into this crazy idea that is solely based on your trauma and history."

Normally, I would have pushed back but I realized I was on thin ground.

"I'll keep this between us if you let it go. But if you insist, I'll have to go to Powers and Edmonson and I don't know what the fallout might be for you. It's almost three in the morning. Get some sleep and forget about all of this, okay?"

I remained silent and he hung up. He saw this as his big

moment, there was no way he was going to let me back into the case unless he had to. As for his veiled threat regarding what the fallout might be for me, I realized in that moment that I didn't care. I didn't care about my real identity being exposed. I didn't care about what my colleagues thought of me or about losing my career. The one thing I did care about was finding Josie Vance. And now I knew that I'd have to do it alone.

The next morning, Antonio texted me to let me know he wouldn't be able to break away from work until midday. Dr. Hoenshell came in to give me my discharge orders and I told him I was on a five-day stress leave from work which seemed to assuage any doubts he may have had about letting me leave. Within the hour, I was in the lobby of the hospital, waiting for an Uber to take me back to the Vance home to collect my car. I didn't risk going into the Sparrow's Nest, I didn't need any more blowback from Grice. I drove down from Palos Verdes, toward the freeway system that would eventually take me to Highland to speak to the Barriage family.

Highland was a dusty, working-class town with residential streets bordered by commercial one-off businesses, like Baseline Buggies Used Cars or Montez Wrought Iron Works. It was punctuated by occasional small-tract developments of homes that all looked the same, like an oasis of new construction and beige spray-on stucco.

The Barriage house was a squat, post-war-style dwelling, painted the color of mustard, with white trim. I knocked on the door and heard footsteps on the other side.

Then a woman's voice asked, "Who's there? No solicitors, please!"

"I'm not a solicitor, Mrs. Barriage. I'm Special Agent Emily Ray with the FBI."

I held my identification up to the peephole so she could see it and a moment later the door opened. A woman in her late sixties faced me, her gray hair cropped short. Her face was weathered, and she wore no make-up. In her eyes I could see the resignation and fear of a mother who had lived for years with unanswered questions.

"Is this about Cody?" she asked.

"Could I come in to speak with you? Is Mr. Barriage home by any chance?"

She ushered me in and called out, "Frank, there's a lady here who needs to talk to us. She's from the FBI."

She guided me to a leather couch and sat across from me, her hands clasped together tightly on her knees. Frank Barriage came in, introduced himself and sat stiffly next to her. They both looked as if they had been waiting for this moment for years with a combination of dread and relief.

"I'm here because we were running some DNA searches on remains that hadn't been identified properly in the last few decades and there was a hit through GEDmatch that came back to your family."

"We did that a few years ago. We all did it, the kids also," Frank said, his voice unsteady.

"We got a match, a male between the ages of eighteen and twenty-five that had the genetic markers of your offspring, and a sibling to your other children," I said, gently.

Eleanor's face contorted and she whispered, "It's Cody?"

"Unless you have another son, I'm afraid it is."

Frank grabbed her hand and asked, "What happened to him? We've been looking for him for years."

"It seems he died in a fire and his remains were badly damaged. The DNA was run through CODIS, but he had no felony convictions, so nothing came up. Can you tell me a little bit about him?"

"He was a good boy, just a little confused," Eleanor said, wiping her eyes with her sleeve.

"He got in with a rough crowd in high school, started doing drugs. He stole some stuff from the house... and I finally told him he had to leave..." Frank said, his voice breaking off.

"He was living on the street for a few months, he used to hang out at the big park over on Waterman, the one by the highway up to the mountains. A lot of homeless people lived there," Eleanor continued.

"There were a lot of druggies there and I didn't like it. I told him so and we fought about it. If I hadn't made him leave the house..." Frank struggled to speak but couldn't continue. His pain was palpable, the pain of a parent who had made a difficult choice and faced the worst possible outcome. I could only imagine the regret and blame he had carried for the past twenty years.

"Drug abuse is incredibly hard for families. You did the best you could in those circumstances," I assured him.

"We were supposed to meet him to have lunch at DJs, over near that park. We were hoping to get him into a rehab program. But he never showed up and after a few days, we contacted the police," Eleanor said.

"They didn't put any effort into finding him. Not at all. To them, he was just a homeless junkie," Frank said bitterly.

"You said it was a fire? Was it in a house or an apartment?" Eleanor asked.

"It was an automobile fire. The remains were very scant and... misidentified at the time."

"Did he die in the fire or... was he already... dead?" Frank asked.

"I believe he was dead already."

I didn't tell them that James Tibbs was responsible for their son's death, that he had been murdered, for fear that they might leak Cody's story to the press.

"Can we collect his remains? Who do we contact? I want to give him a proper burial," Eleanor said, her voice faltering.

"I'll have the coroner's office contact you within the week. I just wanted to make the notification in person. I'm very sorry for your loss," I said, rising to leave.

"Thank you for coming. It's better to know than to not, even after all this time," Eleanor said, following me.

"I'm sorry to bring you such painful news, Mrs. Barriage. And I'm sorry to ask this, but could you keep this information private for the time being? We discovered it as part of another case that we don't want to compromise right now."

"That's fine. This is a private family matter," she said.

As I started out the door, she grabbed my arm. "Do you have children, Agent Ray?"

"Yes, I do. Two girls," I said.

She held onto my arm and squeezed it tightly, whispering, "Then you know..."

I nodded and took her hands in mine. She closed the door and retreated into what I knew would be the unbearable grief of parents who had lost a child.

It wasn't hard to figure out what had happened to Cody. Tibbs needed a body to pass off as his own in that burning van, a macabre prop to go with his false suicide note. Most likely he started hanging out at Wildwood Park and the other places frequented by the kind of people who wouldn't be easily missed. Poor Cody Barriage was close enough to his height and weight, same blond hair. I could imagine Tibbs befriending him, manipulating him into a situation where he could make use of him in the worst possible way.

Antonio had already sent me two texts, in the third one he was obviously upset.

> WTF??!! Are U driving? Ur supposed to wait
> for me!!

I'm fine. Making a couple of stops before I head home. See you soon.

We rarely fought but I had the sense that he would not be easily put off this time. On the drive back to La Cañada, I tried the phone number I had for Joe Lavois, but it was disconnected. I called Stephanie.

"Hey, what's up?" she asked.

"I'm following up with Joe Lavois, the guy who bought the Tibbs cabin. The number's disconnected. Can you run a detailed search on him?"

"I'll do everything and get back to you. Ryan said he spoke to you?"

"Yes, he came by the hospital," I said. "Also, can you pull up any building plans or physical property details for the house in Arrowbear? They may not exist any longer but see what you can find."

"I'll get on it before the end of the day. And don't worry, Grice will never know," she assured me.

The drive back home took two hours, traffic was light heading west at midday. I pulled into our driveway and immediately felt my body relax. The past few days had been hell. The girls were still at school and Dolores left a note that Moose had run into a skunk and lost that battle, so she had taken him to the groomer. Then I saw It. It was on the built-in desk by the window, where we put new mail and housekeys.

It was a retractable dog leash. The kind Tibbs used to put on me and Emily. It was beat-up, with scratches and dents in the hard plastic. Everyone in the house knew that we never, ever used these with Moose. It was something I insisted on. How had it gotten here? Inside the house?

The alarm had been set when I arrived and now I hurried through the house to double-check every door and window. The only open window was high on the second floor in the master bedroom with no outside access. Tibbs would've had to be Spiderman to get in that window and with the motion sensors on, the alarm would have tripped. The house was uncharacteristically quiet. I needed a hot shower after a night in the hospital, but I was suddenly uneasy about taking one. The cornerstone of my mental stability was knowing that Tibbs was dead; now that I knew he was alive I would never have peace of mind at home or any place else until he was caught. Or dead.

I sat on the bed and did my box breathing routine. I closed my eyes and repeated Lydia's words in my head.

You're not that helpless child...

It's just shadows, turn on the light...

Turn on the light...

I felt my heart rate slow down after a few minutes but still, I unlocked my Smith and Wesson .38 revolver from the gun safe in the closet and took it with me into the bathroom. I slipped out of my clothes and stepped into the shower, but I didn't linger. I washed off, wrapped myself in a big towel and got dressed in a pair of yoga pants and a tank top with a light cardigan. I grabbed the gun and went downstairs to prepare a cup of tea before I laid out my plan to track down Tibbs. My phone pinged; it was a text from Ryan.

> Turn on the news, Louis Vance has gone rogue on us!!!

I grabbed the remote and turned on the TV in the kitchen as the kettle came to a boil. I flipped through stations until I saw Louis Vance speaking to the reporters camped outside his house. Next to him were Jemmie and Dylan Jones from the Hulu true crime show he had mentioned to me.

"I've taken steps to bring in outside support in the search for my daughter. I am not at all happy with the response from law enforcement. Several key people are off the case now, including a detective and Agent Emily Ray. These people are supposed to be finding my daughter and they're falling apart! I've hired Jemmie and Dylan Jones, who are private investigators, to step in and help us find Josie."

I muted it before the private investigators started speaking. I knew Grice must be losing his mind with this shit show. Then I saw the photo of me from Larissa's article on the news screen. I turned the volume up. A reporter was talking about my disappearance.

"Young Danica Hansen went missing over twenty-years ago in the South Bay, from the same area and three years after Emily Ray, the daughter of real estate developer Michael Ray and his late wife, Andrea. The case received widespread national attention at the time and Emily Ray returned alive eight years later. Danica Hansen's case did not garner the same media attention and journalist Larissa Cinque's story in the Daily Breeze *highlights the class and socio-economic differences between the resources allocated to these cases..."*

I muted the television. I didn't need to hear any more speculation about my disappearance. My hands were shaking as I took a sip of my tea. I feared how Tibbs would react now that Danica Hansen was back in the news. I felt suddenly nauseous and lightheaded. I snapped the rubber band on my wrist a few times to break the reaction cycle.

I hadn't heard Antonio's car pull into the driveway, but I heard his key in the door. I had no time to regroup before he was standing in front of me at the kitchen counter.

"What is going on with you? You're not supposed to be driving, you could've blacked out and crashed," he said, throwing his keys down on the counter.

"They released me. I haven't had another blackout. They needed the room for someone else," I said.

"And the doctor cleared you to drive?"

"He did." I told a half-lie; Dr. Hoenshell and I hadn't specifically discussed driving.

"You know how dangerous it is for you to drive a car? And why do you have your gun out? I saw your location on your phone, what were you doing way out in Highland? You're still working the case, aren't you?" Antonio rarely raised his voice but now he shouted in frustration and fear.

I paused. My emotional circuitry was starting to overload, and I felt the fight-or-flight response coming on.

"I can't just stop investigating this case. Grice is running off in what I'm sure is the wrong direction," I said.

"I know Grice can be an ass and I get it that he wants your job. But this is serious. This is not a typical case for you. The blacking out, the migraines, none of this is normal. It's too much for you to handle."

"It's not, I can manage it—"

He cut me off. "Obviously you can't. If you could, you wouldn't have ended up in the hospital. What does Lydia say?"

"I haven't spoken to her in the past day or two. I've been busy. There's a little girl missing," I said, hearing the edge in my voice.

"I know how you are. I know you get tunnel vision when you're on a case, but this is beyond that. I've been worried since it began. There are so many triggers for you..."

"So, what should I do? Just leave Josie Vance out there? Step back and let Grice follow his theories that I'm sure are wrong?" I pushed back, my own anger overtaking me.

"Maybe he can see something you can't. Maybe you're too close to it. Everyone's talking about the similarities between your case and Josie Vance. And now they're talking about another girl who went missing, a cold case from the same area, a few years later. I saw it on the morning news."

"I know all about it, okay? The missing girl from Redondo Beach. Now, suddenly, everyone is interested in Danica

Hansen, they're going to put new cold case detectives on it, right? Over twenty fucking years later, now they care? No one looked for her at the time!" I shouted.

I was cracking, emotionally, and it terrified me. I wanted to run, to get out of that kitchen, away from the argument, away from Antonio.

"Kids fall through the cracks, I know that's hard to accept, Emily."

"Stop!" I screamed at him. "Stop saying that!"

He moved toward me, reaching out to pull me into him, but I backed away.

"And what is this?" I held up the retractable dog leash. "Where did this come from?" I demanded.

"It was hanging on our gate this morning when I took the girls to school."

"On our gate? Here at the house? We can't stay here; we have to get the girls and move to a safe house!"

I shoved my laptop into its case and put the gun into my purse before Antonio grabbed me by the shoulders to stop me.

"Emily! It belongs to one of our neighbors. Mr. Miller next door found it on the street and hung it on our gate, the cop stationed outside confirmed it. Then a lady two streets over posted about it on Nextdoor. She's coming by to get it before dinner."

"You're sure? It belongs to a neighbor?" I asked, pacing, unable to stand still.

"Yeah. What is going on? I know this case..." He paused, reaching his hands out to try and calm me.

"You don't know anything, okay? You know nothing about me!" I shouted as I pushed him away and ran to the front door.

I was heading towards my car to leave but I'd left the keys in the house. I stood there on the huge expanse of lawn and let my tears of anger and frustration fall as I slumped onto the grass. I could hear Antonio's steps behind me. It had been a very long time since I'd lost control this way, I was so good at keeping all the broken pieces together.

"Sweetheart, let's go inside and talk, okay? Just breathe, it's all going to be fine," he whispered, gently helping me up.

"No, it's not. It's never going to be fine again... because I'm not who you think I am."

The words flew out of me, just like that. I'd said it. I hadn't intended to tell him in this moment, in this way.

Antonio took my hand, tenderly. "Honey, it's time for you to step off this case, okay? We can regroup..."

I put a hand up to stop him. My shoulders hunched forward; it took all my strength to stay standing. I felt total exhaustion, like my body was about to shut down.

"No, I'm not talking about this case. I'm talking about me. I'm not who you think I am. I'm not... Emily Ray," I whispered.

He looked at me with sympathy, with pity. He thought I was having a psychological breakdown.

"Don't look at me that way. I'm not crazy," I said, defiantly.

"Then what are you saying, exactly? I've known you since our freshman year of college. I know you, Emily Ray.'

But as I looked into the deep, coffee-colored eyes of the man I loved, I felt my heart break. He was about to find out that he didn't really know me at all.

TWENTY-FIVE
DAY FIVE: 12:02 P.M.

How do you tell the person you love the most that your whole relationship has been built on a lie?

As we sat across from each other on the big king-sized bed, I could see the bougainvillea blooming in a riot of pink and orange outside in the garden. The sweet scent of jasmine filtered in through the window, a cruel reminder of the beautiful life we'd built together, a life I was about to shatter.

Antonio looked at me, his confusion and concern laid bare. I took a deep breath before I began.

"You know that news story you saw? About the girl from Redondo Beach—Danica Hansen?" I asked.

"Yeah, I know that upset you a lot."

"That's me." My voice sounded strange and thick. "I'm her."

The silence that followed was suffocating. I stared at my hands, unable to meet his gaze but I could feel his eyes boring into me. When he finally spoke, his voice was tight, barely above a whisper.

"What're you talking about?"

"I mean what I just said. I'm not Emily Ray. I'm Danica

Hansen. Tibbs took two girls. And Emily killed herself when we were fifteen..."

"Stop! Don't do this, Emily," he shouted, his voice cracking through the quiet room like a pistol shot. "Please, sweetheart, you need help. You need a break from work and time to recalibrate—"

I interrupted him. "Don't talk to me like I'm one of your rovers or some machine that needs fixing! I'm trying to tell you the truth!"

I began to cry again; Antonio sat back against the bed pillows and stared at me, uncertain and wary. I hated to see that look in his eyes, but I deserved it. I had been living a lie for years and he was caught up in it.

"Tibbs took me three years after he took Emily..."

And I told him the whole story. How Emily died, and I cleaned up. How I escaped and made the desperate decision that set everything in motion. How I had somehow succeeded in becoming the girl that everyone wanted back home. And I ceased to be the girl that no one bothered to look for. When I finished, he stared at me in heavy silence. His dark eyes were opaque and cold. I could feel him pulling away from me, withdrawing from the reality of who I was.

I wasn't ready for the shame that enveloped me, seeing how much I had hurt him. I hadn't even realized that I carried that shame, like a boulder on my back, for so many years. Admitting the truth out loud gave me permission to feel it, to face it. And as painful as it was in this moment, it was a relief in a bizarre way.

Finally, he spoke. "Okay, this is... I don't know how to respond. Part of me thinks that you've lost touch with reality—"

I cut him off. "I haven't. It's true."

"So, all of it, everything has been a lie? Does Lydia know?"

"No, she doesn't. I could never tell her. No one knows, just you."

He stood up and began pacing the room, raking his hands repeatedly through his thick hair.

"It's insane, it's unbelievable, really. I don't know what I'm supposed to think... or do. How could you not have told me something this important? Something that would change our whole life? I mean, *who are you?* Is everything that we've been through, everything that we've made together... just a lie? How did you live every day with that?" he asked, his voice rising.

I felt as if I were made of concrete. There were no words that could fix everything. No heartfelt explanation that would take my guilt away or turn us back into who we had been just twenty-four hours earlier.

"What about our girls? What do we tell them? How do we even do this, Emily... or whatever, Danica? Am I supposed to call you that now? This is like being in a bad movie, like some shit nightmare... I have to get out of here. I have to think... I'm sorry," he said, leaving the room.

I heard his footsteps on the stairway and the back door open and slam shut. I moved to the window and saw him, striding across the big yard and opening the gate that led to the stables. There was a small creek with an outcropping of rocks that ran along the back edge of the property, that was his getaway spot, when he needed to decompress. Like an automated robot, I turned and began to pull out clothes from my closet, packing my belongings to leave a life that I always felt didn't belong to me to begin with. I gathered my toiletries from the bathroom and a framed photo of all of us taken the previous Easter.

After I packed the car, I sent Dolores a text message that I wouldn't be able to get home until later in the week. I couldn't deal with telling her the truth yet and I didn't know how I would ever tell my girls—I needed to figure it out. I called to book a room in downtown Los Angeles as I pulled out of the driveway, watching the gates close behind me.

I didn't bother to fight the tears as I drove away, following the route to the freeway on autopilot. I merged into the ever-present traffic but as I passed the exit for South Pasadena, I veered suddenly to catch the off-ramp, cutting off the driver behind me. There was someone I had to see. It was the person who had been there for me every step of my journey back to life after James Tibbs. The man who took my hand and showed up, who rebuilt a broken child. I needed to see the man I called my dad, Michael Ray.

Fifteen minutes later, I pulled into the parking lot for the Rising Star Memory Care facility in Pasadena. It was located on a quiet, tree-lined street surrounded by luxury craftsman homes. It was a top-of-the-line dementia care home, but despite the luxury appointments, the cruel reality of dementia and Alzheimer's was apparent in the locked doors and the three security officers that were always present.

Michael had started experiencing confusion and agitation at the age of sixty-three. It was early onset and progressed rapidly and within two years, he could no longer live on his own even with an attendant. I visited him weekly now that he was close by and on good days, we would go get lunch at Taco Bell, something he would not have approved of before dementia but now it had become his favorite. I never bothered any longer to let him know I was coming; he would forget it within a few minutes.

I signed in at the office and took the elevator to his room. The housekeeping staff kept everything immaculate, and he had a second-story apartment with big windows that overlooked a courtyard filled with flowers. I found him in his favorite chair, watching TV Land, the retro station that played all the old shows from his childhood and young adult life. He was watching an episode of *Cheers*. I wiped my eyes and pinched my cheeks for color before entering.

"Hi, Daddy!' I said, putting on my happy voice, hoping today would be a good day.

He turned to look at me and smiled blankly, as if he wasn't sure who I was for a moment and then his face lit up.

"Emily! I'm so glad you're here!" he said, rising to embrace me.

"I just came by for a visit. How're you doing? You've been eating well?" I asked.

He settled me into a companion chair and sat back down, still holding my hand.

"Oh, yes. Everything is going quite well. We're going to be pouring the foundation for the new office tower in Houston next week," he said proudly, living in a long-lost memory of his once-busy real estate empire.

"That sounds great. How tall is this one going to be?"

"Thirty-five stories. Gerard Hellman did the architectural drawings, it's really beautiful!" he said.

He remembered many of his former colleagues and things that happened forty years ago. But he had no idea what he ate for breakfast. We chatted about daily life, we laughed at the actors on *Cheers* until his attendant, Janetta, came to take him down to lunch.

"Are you going to stay to eat with us today, Ms. Ray?" Janetta asked.

"No, I'm in the middle of a case, I just wanted to stop by and say hello," I explained.

"Okay, well, I'll give you a minute, I have to take Mr. Robin down as well," she said, closing the door behind her.

I leaned into Michael. I knew he wouldn't understand what I was talking about, but I had to say it out loud anyway.

"Daddy? I have something to tell you," I said.

"That Ted Danson is funny in this show. Did you know that he wore a toupee? I heard that once, but I didn't believe it," he said, smiling.

I squeezed his hand tightly and whispered, "I'm not her. I'm not Emily."

He looked at me with such clarity and kindness and whispered back, "I know. I always knew that honey."

I froze. I knew he couldn't have meant what he said but it shook me to my core to hear those words.

He smiled and touched my cheek. "You look just like her."

I nodded. I could barely speak but I managed to say, "I do. I look just like her."

I started to cry. I didn't want to upset him, but I couldn't help it. I knew in his confusion he had no idea what he was saying but in a strange way, it made me feel that he'd forgiven me.

"Don't cry, honey. It's all okay. We're going down to lunch now. I hope it's grilled cheese. Shall we go?"

He stood and grabbed hold of his cane and took my arm. We walked down the long hallway; he slipped his hand into mine. It felt so frail and small.

"You're a wonderful girl. I thought I had lost her forever, but you came back to me. That was the happiest moment of my life, you know?" he said.

"It was the best moment of my life too, Daddy. The very best moment."

TWENTY-SIX
DAY FIVE: 3:10 P.M.

I checked into my hotel room and opened my laptop. I felt like I had been through ten rounds of a heavyweight fight, but I had work to do. Stephanie texted that she had sent over everything I had asked for. Joe Lavois had worked with several different plumbing companies over the years, usually in two- to three-year stints, which struck me as odd. I scanned the list of his former employers: O'Malley and Sons Plumbing and Heating, Logan Broward Plumbing, Rooter King, Glendale Commercial Maintenance Company, and a dozen more. Most tradesmen don't move around that much when they land a good gig.

Glendale Commercial Maintenance jumped out at me; it was where Garvey Tibbs had worked for many years. It was a possible point of connection. The company was still active. I called but got a voicemail message. Reviewing Joe Lavois' information, I saw that in the past year, he had changed his mailing address from the Long Beach house to a post office in Running Springs.

I opened the email attachment that Stephanie sent of the building plans for the Arrowbear cabin. It had been built in 1964. It was small, an A-frame with two bedrooms on an upper floor and a bathroom. Downstairs consisted of one large room with what looked to be a galley kitchen, a dining area and a fireplace. There was a small bedroom downstairs as well and like many mountain homes, the cabin was raised with a build-up underneath it.

Everything seemed to be connected to the house in Arrowbear. There were too many coincidences: the location where Tibbs staged his death, the proximity of a safe house nearby, the character of the mountain communities that made them a perfect place to hide out. Even the messages sent from the post offices in Victorville and Hesperia fit. Those communities were not that far if he drove down the back side of the mountain and it would create a distraction if it diverted our attention.

I hadn't heard back from Glendale Commercial Maintenance and decided to pay them a visit. On my way to their office, my phone rang, and I saw it was Lydia, but I didn't answer. I felt bad for avoiding her, but everything had moved so fast in the past few days, I couldn't manage talking with her yet. I texted a quick message:

> I'm in the middle of it, all is well. Call you later.

I arrived at Glendale Commercial Maintenance, which was in a small office building that also housed the Armenian Relief Society and a storefront kebab house. I had a photo of Joe Lavois that I had pulled from the internet. It was over ten years old and showed a lanky, dark-haired man with a thick mustache. I also had a photo of James Tibbs in his twenties. The hallway to GCM had the musty smell of old manila folders and cardboard. In the office I found a young Armenian woman seated at a receptionist desk, with the biggest false eyelashes I had ever seen.

"Can I help you?" she asked, peering out at me through a forest of black synthetic fibers.

I introduced myself, flashing my FBI badge, and asked to speak to someone in management. She went through a door and came back a moment later with an older, heavyset man. He extended his hand and gave me an excessively firm shake.

"I'm Ben Hendry, owner/operator. How can I be of service to you?"

"I have some questions about a couple of former employees. Joe Lavois and Garvey Tibbs."

"We can talk more easily in my office," he said, ushering me down a hallway. Once in his office, he gently closed the door.

"I didn't want to talk in front of Anahit. Her dad is still in contact with Lavois. Joe worked here off and on over the years. He's a good plumber but he's difficult. I've hired him back a few times when I was short-staffed, but he never lasts very long. He hates having to answer to anyone," Hendry explained.

"Did he ever work here with Garvey Tibbs?" I asked.

"Good old Garvey! Yeah, they worked here together when Lavois was young. They became quite the friends, too. Joe didn't have much family, and he was always going over to Garvey's for dinner and holidays. But I think they were in some shady business together."

"Shady in what way?"

"When they worked together, material would disappear. Not in large quantities but over time, I started to notice it. And they always had electronics for sale, like the ones that fall off the back of a truck. You know what I mean?"

"Were you ever acquainted with Garvey's son, James?" I asked, sliding a photo of Tibbs across the desk.

"Jimmy Tibbs, yeah. Garvey used to bring him on jobs sometimes. Always during the week, when the kid should've been in school. They were a strange pair, Garvey and his wife. And their kid turned out to be nuts! He kidnapped that little girl years later," he said, shaking his head.

I felt a quickening in my body; I was getting closer.

"So, you think it's probable that Joe Lavois knew James Tibbs?"

"More than probable. They definitely knew each other. Lavois is about twelve years older than Jimmy was. The kid thought Lavois hung the moon."

"And what makes you think your receptionist is in contact with Lavois?"

"Her dad works here, and he and Lavois are cut from the same cloth. Kind of like Garvey, always bitching. Malcontents, my wife calls them."

I thanked him for his time and on the way out, Anahit of the eyelashes waved me over.

"Have you talked to Joe Lavois? My dad has called him a few times and he hasn't called back or anything. I'm kinda worried, it's been a long time. He was moving up to that cabin, out in the middle of nowhere."

"I haven't but if I do, I'll tell him to give you a call," I said.

"He's kind of grouchy but he's hot, even for an old guy!" she giggled.

I'm always surprised at the incredibly low standards some women have. How would a guy twenty years her senior, a malcontent and petty thief with a porn mustache, be described as hot? Aside from Anahit's poor choice in men, I had gotten valuable information that established a close link between Tibbs and Lavois. The way Hendry described Lavois' character, it wasn't a stretch to imagine him helping Tibbs stay under the radar.

On my way back to the hotel, Ryan called with an update. "Things are heating up in Victorville. We've got a guy on the run. His name is Tyler Murray. He was released from prison a few months ago. We've searched his trailer and his storage space. We found child pornography videos and other stuff. A neighbor says she saw him with a little girl in his car. And we finally got camera footage of him from several weeks ago in one of the post offices where the drawings were mailed. Once we get good intel on his location, we'll move on him."

"What's going on with the private investigators?

"They're driving everyone crazy. They have their online community of sleuths digging into the case and posting about it, you know, searching for clickbait. I'm sure Grice regrets taking the whole thing on himself; he looks like he's ready to blow."

"Did you have a chance to show the surf shop owner the photo of the blue sedan?"

"I did it this morning. She said it's the same kind of car that she saw in the alleyway. What about Tibbs?"

"He definitely faked his death. The DNA wasn't his, it's a match to another young man who's been missing for years."

Ryan let out a low whistle. "Oh fuck! He could really be our guy. What's going on with Lavois?"

I filled him in on the Joe Lavois–Tibbs connection and my suspicions about the Arrowbear house.

"I'll be going up there to get a better sense of what we're dealing with," I said.

"Whoa! You can't go alone, it's way too risky!" he said.

"I'm just checking it out and I plan to take backup."

"Who? The whole team is out here in bumfuck and you're on leave."

"There are other people I can call on besides the FBI."

"Well, let me know if you need me. I'll be there as fast as I can," he offered.

"How would you work that with Grice?"

"Let me worry about that. Just keep me posted. Gotta go, Diaz is calling..."

Back at the hotel, I felt the familiar anxiety and restlessness coming over me. I went to the hotel gym and got on a treadmill. I set the speed and incline levels high, to make it as hard as I could stand it. As my feet pounded out a steady rhythm, I remembered a family trip to Disneyland last year. How we'd been on the Peter Pan ride when it broke and we got stuck in our flying boat, in mid-air, for over an hour. Antonio and I made up stories about Tiger Lily and Tinkerbell to keep the girls entertained. Just the memory of it made me cry again. How could I have ruined everything? I pushed through the tears, running harder until I was exhausted, my clothes wet with sweat. I showered and refocused my mind on the case. I couldn't fall into a pit of sadness and self-pity. I had to bring Josie Vance home alive.

I ordered tuna salad and sparkling mineral water from room service. I studied the floor plan of the Arrowbear cabin until I had it memorized and then searched the area on Google Maps to see how close the neighbors were. A handful of houses were nearby but no houses on either side. I drew a map of the route I'd use to approach and how many exit points there were to escape the area if need be, then checked the Caltrans website to see if there was any major road construction or closures in the area but it was all clear, which meant I'd be heading up there tomorrow to find Tibbs.

I'd go up in the evening; moving under the cover of darkness would arouse less attention from neighbors or small-town busybodies. Part of me wanted to rush up there and confront Tibbs immediately. But it wasn't just about me; he had Josie and I needed to make a careful plan to ensure her safety. Near midnight, I called room service to pick up the dishes and prepared for bed.

A few minutes later there was a knock at the door, and I assumed it was room service but when I opened it, Antonio was standing in front of me.

"How did you find me?" I asked, feeling my chest tighten.

"Location services on your phone. The phones are linked so I can see where you are."

"I forgot to turn it off. Do you want to come in?" I asked.

He walked past me into the room and remained standing.

"I have something to say. Please don't interrupt me, I know you're going to want to but please don't," he said, with such seriousness that I knew it was the "our marriage is over" talk.

Two steps from the abyss...

"Okay, I'm listening."

"I'm sorry for the way I reacted earlier... I was completely shocked. But today I've been following that news story on Danica Hansen... I mean, your story. The second installment is online now—that girl's a good reporter, by the way—and it broke my heart to read it. I knew all about Tibbs and what you went through with him but to find out that before him, you were such a little girl, living in such an awful situation... and that no one even looked for you for so long..."

His voice broke off. I knew that he was struggling to hold his emotions in check. Like most men, he hated to give in to crying and I saw that he was close to it. I wanted to reach out and do something to help him. But I didn't.

He continued, "It just made me... furious and sad. I wish you had told me earlier, years ago, because I would've helped you carry that secret. I wish I had been able to help you with it. I can't imagine how hard this has been for you, for so long."

"I lied to you, to everyone. Everything I've done has been a fraud—"

He interrupted me. "No, it hasn't. Everything you've done, you accomplished with your own skill and resilience. It doesn't matter if your name is Emily Ray or Danica Hansen or... Kermit the Frog. I know who you are and how you're made. None of that is fake. You were just a kid when you made that decision. And who wouldn't do what you did—if they could get away with it? How many people would happily trade in the shitty hand they'd been dealt and become someone else?"

We stared at each other for a beat, unsure how to proceed.

"I thought you would divorce me, that everything would be over now that you know," I finally said.

"Divorce you? I love you more than anything in the world. You're my wife, I can't do this life without you, Emily... I'm sorry, what should I call you?"

He moved toward me and pulled me into an embrace as I started to cry. His arms wrapped around me, and I buried myself into his shoulder. He knew my secret, the worst thing I had ever done, and he still loved me.

I had spent so long being Emily, transforming into the girl that everyone cared about because on some deep level, I felt that was the only way anyone would ever care about me. I didn't deserve what Emily had—even Tibbs used to say that she was the special one and I was nothing—and if anyone knew the truth, I would go back to being the invisible, worthless person I had been. But I was wrong.

Now I was in the tight embrace of a man that I adored, the father of my children, and I was safe. I didn't have to pretend any longer. We stood there, unmoving, until my heartbeat slowed down, my breathing steadied. Antonio pulled back and smoothed a loose strand of hair into place.

"Shall we go home?" he asked.

On the drive back through the quiet city streets, I filled him in on everything I had learned in the past forty-eight hours, about Cody Barriage, Tibbs being alive and how I feared I was his real target.

"What do you think he'll do now? If he thinks you're off the case?" he asked, his hand resting protectively on my thigh.

"Either he thinks he's won, or he'll make some dramatic gesture, especially with all the Danica Hansen information being out there. I'm pretty sure he's going to expose me. I just don't know how," I said, entwining my fingers with his.

"Who's going to believe him if he says that you aren't Emily Ray? He's a psycho, a criminal."

His words brought me up short. It hadn't occurred to me that if Tibbs were to reveal my identity, he would not be believed. Upon the realization that he was alive, I'd had a knee-jerk reaction, as if he still had power over my life. Antonio was right. It would be seen as the rantings of a crazy person.

"What do you think I should do?" I asked.

"Nothing, for the moment. You don't have to reveal yourself to find Josie unless it's imperative. I'm with you, whatever you decide," he said, kissing the back of my hand.

I reached out to touch his curly hair, giving it an affectionate little tug. He laughed softly.

"What're you doing, crazy girl?"

"I just love you," I said, quietly.

"Love you more."

Tibbs was powerless over me now. I had someone to help me carry my secret, a safe place to put that weight down. For the first time in my life, I felt free.

TWENTY-SEVEN
DAY SIX: 7:42 A.M.

After a few hours of sleep, we got the girls up and ready for a day at Art Camp. As they ate their French toast, they shared furtive glances and giggles, until Antonio asked, "Okay, what's up with you two?"

"Mommy and Daddy had a date night!" Juli shouted.

Eliza made kissy sounds at us as Dolores packed their lunches, with a wink. As she ushered them out to the car, I knelt down and pulled each one into a hug.

"Do you know how much Mommy loves you?"

"Maybe a little?" Eliza asked with a sly smile.

"More than the whole big universe and beyond!" I said, kissing them wildly. They laughed and pulled away. I looked into their hazel eyes, wondering how the day would play out, if I would come back safe and sound. I pushed the thought away and clutched at their squirming bodies.

"Remember me? I'm the tummy monster!" I said in my best scary voice.

"Stop! You're tickling us!" Juli objected, loving every minute of it.

I waved as Dolores pulled into the street, and the gates

closed, then went back inside to make a fresh pot of coffee while Antonio packed his briefcase for work.

"So, what's the plan for today? If you're heading up to the mountains to find Tibbs, I don't want you in a confrontation alone with him. I think I should go with you," he said.

"Honey, you wouldn't know what to do in this situation. And you're not good with firearms, if it comes to that," I said, gently.

"But I should be there to protect you," he insisted.

"If you're there, it will distract me and I'll be worried about your safety."

"Em, I'm the husband, it's my job to keep you safe."

I smiled, his eyes were so earnest and kind. I reached out and took his hand.

"If this were an old John Wayne movie, you would ride in with guns blazing and save me from the bad guy. But I don't need that kind of saving—"

He started to interrupt me, and I stopped him. "You protect me every day by giving me a safe place to exist, with all of my faults, and by having my back, especially now. But this is professional, I'm trained for this kind of thing... and I'm much better with a gun than you are," I said.

"I know, you're kind of like the family sniper," he said with a laugh.

"I have a gut feeling I'm right about Tibbs and he's up there. I came up with the plan last night, I'm taking backup. So, don't worry, I wouldn't dream of going up there alone," I assured him.

"What kind of backup?" he insisted.

"I'm reaching out to Detective Whirt and I'll probably contact the local sheriffs once I'm up in the mountains. And I've been getting intel updates from Stephanie Leedom so I'm well prepared. And Detective Ryan offered to come join us as well."

"What if Tibbs has an arsenal of weapons? Like an AR-15?"

"I'm not going to get into a situation where he will have a

clear shot at anyone. It won't come to that, I promise. I love you but I need you to trust me," I said, taking his hand.

"Well, I don't like it but I know there's no stopping you when you get like this. Call me with regular updates or I'll call the local police myself. And keep your location on your phone so I know where you are at all times," he said.

He kissed my forehead and held me close for a long beat.

"You have to come back to me," he whispered.

"I always do, don't I?"

He left and I settled in with a cup of fresh coffee. I would wait until nine o'clock to call Whirt. I was certain he would want to be part of catching Tibbs after all these years. I was scanning the front page of the *Los Angeles Times* when I got a call from Larissa Cinque.

"Agent Ray? I'm sorry to bother you but Detective Whirt told me you're on leave from the Vance case for a few days?"

"Yes, I am. How can I help you?"

"I know it's a shot in the dark but today I'm scheduled to talk with Danica Hansen's aunt, Janelle Morris. And later with her dad who's in prison, on a Zoom call. I was wondering if you might review the questions I'm planning to ask them, just to be sure they're on target?"

At the mention of Janelle's name, I froze. A wave of memories flooded my mind; the musty smell of the trailer, the lingering scent of burned microwave popcorn, the constant blathering of voices on the TV. That small, cramped dismal backdrop of my childhood, I felt as if I were back there again. I had buried any recollection or feeling from that time the night I ran to freedom, the day I became Emily Ray. I had never wanted to revisit it but now I suddenly wondered what Janelle told herself and others about my disappearance. The woman who had failed me so spectacularly as a child that I'd ended up in Tibbs' nightmarish grasp.

I heard myself saying, "I'll do you one better. How about if I join you for the interviews? To give you some FBI backup?"

"Really? That would be amazing! Danica's aunt still lives in the same trailer park in Torrance. I can send you the address. It's called Beach Palms. I'm meeting her at noon and then my Zoom is scheduled with Glen Hansen at 1:30."

"Okay, I'll meet you there just before noon," I said.

I didn't need directions to the Beach Palms Trailer Park, I could find it in my sleep. I knew it was risky, but this chance would never come again. My whole life I had been terrified of being exposed, of stepping back into that miserable world I left behind. Now, I was ready to walk right into the fire and face it.

You're not that little girl any longer...

Turn on the light...

Before leaving for the South Bay, I booked an Airbnb in Arrowbear for an evening arrival, using a different name. At 9 a.m. sharp, I called Whirt.

"It's Emily Ray. You want to go help me catch James Tibbs?"

"James Tibbs? What the hell?"

"Long story, I'll fill you in on the way. We have to go up to Arrowbear, above San Bernardino."

"What the fuck? He's alive? Do you think he has Josie Vance?"

"Yeah, I do. I don't want to go alone, and I thought you'd enjoy taking him down, after all these years."

"Catching that motherfucker would make everything worth it. What do I need to do?"

"Be at my house by six tonight. And pack your firearms," I said.

"Who could resist an invitation like that?"

.   .   .

I coasted through mild traffic to Torrance and parked across the street from the Beach Palms Trailer Park. I watched and waited. There was a stucco wall on either side of the main driveway, covered in plaster that resembled a cake with too much frosting. At Christmas, the park management hung a ton of lights at the entrance and hired a local guy to play Santa in the clubhouse for the kids. I had forgotten about those times, the small, happy moments of living with my aunt.

The trailers ranged from the nice ones, decorated with neat, tidy fences, and hanging flowerpots, to the ones with sheets of plywood on the exterior walls. Janelle's trailer was rundown and shabby, a flower bed filled with faded plastic tulips and gladiolus from the Dollar Tree. Larissa arrived and I crossed the street to meet her.

"Agent Ray! I got two parking passes for us," she said.

"I left my car across the street. Does Ms. Morris know we're here?" I asked.

"I just texted her. She should be out in a moment. That's her trailer, the beige one," she said, pointing to it.

As we approached her trailer, my heart hammered in my chest. I could see myself, as a child, wandering around this shabby park, unsupervised and locked out because Janelle was drinking at the Shoreline bar. Or waiting alone in the chilly trailer, a stale box of crackers and warm soda for my dinner when she forgot to bring food home. The door to the trailer opened and Janelle walked out. She was older now, dressed in ill-fitting skinny jeans and a tight Jason Aldean T-shirt, a pathetic attempt at youthfulness. Would she recognize me, after all these years? I braced for her reaction, but she looked right through me, her eyes dull and flat.

"You're the reporter, right?" she asked, waving to Larissa.

"Yes, Ms. Morris, and this is Special Agent Emily Ray from the FBI," Larissa said.

I extended my hand and Janelle took it, giving me a skeptical once-over.

"I didn't expect no one else but you," she said.

"I invited her to join me, in case you remembered anything that might be useful," Larissa explained.

"Fine by me," Janelle said, ushering us into her trailer.

I saw that not much had changed in twenty-three years; it was still crowded, disorganized and dirty. She motioned for us to sit at the small dining table that had cigarette burn marks on it. I remembered how she would dangle her lit Marlboro while talking on the phone, oblivious until the smell of burning wood caught her attention.

"So, what'dya want to know about Dani? She was here with me 'cause her mom took off with that deadbeat Jedidiah and they went to Texas. She didn't even know that asshole had open warrants out there and he got picked up within a couple of weeks. It was a fucking mess," she snorted as she laughed.

"And Danica disappeared on a regular school day, correct? Do you have any recollections of that day?" Larissa asked.

"Nah, she was bugging me to take her to the bus station to meet her mom. She thought Amber was gonna come to get her 'cause she'd sent a postcard. Now, I know my sister and there was no way she was coming on a fucking bus to get Dani and I told her so. But she had to go and wait for Amber. And then she never came back. If she'd a stayed home, she wouldn'a disappeared."

"How often did Danica wander around unsupervised? It sounds normal for you to let a ten-year-old go to the bus station alone," I interjected, waiting for her reaction.

"Dani did what she wanted, there was no way I coulda kept her home. She always went all over the neighborhood on her own. It's just the way it was back then," she said, defensively.

"Really?" I asked, challenging her version of the past. She

made it sound as if I were a hard-to-control child, rather than one she rarely thought about or cared for.

Larissa shot me a nervous glance and interjected, "So, you didn't realize that Danica was missing right away, correct?"

"Well, I thought Amber had come and got her, when she didn't come back. I thought she was with her mom. When Amber called me a few weeks later asking for Dani, I went straight to the police," Janelle said.

"So, you never confirmed with your sister that she had picked Dani up?" Larissa asked.

"Why would I have done that? I didn't keep tabs on her. She wasn't my kid, y'know." Janelle shrugged.

"I saw in the police report, they thought she might have been a runaway and you agreed. Did Danica do anything prior to her disappearance to lead you to believe she was a runaway?" I asked.

"She had taken off a few times before. When she got mad at me or something," she lied, lighting a cigarette and taking a deep drag. I felt a surge of fury and resentment at her callous deceit.

"So, your ten-year-old niece disappears, you never check with anyone to see if she's safe and then you tell the police that she probably ran away? So, they won't treat her case with any urgency?" I asked pointedly.

"I did my best, once I knew she was gone! I loved that little girl," she protested.

"Did you get foster care money for taking care of Danica?" I asked, looking at her square in the eyes.

"No, I never got nothing like that, but I shoulda," she said, casting her eyes down, her hand scratching at her collarbone nervously. "They said some bullshit that I didn't have the right kind of house for foster care. Amber didn't want her going back to the system, so she dumped her with me."

I felt the seething rage bubbling up inside me, to hear her self-serving excuses and lies. I stepped outside. Maybe I had hoped Janelle would show some remorse for what had happened, but I was wrong. She sat there, lighting one cigarette after another, presenting herself as a devoted aunt who had been tormented by my disappearance. Leaning against her weather-beaten trailer, I realized that I'd wanted Janelle to admit to how she'd neglected me, but it was never going to happen. All I got was confirmation that she was the same dysfunctional, selfish drunk she had always been.

After realizing there would be no bombshell revelations, Larissa was ready to leave. Janelle seemed to expect that she might get some cash for the interview and her annoyance was clear as we walked away.

"What do you think? She's really a screw-up. How did Amber think leaving Dani with her was a good idea?" Larissa asked shaking her head sadly.

"You'd have to ask her, but this is a very common scenario. People neglect and abuse their children all the time."

"I guess. Amber's living in Alaska now, won't talk to anyone about Dani's disappearance. I tried to contact her, but she's hooked up with one of those doomsday prepper guys who live off the grid in the middle of nowhere. Sounds horrible," Larissa said, unlocking her Honda Civic. I was surprised to hear any news of my mother, but her living in Alaska, following another loser, wasn't unexpected. I had no interest in her at this point. Still, it had been a heady afternoon so far and I felt like I was on a second-rate roller coaster that might come off the track.

"So, how are we doing the interview with Glen Hansen?" I asked, trying to steady my nerves.

"If you meet me at the *Daily Breeze* offices, I can log into the Wi-Fi and we can use one of the conference rooms."

The *Daily Breeze* offices were in Hermosa Beach, a short drive from Torrance. Their newsroom looked like any other mid-sized regional newspaper, and I got a pass to enter with Larissa. We moved among the desks to a small conference room.

We had fifteen minutes before the Zoom call with my father from San Quentin. Prisoners were allowed one video call a month and the fact that Glen Hansen agreed to use his one call to speak to an unknown reporter told me he didn't have much contact with the outside world.

Larissa logged in and we waited for Glen Hansen to join the call. I was nervous, I hadn't seen or spoken to my dad in many years; he was a stranger to me. I felt a wave of panic; this was too much to deal with. Lydia was right, I overestimated my resilience and now I felt like that six-year-old girl I had been the last time I saw my dad. I remembered the confusing mix of emotions when my mother told me he would be gone for a long time, and I should just forget about him. I recalled his rare sober moments, when he took me to a small traveling amusement park and won a stuffed hippo for me at the ring toss game. The time I got a piece of broken glass in my foot and he gently extracted it; as he leaned over me, I smelled a mixture of tobacco and whiskey that clung to him. These long-buried memories came rushing back at me as I tried to sit calmly in the *Daily Breeze* office, waiting for Larissa to make the connection. I couldn't keep still, my legs were restless, fidgeting as my anxiety grew.

He wasn't just a witness to interview in an investigation. He was my own father. Did he remember me? Was I just a faded image of a long-lost period of his past? Did I matter to him, ever?

The screen came to life and a window appeared, showing the face of a man who shared my almond-shaped blue eyes, my aquiline nose, a dimple on one cheek. I was shocked by how much I looked like him, now that I had grown up. Glen Hansen barely resembled the man I'd known as a child. He was gaunt and pale, with deep circles under his watery eyes. He ran his hands nervously over his slicked-back ponytail, his fingers were scarred and knobby. Prison had hollowed him out; his blue shirt hung on his bony frame; he looked as if a strong breeze would knock him over.

"Hello, you must be Miss Cinque," he said politely.

"Yes, we're in the *Daily Breeze* offices right now. This is Special Agent Emily Ray with the FBI. I invited her to join us," she said.

"Are the feds getting involved in looking for Danica? I heard they're putting new detectives on it," he said.

"Not at this point, but the more information we can compile, the better," I lied, eager to appease him, as I had done as a child.

"So, Mr. Hansen, you were incarcerated already when Danica went missing, correct?" Larissa asked.

My father shifted his weight and worked his hands into fists, nervously.

"Yeah. I fucked up. I got put away and left Amber with Dani but she wasn't cut out to be a mother. She just wanted to drink and party, and she never did right by the kid. Neither did I. I was a shithole father..." His voice trailed off.

I felt a shift inside, a flickering of compassion that I was unprepared for. With Janelle or my mother, it was easy to stay shut-off, emotionally. All they had to offer were excuses and self-serving lies. This was moving in a different direction, and I felt like I was balancing on a steep ledge, holding my breath.

"How did you find out she was missing?" Larissa continued.

"They didn't even know she was gone! Amber and that drunk-ass sister of hers, they didn't even know she was missing. When they found out, weeks had gone by and the cops had no clues, nothing. I found out from the warden, and I called Amber but she wouldn't talk to me. I was just stuck, nothing I could do and no information," he said, his voice getting tighter and more agitated as he spoke.

"Did you have a close relationship with your daughter?" Larissa asked.

"No, I was too busy with my own bullshit, getting in trouble. But Amber was no help. She never let me see her when I had the chance. I tried a bunch of times to take her to the park or something, but Amber would always mess it up."

"So, you really had no idea she was missing and then you couldn't do anything. That must've been very frustrating," Larissa said.

"I'll tell you, Miss Cinque, there's a lot of rough shit that goes down in prison. But that was the worst thing that ever happened to me. To know your little girl is lost and you can't do nothing to help. And they never found her..." His voice broke, and he covered his face with his hand.

My mom had always told me that my dad had no interest in me. Watching him suffer now, knowing the helplessness he felt years ago, was more than I could manage. Tears welled up in my eyes and I had to turn away to hide them, breathing through clenched teeth to calm my heart rate, regain my composure.

"Do you have any questions, Agent Ray?" Larissa asked and I shook my head, silently. I didn't trust my voice not to falter.

As she was winding down the conversation, my father turned to me. "She said you're with the FBI, right? Can you all do something to help find her? I know she'd be grown by now but maybe there's something you can do, miss? I just want her to be found, even if it's just, you know... whatever might be left of her, somewhere..."

He fought back tears, rubbing his hands over his eyes. If there was ever a moment I wished I could tell the truth about who I was, this was it. My own father was broken and begging for help to find me. And I was sitting right in front of him.

"We'll do whatever we can, Mr. Hansen," I said, my voice cracking, before excusing myself to use the restroom.

In the bathroom, I locked the stall door behind me and rested my forehead against the cold tile on the wall. I felt overcome with regret that he had suffered so much at my disappearance. Of my small, dysfunctional family, it seemed that he was the only one who really cared about me, and I never even knew it. I splashed cold water on my face and adjusted the claw clip holding my hair, putting my professional persona back in place. When I emerged, Larissa had logged out of the call.

"Wow! That was intense. The poor man, I feel so bad for him. They didn't even tell him," she said.

"I know. It was... really sad," I managed to reply.

"What do you think happened to Danica? It's weird that they never found anything related to her."

"That happens a lot more than you think. Some kids just vanish, most likely they met with foul play."

"That poor little girl never stood a chance."

"No, she never did."

"I'm going to stay on top of this with the Redondo PD. We're going to find out what happened to her. Can the FBI get involved in cold cases like this?"

"Sometimes. It's not my division," I said, with a growing sense of unease.

"Maybe you could ask them? The more we publicize this, someone is bound to come forward with information about her," she said, climbing into her car. I touched her arm to stop her.

"Larissa, I know your intentions are the best but don't get too optimistic. The fact that no one has heard anything about this girl for over twenty years doesn't point to a positive outcome. She was probably picked up by some predator and she's most likely dead at this point," I said gently.

"But she could be like Steven Stayner, who came home years later," she protested.

"She could, but it's not likely. It might just lead to more suffering for Glen Hansen and I don't want you to deal with that. It's not easy and it's better just left alone."

"But what if we could help find her, after all this time?"

"You'll probably come up empty-handed with more questions than you started with. And if by some miracle she's out there living her best life, do you think she wants to be found?"

"What are the chances of that, realistically?"

"Not good at all," I said.

She sat back in her car and sighed. "Thanks for your advice. I'm still going to pursue it. Someone might know something."

I watched her drive away. She was right, someone could come forward with information, someone who knew the truth. Someone I had to catch and kill before that happened.

TWENTY-EIGHT
DAY SIX: 3:10 P.M.

On the way back home, I reviewed my plan again and again. Antonio was out and the girls had gymnastics in the afternoon so I wouldn't get a chance to see them before I left. With the turmoil that we had gone through, it was a relief to me that they were not affected by it; their lives and activities continued as usual.

I took the stairs two at a time when I got home and pulled my undercover bag from the closet. It held a couple of wigs and glasses, a pair of faded polyester stretch pants and an old Dodgers T-shirt. I packed a large duffel bag with battery-powered bolt cutters, two crowbars, Ryobi skill- and chainsaws, a long axe, and a heavy mallet. In a leather gun bag, I put my Glock, a Sig Sauer, the Smith and Wesson revolver and two hunting knives. From a small, locked fridge in the laundry room, I took out a vial of methohexital, a fast-acting sedative for intra-muscular injection with a syringe. If Tibbs and I were going to have a rendezvous, I was ready.

Whirt arrived at six sharp, stepping out of his car to take in the yard and house.

"Wow! This is some spread. The FBI pays better than I thought," he said.

"It doesn't. This was a gift from my dad."

I took him inside and explained about Cody Barriage and the DNA, how the messages sent to the team after Josie was taken had to be from Tibbs. He was our suspect.

"This is like some serious *Criminal Minds* shit here!" he said. "Who gets to catch a creep like this after so many years? It was worth it getting kicked off the case. Does Grice know you're doing this?"

"No, I'm officially on leave so I'm going completely rogue," I said.

"Good for you. Just hope they don't fire you," he said. That was a very real possibility, but I didn't care. I had to find Josie and bring her home, no matter the cost.

I called Antonio and filled him in, letting him talk to Whirt to prove that I had backup before we left.

"Drive safely and keep me posted, no matter what. If I don't hear from you, I'll call the local police. And the National Guard!" he warned.

Whirt and I made the long trek to San Bernardino and then up Highway 330, just as the sun was beginning to set. The Scotch broom had started to bloom, lining the way with brilliant yellow bushes, amid the rocky hillsides. The California sunset bathed everything with a soft, pink glow. When we reached Rim of the World highway at the top, the road narrowed, and the terrain became more rugged. At Arrowbear Drive, we took a right turn to a park with a baseball diamond. There was a lone guy fishing at the edge of a small lake. It was clearly the center of town and there wasn't much to it.

We continued on residential streets that twisted and looped into the kind of dead ends that we had to back out of, they were too narrow for a U-turn. Many of the homes were shabby and rundown, with peeling paint and half-collapsed entryways. It was an end-of-the-line kind of place that felt like you might get a gun pulled on you just for being an outsider.

GPS didn't work in the mountains and after a few mistakes, we finally found the Lavois cabin on Hookbill Road. It was a small blue and white house perched at a crooked angle on a corner. A blue Nissan Sentra was in the driveway; it was the car registered to Lavois. Our Airbnb was nearby, strategically located on an access road above the Lavois home; we had a clear view of the entrance, driveway and side lot.

Our rental was a simple, neat affair with two small bedrooms done in Hobby Lobby decor. We settled in and unpacked; I stashed the duffel bag with my firearms while Whirt fiddled with the television remote.

"Damn it, I can never figure these things out! Why are there so many buttons that don't make sense?"

"Give it to me. What do you want to watch? The Wi-Fi password is posted in the kitchen," I said.

"Everything is so complicated now, for fuck's sake..." he muttered as he walked off.

I unpacked my dinner: tuna fish sandwiches, sliced cucumbers and strawberries, a banana. Whirt came back in, having changed into sweatpants, holding a takeout menu from Domino's.

"Are you eating that bird food again? I saw you every day on the case, always the same. It looked like grass cuttings on bread," he ribbed me.

"For lunch it's watercress and cream cheese. If it's dinner on the road, it's tuna fish," I explained.

"Don't you ever have a big juicy In-N-Out Burger? Or a large order of greasy onion rings?"

"No, I don't. I always eat the same things. I have routines. My brain loves them," I said, relishing a bite of my sandwich.

"Well, I'm ordering a pizza from Domino's. Cheese and

pepperoni. The wife makes me add vegetables but I'm unsupervised tonight!"

Stephanie had sent me the contact information for Joe Lavois' daughter in Oregon. Since that was his last known destination, I called her to confirm. She answered in two rings; I heard a toddler crying in the background.

"Hi, I'm a friend of Joe Lavois, I'm trying to get in touch with him about a plumbing job?" I asked.

"He's not here. I haven't talked to him in over a year. He moved to that cabin in the mountains so I'd try his cell but he has crappy service up there," she said irritably, eager to get off the phone.

"Do you know where I could reach him?"

"No idea. He always says he's coming to visit but never shows up. The story of his life." The toddler's cries became louder. "Look, I've got a baby to deal with. Good luck finding my dad, he's hard to pin down," she said before hanging up.

"Let me guess. Lavois isn't with his daughter?"

"She hasn't spoken to him in over a year. He seems to have lost contact with everyone," I said.

"No kidding. It's hard to keep in touch when you're dead. I'm gonna go pick this pizza up, they'll never find this place. You sure you don't want a choco lava cake?" he asked.

"Just go! Hurry back."

He left and I stationed myself at the sliding door to the deck with my binoculars. I sent a quick text to Antonio, letting him know that we had arrived safely. The Lavois cabin was completely dark, no sign of life or movement. I wondered if maybe I had it all wrong. I saw a family of racoons waddle up the driveway to explore the trashcans, climbing on one and tipping it over. They rummaged through the garbage inside, chewing scraps of food, which meant someone had put fresh trash out; the house wasn't vacant. Suddenly, a motion detector light came on and the door opened.

A wiry, compact man with close-cropped gray hair stepped out, holding a large plastic trash bag. He waved and shouted at the racoons, scattering them. He wore jeans, sneakers and a hoodie. I sat stock-still, praying his face would be visible in the exterior light. He took the trash bag to one of the plastic bins and secured it with a bungee. His gait was shuffling, unsteady. When he turned back to the house, the light fell across his face. My breath caught in my throat. It was Tibbs, now in his forties, his pallor faded to a grayish yellow. His eyes were prominent, ringed with dark circles; his face was gaunt. I broke into a sweat and nausea hit me. This wasn't a flashback; it was the real thing. I was right, he was alive. I felt adrenaline shoot through my body. Now it was my turn to watch and wait. This time I was the predator.

TWENTY-NINE
DAY SIX: 7:05 P.M.

When Whirt returned, I was laying out all of my tactical gear. My black RVRC Hypershell hiking pants and a fitted, long-sleeve T-shirt were folded on a chair in my room; my bullet-proof vest hung on a hook. I was checking the firearms and loading ammunition as Whirt hung in the doorway, watching me.

"What's up? You look ready for war," he said, already chomping a warm slice of pizza.

"Tibbs is there. I saw him taking the trash out."

Whirt froze, his pizza slice dripping oil onto his sweats.

"You're sure it's him?"

"I'm sure. Josie has to be in that house. We have to get her out safely."

"Okay, when? Tonight? Right now?" Whirt asked.

"No, I need a better sense of the area, the neighbors. And if he has any schedule, coming and going."

"No warrant?"

"No. I'm way past that. I'll be fired for doing this and you're retired. I'm not worried about protocol. We need to get Josie."

"And say it all goes smoothly—which I doubt—what next?"

"We call in local law enforcement to arrest Tibbs. We get Josie over to the local hospital for evaluation. We call her parents, Tibbs gets locked up and we all live happily ever after," I said.

"The place could be booby-trapped. He has to be prepared for us to show up. He could have an arsenal of weapons in there, even military-grade stuff. I say we call in the local sheriffs as backup."

"No, because if they check with my superiors, it'll be over, and we could lose him."

"So, it's just you and me?"

"Whirt, if you're nervous I can do it myself. You can stand guard from here."

"No way I'd let you do it alone, we're going in together. What's the plan?"

"We'll take turns keeping an eye on the house, to make sure he doesn't leave with Josie. If he goes out alone, we move in and get her. If he doesn't, we'll have to immobilize him so we can find her."

"Are you prepared if she's... not okay?" he asked, cautiously.

"If he's hurt her... or worse? Yes, I'm prepared for that," I said.

"How do you think you'll handle it?"

I paused, weighing whether or not to trust him. Finally, I said, "No matter how this goes down, I'm going to kill him and make it look like a good shooting."

Whirt stared at me for a long beat, then nodded his head.

"I'm fine with that," he said.

It was an uneventful night. There was no sign of Tibbs again, no lights from inside the house. I thought of Josie in there, alone in total darkness with that madman. I told myself she was still alive, she had to be, and we would save her in time. By morning, a few residents emerged to walk dogs or exercise. An Edison truck pulled up on an adjacent street to work on a power pole. We'd have to wait until things quieted down to make our move.

I heard Whirt's voice from the kitchen. "You won't believe this! Check out the KCAL news!"

I pulled it up on my phone and saw a glut of news reporters outside a strip mall in Victorville. Front and center were Jemmie and Dylan Jones, the internet sleuths.

"We're outside a storage facility here in Victorville where the police and FBI are on the hunt for an alleged child kidnapper, Tyler Murray, who's suspected of taking Josie Vance several days ago in Palos Verdes. According to private investigators, Jemmie and Dylan Jones, the suspect has been traced to this storage facility..."

Jemmie Jones thrust herself toward the microphone as Whirt came in with two cups of coffee.

"Can you believe this clusterfuck? Grice has to be losing his mind!" he said.

"Louis Vance must have orchestrated this. But it's good for us."

"How so?" he asked.

"We know Tibbs is following the case. This throws him completely off our scent. He thinks we're in Victorville chasing shadows. He might get lazy or cocky. Or both," I said.

"I'll take over the watch," he offered.

"Thanks, I need to catch a few Z's. Wake me up if anything moves."

In my bedroom, I texted Lydia. I felt terrible for avoiding her but I didn't want her to know about the blackouts or that Tibbs was still alive. She would have pressured me to step away from the case and I couldn't do that, not when we were so close to catching Tibbs.

the vance case is heating up, we're very close.
Lots to talk about, soon. XO

> *I'm worried, I spoke to Antonio. you need to step back Emily!*

I didn't respond. I slipped under the covers and fell into a fitful sleep. When I woke a few hours later, Whirt was still at the window, watching the Lavois cabin.

"No sign of him?" I asked.

"*Nada*. It's dead as a doornail. You sure you saw him?"

"I'm sure."

I heard a car approaching, I expected it to pass by but it pulled into our driveway.

"Who the hell could that be? No one knows we're here." I unholstered my Glock, just in case.

"Don't know. I guess I should open the door and find out," Whirt said, nonplussed. A moment later he returned with Ryan, dressed casually in jeans and a T-shirt.

"Hey, I thought you might need a little extra backup. Whirt texted me," he said, smiling broadly. "I brought the extra firepower and other goodies."

He set down a duffel bag filled with his own tactical gear. We locked hands; I was genuinely glad to have him there.

"Did I mention that I was with Special Forces for three years?" he asked.

"Really? Now I have more respect for you, despite the girly Starbucks addiction," Whirt said.

"What about Grice and Victorville?" I asked.

"We took that Tyler Murray guy down a couple of hours ago, so I was still in the area. Murray didn't have Josie but he had his ex-girlfriend's kid. Little girl about five years old. The asshole took her as payback when the kid's mom dumped him," he said.

"How's Grice taking it?" I asked.

"Not good. And those Hulu private eyes took off once they

saw that Grice got it wrong. What's up here? Whirt says you're closing in?"

"Tibbs is alive, I saw him. Living in Joe Lavois' cabin."

"We're waiting to make a move. We're going totally rogue on this," Whirt said proudly.

"Ryan, you were never here, okay? Our careers are over, but you don't want any repercussions from this. So, keep your head down," I said.

"I'm here to back you two up, just tell me what the plan is. What if we have to confront him?"

"All I have to do is get close enough to jab him with a needle. The drugs will do the rest, he'll be out in seconds. There's three of us, only one of him," I said.

"So, we're going way out of bounds, right? Drugging a suspect, illegal entry. Everything will be thrown out in court," Ryan said.

"Yep. But I'm pretty sure Lavois is dead, and Tibbs did it. We know he killed Cody Barriage and there's no statute of limitations on murder. Josie is the main objective here."

"Hey, a neighbor is moving around," Whirt said and I saw a white-haired woman emerge from the house next door to Lavois, to toss birdseed. I looked through the binoculars as she chatted nonstop on her cell phone, watering plants, sweeping up dust.

"Okay, Whirt. We're going birdwatching. You're my dad," I said, tossing him a small bird guide. I pulled out my dowdy undercover clothing.

"Your dad?"

"Yeah, what else would you be, Boomer?" Ryan asked with a smirk on his face.

I put the short auburn wig on, with the glasses. I handed Whirt a can of bear spray.

"Take this. You'll look like a flatlander who's afraid of the woods," I said.

"I am a flatlander afraid of the woods," he replied, before putting on a large sun hat.

We looked like tourists trying to fit in. Ryan stayed to keep watch on the Lavois cabin. Whirt and I left the house and headed toward the lady on her deck. I carried a large map. We were so close to the Lavois cabin, I could've looked in the windows if they weren't blacked out. I knew Tibbs had to have made peepholes to see outside, just like he did in the Glendale house. Was he watching us now?

"What're you going to say?" Whirt whispered.

"I'll ask directions, she looks like a chatty Cathy," I replied as we approached.

"How d'you know that?" he asked.

"One car in the driveway, no wedding ring, elderly woman probably lives alone, who's been blabbing non-stop on her phone. She's a talker."

"Wow..." Whirt said, under his breath.

"Excuse me," I asked loudly, "is this the way to Green Valley Lake?"

The woman laughed, hanging up her phone. "Green Valley Lake? That's about five miles up the road and on the other side of the highway."

"Oh, darn! We heard they have the dark-eyed junco," I said.

Whirt interjected enthusiastically, "And the pygmy nuthatch!"

"Are you birders?" she asked, with a huge smile.

"Yes, ma'am, we are. We came all the way from Yorba Linda," Whirt said.

"We have a lot of species up here. Have you been to the scenic overlook? It's at the ski area. My name's Sue Allen," she said.

"I'm Katie Gaines and this is my dad, Henry. We're not going that far, just staying close to our rental. This sure is a pretty area. Are there many homes for sale?" I asked.

"Oh, quite a few. A lot are vacation homes, so they're empty most of the time."

"Yeah, I noticed a lot seem to be closed up for the season, no sign of life. I sure wish they'd sell, I'd buy one in a minute," I said, glancing at the Lavois cabin. She came down from her deck and met us in the driveway.

"We have a lot of people who want to live off-grid, you know? They just want to be left alone, and I can understand that," she said conspiratorially.

"Hell! I feel that way all the time!" Whirt said loudly, with a robust laugh. I shot him a warning glance.

The woman continued. "There's an adorable house just up around the corner on Elm. It's white with yellow trim. I know the realtor, you should call about it," she said.

"I will. This one could use a little makeover," I said with a laugh, gesturing to the Lavois house.

"Oh, that one belongs to a plumber fellow from Long Beach. He moved up here when he retired but he had to go see his daughter a few months ago. His cousin keeps an eye on it but no one sees much of him. He's not well." Her voice dropped to a whisper.

"Oh, that's too bad," I said sympathetically.

She leaned in close to us. "I think he has the cancer. He lost all his hair for a while last year and he's gotten way too thin. He's been up here for years helping his cousin out. One of those quiet types."

"That's a shame. I'll pray for him," I said in my most sincere voice. As always, I was amazed at how easily people share information with total strangers.

Whirt and I continued up the road, searching for birds.

"Jackpot! The cousin has to be Tibbs," Whirt said when we were out of earshot.

"He's sick, probably dying, and he wanted to go out with a big bang," I said.

"And he wanted to fuck with your head as his last hurrah. I'm going to enjoy catching this asshole..." he muttered.

We continued our ruse of birdwatching, walking the streets of the neighborhood, talking loudly and making conversation with anyone we ran into. We scanned the entrances and layout of the Lavois cabin. There were several hiding spots, just out of the sightline from the front door, that we could utilize to ambush him quickly. A crawl space under the front porch, a blind spot behind a small storage shed, a large pile of stacked pallets.

My phone buzzed with a text from Ryan.

> movement in the second-story window foil
> pulled back

I felt my heart rate quicken.

THIRTY

DAY SEVEN: 5:15 P.M.

After the first flush of excitement, the rest of the day was uneventful. There was no more movement at the Lavois house until late afternoon. I was keeping watch at the window when the door opened and Tibbs emerged.

"He's leaving!" I said, waving Ryan and Whirt to the slider. We huddled, watching him shuffle to the Nissan and fumble with the key.

"Man, he looks like a ghost," Ryan said.

Tibbs climbed in and started the engine; it made a whining sound as he backed out and drove off. I was already dressed for the takedown, and we all had our weapons at the ready. But there was still an Edison truck just up the street, with a worker in a cherry picker, high up overhead. He could see the whole area and would surely call the police if he saw three heavily armed people breaking into Lavois' cabin. Sue Allen was still on her deck, setting out food for the wildlife. It wouldn't be dark for another few hours.

"What'd we do?" Whirt asked.

"We wait. The Edison guy is a problem, there are too many people still out," I said.

"God! I just want to run in there and find Josie!" Ryan said.

"Me too. But we can't risk the whole thing," I cautioned him.

Night fell, the streets became quiet and empty. Only wild animals moved freely about. Tibbs hadn't come back. We couldn't wait any longer.

"It's time. Let's go," I said. Adrenaline pulsed through my body; I felt invincible, I'd waited a lifetime for this moment.

We had our hiding places scoped out in case Tibbs returned before we got in. If he found us inside, I would take the lead in dropping him, with Ryan as my backup, while Whirt handled Josie. Ryan carried the duffel bag of power tools as we moved silently through the woods, across the street and down a small ridge to the Lavois cabin. We had silenced our phones, I had the methohexital and syringe in my fanny pack, my loaded guns with the holsters open. In the driveway, I pulled the trashcans over to spill the garbage, betting on the idea that Tibbs would stop to clean it up, buying us some time. Ryan deftly moved to the side door and unscrewed the boards blocking it. He was at work on the lock when I saw headlights approaching. I signaled to them to get into place. I crawled under the porch, balancing on my knees, ready to spring out at the right moment. Whirt was behind the storage shed, Ryan crouched by the woodpile. The headlights swung into the driveway, and I inched forward. The car came to a stop, the door opened and Tibbs stepped out, carrying a plastic bag.

He saw the trash strewn across the driveway and cursed, "Fucking racoons! Making this fucking mess every night..."

When he stooped to gather the trash, I made my move. I shot out and jumped behind him, slamming the butt of the gun into his neck, hitting his carotid artery. He fell to the ground briefly, and Whirt joined me in wrestling him down. He fought back hard, Whirt clapped a hand over his mouth to silence him and I saw Tibbs twist his head and bite down aggressively on

Whirt's wrist. Whirt pulled his hand back as blood spurted out dangerously. I jabbed the methohexital into Tibbs' neck, pushing down on the plunger. He struggled for a moment, and I saw the recognition in his eyes staring up at me before he went limp and lost consciousness.

I fished his keys from his pocket while Whirt and Ryan helped me hoist his dead weight up to carry him inside. We executed everything in less than ninety seconds and then the front door closed behind us. Since Tibbs kept the interior lights off, I lit several candles I had brought, placing them around the room. I checked Whirt's wrist, the bite had hit close to his radial artery and the blood was running steadily.

"You need to get this checked out. It has to be sutured up," I said.

"I'm fine." Whirt winced in pain as he shook me off.

"Stay still, old-timer," Ryan cautioned him, grabbing a first aid kit from his duffel. He squirted disinfectant on the wound, deftly wrapping it tight in a clean gauze. Tibbs was still an unconscious lump on the floor. We looked around the darkened room, the candles casting weird shadows on the knotty pine walls.

It was sparsely furnished. A mismatched couch and armchair, a small table with two wooden folding chairs. A large bookcase and an armoire. We got Tibbs into a folding chair and handcuffed his wrists behind him. I zip-tied his ankles to the legs and his head rolled forward onto his chest. He would be unconscious for the next seven to twelve minutes. We spread out into all the rooms, calling for Josie, but we got no response.

"Pull all the furniture away from the walls and look for a door. There's a build-up underneath the house," I said, yanking the bookcase out to find a blank wall. We pulled everything away but found nothing.

"There's no sign of her. What now?" Whirt asked desperately. I saw a dark blood stain growing on his wrapped wrist.

"Check the closets and the kitchen cabinets, look for a false wall or a space under the floorboards," I said, my eyes darting around frantically.

We opened all the closet doors and pushed past winter coats and boots but found nothing. In the kitchen, Ryan stuck his head into the pantry, sweeping canned goods and canisters aside.

"It's here!" he shouted, tossing food items onto the floor as he yanked a wooden shelf from the wall. We removed all the pantry shelves, and we saw it: a roughly carved door in the drywall, attached with hinges and bolted shut.

We cut through the bolts and pried the door open. I steadied myself as we descended. It was like a horrible déjà vu, walking back into the nightmare of my childhood. My rage was building up, uncontrollably, like a volcano bubbling into life. My mind was laser focused. We stepped into a dark, dank room with a dirt floor. With the flashlight, I saw a pile of plastic sleds, an old lawnmower, a shop vac. Shovels and other tools were scattered in the dirt. Plastic tarps were stretched along the walls, at their edges I could see black soundproofing foam hung underneath them. We had the right spot; this was how Tibbs had outfitted his bunker in the Glendale house. I heard a small whimper and scanned the room with the flashlight, then I saw her. She was obscured behind a pile of boxes, just the toe of her small sneaker was visible.

As we drew closer, we saw Josie Vance duct-taped to a chair in a corner. Her small wrists and ankles were secured with zip ties, a gag stuffed in her mouth. Tears spilled from her eyes, and she was shaking. I ran to her, kneeling to cut the zip ties with my Bowie knife.

"Whirt, go keep an eye on Tibbs while we get her loose!" I said as I carefully removed the gag from her mouth. Stroking her hair, I whispered, "You're okay now, Josie. I'm with the FBI, these are the police. You're safe. You're getting out of here."

She cried and struggled against the duct tape on her wrists.

"I want to go home!" she sobbed.

"Don't worry, we've got you now. You're going home tonight. Your mom and dad will come for you. You're safe now, honey," I said, pulling her small body into my arms to comfort her. I felt her slim shoulders heaving up and down as she gulped in air between sobs.

We had her. She would be going home alive. I carried her up the stairway as Whirt was calling in for backup from the local sheriffs. Tibbs still hadn't regained full consciousness, but his head was lolling from side to side. When Josie saw him, she let out a cry and buried her face against me.

"He can't get loose; he can't hurt you ever again. Okay? He's never going to come back. Just don't look at him. Go with Detective Whirt, he's going to call your parents."

I pulled Whirt aside and whispered, "Take her out of here, have the paramedics meet you out by the highway. She needs to get away from him. And have them look at that wrist."

Whirt took Josie's hand before picking her up and holding her against his chest.

"My name's Ed. I have a granddaughter about your age, her name is Monica. Let's go to the car so we can call your mom and dad, okay?" he said softly.

Josie continued to cry and hid her face as Whirt carried her out. Ryan's shirt was stained with sweat as he shook his head.

"I can't believe we found her. And that's him? The same freak who took you?"

We looked at Tibbs strapped to the chair, blinking his eyes as he was coming to.

"The sheriffs are on the way. You should get out of here, Ryan. He's not going anywhere. I can handle him."

"You sure? I can wait outside," he offered.

"No. You can't get caught up in this. You can go. Thanks for everything," I said, pulling him into a hug.

"Call me when you're done here, okay?" he ordered.

I nodded and he slipped out the door into the night. I pulled up the second folding chair and set it across from Tibbs. The candles flickered. I trained my Glock on him, resting it on my knee.

Tibbs struggled to keep his head up and as his eyes adjusted, he saw me seated across from him. Now that I had time to take him in, I saw that he was a bag of bones. His skin had a distinct yellow tint to it, indicative of liver failure or perhaps hepatitis. The dark circles under his eyes were deep, almost purple. He was seriously ill.

"Hello, James," I said.

He shook his head and glared at me as he hissed, "Lying bitch!"

He pulled against the chair and almost fell to the floor. I laughed, knowing it would infuriate him more.

"How's it feel? To be the one tied up, helpless? I've waited a long time to see you this way."

"It's over for you, they all know now that you're a liar..." His voice was raspy and low.

"Do they?"

"You're off the case..." he insisted. He darted his eyes back and forth, like an animal caught in a snare. The edges of his mouth were wet with saliva.

"If I'm off the case, what am I doing here? With you strapped to a chair and a ton of cops on the way?"

"I saw on the news. You're out! You're over!"

"No, they lied because we knew you would believe it. And you did, you stupid fuck," I chuckled.

He hissed at me again, his fingers working hard against the handcuffs. "You're nothing! You're not her. You wanted to be her because you're trash but you're not her, you're not her... I should have let you burn..." he mumbled.

"You must've been shocked when Emily turned up, living

her best life. Big FBI agent, catching freaks like you. Having it all, right? While you had to live up here, hiding like a stray dog," I said. I knew he couldn't take being ridiculed and I saw the rage building in him.

"It's not your life, it's her life! You stole it, you're nothing... they didn't even look for you..."

He spit furiously at me, the glob of wet mucous falling short on the floor between us.

"I've always been curious, Tibbs. Why'd you let me go? Was it too much that you drove Emily to her death?"

"I didn't kill her! She killed herself, it wasn't me!" he tried to shout but dissolved into a fit of coughing; I saw bloody spittle on his chin.

"You can lie to yourself, but you killed her, it was all you."

"Shut up!" he screamed.

"What about Cody? And Joe Lavois?"

He grinned manically. "It was easy. After I found that junkie to go in the van, I came up here. No one even knew I was in the cabin. It was perfect, until some bitch from the county came sniffing around. That's when I needed Lavois."

"So, he was on board with you hiding up here?"

"Sure. He thought it was cool. He thought he was getting a free cabin. It worked fine until he decided to move up here for good, stupid asshole," he said, struggling to breathe.

"Where is he?"

"No one will ever find him. This is a big forest."

"So why now, James? Why take Josie and play all these games with me?"

"Because you thought you got away with it. I saw you on the news, how they gave you that award and they treated you like a hero. You're trash, that's all you ever were. I've been waiting for the right time... but then it started to run out on me..." He panted heavily, his voice failing.

I could see the physical toll it took for him to fight back, to talk. The sweat dripped from his hairline into his eyes and he tried to shake it off. He almost lost his balance in the effort as he struggled to continue.

"I was afraid I'd die before I could take you down. But I planned and I found the perfect little girl, just like Emily. I planned everything so I could make you pay and let them know that you're a lying bitch. And now you're gonna lose everything! I sent another message today, telling them who you really are..." He began to laugh.

"Really? And who's going to believe you? Everyone knows you're a nutcase and a criminal. You look like hell, Tibbs. Your skin is yellow, even the whites of your eyes. I've seen dying people before. Is it cancer? Kidney failure? Those are hard ways to go."

"Shut up!"

"It's got to be rough; how can you go to a doctor if you're supposed to be dead? So, I guess you just live with it? Knowing every day that your body is rotting and there's nothing you can do? Was this your last big hurrah, trying to ruin my life? And you failed miserably, didn't you? Like everything else."

"Fuck you!" he shouted.

"No, as I recall, you were never able to do that," I said dryly and he tried to kick out at me, knocking himself to the floor where he rocked against his restraints.

I crouched over him, leaning my face in close to his. "Look at you, struggling like a cockroach. You pathetic piece of garbage. You thought you were going to beat me?"

He writhed on the floor as I stepped back to watch him. The satisfaction I felt was palpable. The power I had over him was like poison running through my blood, but it was a sweet, delicious poison. I could taste it; I pulled my revolver and cocked the hammer, resting the barrel against his sweating temple. He squinted his eyes shut. I heard sirens approaching in the distance and in that split second of my hesitation, Tibbs suddenly pitched his body forward with a guttural scream and pulled one of his hands free from the handcuffs.

I jumped back and saw that he had dislocated his thumb to get loose and he lunged for me, grabbing my leg and knocking me off balance. I fell to the floor and felt his hand on my ankle, reaching for my Bowie knife. I kicked at him as he grabbed it and plunged it into my flesh. I pulled back in pain and when he rolled over toward me, I fired my Glock into him, unloading a full magazine, the weight of my rage taking over until the clip was empty. The bullets tore through his chest, knocking the gun from his hand. I hit his aorta, the blood gushing out in large spurts like a geyser until it stopped. His body flopped over; the life went out of him instantly. His head rolled against the floor, his eyes open. I sat up, covered in his blood, stunned.

The sirens were closer now. Whirt texted me and Ryan that Josie was at the local hospital and her parents were on their way. I texted back, including Antonio in the message:

Tibbs is dead. It's over.

I heard the sheriffs pull into the driveway. I sat down, took off my FBI badge and laid it on the kitchen counter. I set my Glock next to it and arranged my other weapons in a neat row. And I waited.

THIRTY-ONE
DAY SEVEN: 10:17 P.M.

I sat in the darkness, at the back of the ambulance, wrapped in a blanket, my wrist in a sling. I had a nasty gash on my calf from where I struggled with Tibbs and an EMT had wrapped it so tightly it throbbed. My chin was bruised from falling and now that the adrenaline rush was over, my whole body hurt. The sheriffs and police swarmed the area, neighbors stood outside, shocked by the flashing lights, the crush of police presence. The bureau had dispatched agents from the Riverside and San Bernardino offices who interfaced with the local cops and the forensic team. Tibbs lay on a stretcher, in a black body bag, waiting for the coroner to arrive to claim him.

I gave my statement to the young deputy sheriff who arrived first; he blanched when he saw Tibbs' lifeless body in a river of blood and me looking like someone from a horror movie. My phone had been buzzing for the last hour and a half, but I didn't answer it. My husband was en route to pick me up. I was in a mild state of shock that it was finally all over. A female agent from the FBI regional office in western San Bernardino County approached and sat next to me.

"This was quite the takedown, Agent Ray," she said.

"Yeah, it was. What's your name?"

"I'm Special Agent Kristen Griffith, from the regional office here in San Berdoo," she said, using the local slang to refer to the rough and tumble county.

"I gave my statement to the deputy. I'll do an interview with you or anyone else once I get this wrist checked out. It hurts like hell."

"I can have you taken to the local hospital for an evaluation. I just wanted to ask—they said you're on leave from this case, right?"

"That's right. My SAC took me off the case. I suspect I'll be fired now."

She leaned in with a smile. "Fired? This is starting to blow up already on social media! The rest of CARD was out in some dog-patch town chasing the wrong guy and you caught Tibbs and saved the kid on your own? Everyone's saying you're like the Terminator! They'll make a movie about you!"

She showed me her TikTok feed with stories about the case and rescue. I suspected that Ryan was the one who spearheaded this campaign so quickly.

"Don't worry, Agent Ray. No way they're letting you go after this. You're an icon!" she said with a wink as she corralled a deputy. "Please take Agent Ray to the local hospital for evaluation. She's done here."

The coroner had arrived. As I walked to the deputy's SUV, I saw them wheel Tibbs' lifeless body out of sight and into the white van. We both pulled out at the same time, our SUV following the van like a funeral cortege until our paths diverged. They turned and disappeared, heading down to the city lights below, to the place of the dead. We continued to face the living.

When we pulled into the parking lot of the small Mountains Community Hospital, there were already a few reporters who had made their way up. I knew that number would grow before morning, especially with the sensational details of the case. I kept my head down, ignoring the shouted questions, and went into the ER to find a group of cops and FBI agents in the waiting room, several of them congratulating Whirt, who stood among them like a hero. I caught his eye and gave him a thumbs-up; I was happy to see him basking in the respect and recognition he deserved. He had come full circle, and his retirement would include a commendation from the chief and a lot of press coverage. He'd be invited to speak to cadets at the academy, all the perks of being a storied detective. I doubted he'd have time for that cruise with his wife.

A nurse led me into the treatment area. In the only private room, I glimpsed Josie Vance and her parents, who must have had a police escort with flashing lights to get here so quickly from Palos Verdes. I sat on a bed and waited for the doctor to check me out. Before he could, Melanie Vance stuck her head around the curtain.

"Agent Ray? I want to thank you for finding Josie, for being the one who knew where she was... you're amazing, really... How did you know?"

"I just followed the information we had and knew how to interpret it," I said wearily.

She started to cry and took my hand. "I'm so sorry we doubted you. Lou is so embarrassed about those Jones people, he's too mortified to come over here. We owe everything to you."

"Can I talk to Josie for a minute?" I asked gently.

"Of course," she said. I followed her to the private room and found Josie under a plushy blanket, with a new stuffed toy. The abrasions on her arms and legs were wrapped in bandages. Louis sat next to her, holding her small hand in his.

"Josie? It's me, the agent who found you with Detective Whirt. Are you doing okay?"

"Yeah, I'm tired," she said in a weak voice. I assumed she'd been given a mild sedative.

"You're a very brave girl, you know that? James Tibbs is a

scary man. He took me when I was your age and he kept me for a long time. But there were a lot of people looking for you, even when you felt all alone. We were out there, and we were not going to give up until we found you. I want you to know, he's gone. He's never coming back."

"Is he dead?" she asked.

"Yes, he is. He really is. He's never hurting another little girl again."

Her eyes fluttered, she was falling asleep which was the best thing for her. Louis reached out to shake my hand.

"Thank you for everything, Agent Ray," he said stiffly.

"Can I give you a word of advice?" I asked.

"Yes, anything," Melanie said.

"Don't trot her out to reporters to tell her story. They'll bombard you with calls and offers, but just let her recover quietly. This is her story, and she has a right to decide when and if she wants to tell it when she's older. Protect her, okay?"

"We will. We're making some big changes after this," Louis assured me.

The doctor signaled to me and after X-rays, determined that my wrist had a hairline fracture and needed a cast. It was setting when Antonio burst through the doors and ran to me.

"You're okay? He didn't hurt you?" he asked.

"Just a little banged-up. He fared far worse," I said.

"They told me that you killed him."

I nodded. He embraced me and whispered, "It's all over now, Em."

And this time, it really was. There would be no monster suddenly appearing, no troll to climb out of a cave and pull me back in. Like a character in an old folk tale, I had gone into the chaos of the forest, and I had slain the dragon by my own sword.

. . .

A few days later, I sat waiting for my meeting with SAC Powers in the Westwood offices of the FBI. I was curious to see how it was going to play out. I knew I'd be reprimanded for breaking with protocol, but it was hard for the bureau to argue with results. Josie Vance was alive and safe with her parents. In the end, the meeting was brief. I was put on an extended leave while my conduct was reviewed but it was clear that I was not leaving the FBI unless it was my choice. I rode the elevator down to the first floor and passed the security guards at their screening stations. I walked into the bright sunlight and saw the members of the CARD team gathered by the gray FBI sign in the front courtyard. Diaz held a big bouquet of flowers. Grice was conspicuously absent.

"Agent Ray!" Stephanie shouted, calling me over.

The team circled me, and Izzy said, "We couldn't really do this upstairs with the top brass around, but we wanted to congratulate you."

Diaz gave me a quick hug and said, "You're the shit, Agent Ray, pardon my French. I hope you like freesias, my mom said they smell the best."

I smiled and took the flowers, shaking everyone's outstretched hands.

"I knew she would do it, I never doubted her once. There's a reason she's the head of this team," Stephanie said.

"Thank you, guys. It means a lot to me. I never wanted to make the team look bad, I just knew that Tibbs was our suspect, and I had to move on him. It wasn't a big deal," I said.

"Not a big deal? When we were out at a storage place in bumfuck Victorville thanks to Grice and his big ego? Take the credit, you earned it, homegirl," Diaz said.

That was a first. I'd never been called homegirl before, and I liked it.

. . .

I made an appointment for the same day to meet with Lydia at her office in Pasadena. I had avoided her during the most intense days of the case, and I knew she was upset. I arrived and leafed through the magazines absentmindedly. After a few minutes, she came out and I could see immediately that she was not happy.

We went into her office, and I sat on the big, chintz-covered couch, the room decorated with pastel prints of landscapes. She took her spot across from me and I suddenly felt as if I were a teenager again, unsure how to proceed.

I smiled nervously, shrugged and said, "If I had told you it was Tibbs, you would've insisted that I leave the case."

"You're right, I would have. It was so dangerous for you to be in that situation."

"I know. But I had to find Josie, that's my job. And I couldn't let my own issues stand in the way of that."

She looked at me for a beat and I saw her soften. "I admire your dedication to your work, but you're not made of steel. You're not Supergirl, even if you sometimes think you are. You lived through something that most people would not be able to survive. You must respect that and take care of yourself."

Her words hung in the air; I was thinking of Emily, the fifteen-year-old girl who lost that struggle to survive; the girl who couldn't endure another day with James Tibbs. Sitting in that peaceful, quiet office, I could picture her face so clearly. I thought of the days we spent together in that house of horrors. The laughter we shared at silly cartoons, the fear we fought against when Tibbs went into crazy mode. I could still feel her thin frame against my spine as we slept curled together for comfort in those terrifying times. I wondered if she was at peace now. It sounded strange but I had felt her presence so much in the past few days, as if she were hovering around me, letting me know she was there.

I wanted to tell Lydia the truth about me. I wanted to

unburden myself and tell her the strange and awful story of Emily's death; how I kept her alive for myself and Michael Ray by taking on her identity. But I wasn't ready. The day would come, but I wasn't ready yet.

"I'm sorry I stayed out of touch. I just knew that I had to keep moving forward and I couldn't let anything pull me off-course. They've put me on an extended leave but I'm pretty sure I'm finished with CARD. There are no more demons to chase," I said confidently.

She didn't even try to hide her relief as she grabbed my hand and held it tightly.

"As awful as this was, if it pushes you to move into something else, then it was a good thing. I'm so happy you're safe, Emily. I was really afraid of losing you," she said.

"That's not happening. You're stuck with me forever."

EPILOGUE

I rose late, as I had become accustomed to in the past weeks. Being on leave from work was a welcome change. I got used to picking my girls up from school, helping with class projects. I was able to cook dinner with Dolores and be at the table on time instead of eating a plate of food covered in foil after everyone was asleep. The guns stayed locked up, I didn't have to go through the daily ritual of securing them or feeling their heavy, lethal weight on my hip at all times. I read a few books, signed up for a painting course at the community college. My life was shifting into something I hadn't expected, and it was good.

Whirt received a special commendation from the mayor, and they hosted a fancy retirement dinner for him at Nelson's by the beach. Larissa Cinque won a local news award for her coverage of the Josie Vance case and upon graduation from USC, she got hired by the *Los Angeles Times*, her dream job. They put her on a high-profile investigation of an international trafficking ring, and she had to put the Danica Hansen story on hold. She had new stories to tell. Tibbs had sent a final message, disclosing that I was actually Danica Hansen, but like Antonio predicted, it was dismissed as the rantings of an unhinged lunatic.

Ryan decided to join the FBI and was undergoing the recruiting process. He wanted to work with CARD, and I had given him the highest recommendation. The cold case detectives from the Redondo Beach PD who had been on the Danica Hansen disappearance didn't come up with anything and ultimately, the case got filed again as unsolved. She receded from memory. I had weighed the options and decided that I had no good reason to bring her back to life.

It was a Sunday; Dolores was taking the girls to a birthday party for one of their classmates. Antonio and I stopped at the florist and picked up two special order wreaths, made from plumerias, roses and gardenias. Their sweet fragrance filled the car as we made the long drive to Palos Verdes. We didn't talk, we just listened to "The Old Castle," a classical piece by Mussorgsky, a favorite of ours.

We arrived at the overlook to Lunada Bay, pulling into the gravel, crunching under the tires of the car. There was a stairway down to the beach, not easily visible but known to locals. We walked down with the wreaths and stood at the water's edge. From my pocket, I pulled two small photos, one of Emily and one of me. I affixed each one to a wreath.

Antonio slipped his arm around my shoulder. The sun was high in the sky, the water slightly rough.

"You ready?" he asked.

I nodded, slipping off my sneakers and rolling up my jeans. I waded into the shallow waves, the cold water lapping at my ankles. In each hand, I held a wreath and when the waves pulled out, tossed them into the sea. They floated as the water receded, carrying them off.

The wreaths bobbed on the white caps until a large wave pulled them under and they disappeared. Two little girls, who had fallen into the abyss. Two little girls who had vowed to stay together, had become one. They were both free now.

We all have them.

Secrets.

A LETTER FROM THE AUTHOR

Dear Readers,

Thank you so much for reading *My Name Is Emily Ray*! If you want to stay in touch with other readers and keep up to date on my new releases, please sign up for my email newsletter which will have the latest information on the Emily Ray series and more.

www.stormpublishing.co/michele-dominguez-greene

If you enjoyed the book and could spare a few moments to leave a review I would greatly appreciate it. Even a short review can help build an audience for a new book and ensure that it reaches as many readers as possible. Your support as readers is the lifeblood of any new book. Thank you so much!

I wrote *My Name Is Emily Ray* because I was fascinated by the emotional journey of people who survive complex trauma. Why do survivors react in different ways and what are the conditions that make a character like Emily become a driven perfectionist, determined to overcome her past? As part of her motivation, I added in the element of stolen identity—that a desperate, youthful decision can turn her life in a wildly different direction. That opened up a whole new area to explore: Why do we perceive some people as more worthy than others? Why are some children valued and some discarded? And what happens when a young girl flips the narrative of her own life? As much as the book is a suspense story, with the kidnapping of Josie Vance and the FBI's search for her, it is also an emotional and psychological journey for a woman who thinks she has her life safely compartmentalized until that coping strategy doesn't work any longer and she has to face her own hard truths.

Emily Ray is a thoroughly modern woman, with a modern marriage and family life, which brings challenges that are not easy to navigate. I think a lot of women feel those pressures, balancing how to be true to their own dreams and still fulfill their roles as spouse and parent. In Emily's case, the demands of her work carry huge consequences, any mistake can have tragic repercussions. Like any art form, a novel should reflect back our own struggles and triumphs, the precarious nature of the human condition and I hope that Emily's story resonates with readers in this way.

Michele-Greene.com

 facebook.com/MGreeneArtist

 x.com/MicheleDGreene

 instagram.com/micheledgreene

ACKNOWLEDGMENTS

I would like to thank Robert Loosle (FBI SAC Los Angeles, retired), Carlos Narro (FBI, retired) and Robert Clark (FBI, retired) for their input and advice. I would also like to thank the entire team that runs the FBI Citizens Academy for the invaluable information that they provided.

Tremendous gratitude to Lydia Glass, Ph.D., for her input regarding complex PTSD.

Many thanks to my son, José Daniel, for his understanding when I was holed up in my home office writing for hours and I forgot to pick up dinner or dry the laundry. Your maturity and support for me during this process made it possible for me to write and sell this book. You are my treasure, the light of my life.

Without the guidance and belief of my amazing agent, Jill Marsal, I would not have realized this dream, and my editor, Claire Bord, made this a much better book and made me a better writer. Heartfelt thanks to these incredible women.